Praise for

Sharon Gillenwater

"There's something infectious about Ms. Gillenwater's slice-of-life writing style. Her enthusiasm for life, love and the Lord draws readers in and causes their hearts and imaginations to soar."
—*Romantic Times* on *Highland Call*

"Gillenwater's latest is highly agreeable, with intriguing...characters, a light Christian message, and heavy doses of adventure and intrigue. It should prove popular."
—*Library Journal* on *Highland Call*

"Sharon Gillenwater sweeps her readers up in a powerful mix of characters and settings and never fails to deliver a heart-touching tale of love and faith."
—Annie Jones, bestselling author of *The Snowbirds*

"Sharon Gillenwater's novels contain an irresistible blend of adventure, inspiration, and romance that never fail to touch the heart. Her lively dialogue, passionate characters and engaging storyline will make you want to devour this book in a single sitting. Jump right in and enjoy!"
—Diane Noble, bestselling author of *Phoebe*

Sharon Gillenwater

Twice Blessed

Published by Steeple Hill Books™

STEEPLE HILL BOOKS

ISBN 0-373-78516-X

TWICE BLESSED

This edition published by arrangement with Steeple Hill Books.

www.SteepleHill.com

Printed in U.S.A.

To my Lord Jesus Christ who forgives,
forgets and gives new beginnings.

To Justin and Erin—
may God bless your marriage and deepen your love
and friendship more with each passing year.

And in loving memory of Uncle Bruce,
whose teasing and bluster didn't hide
a heart of gold. You are missed.

And He died for all, that those who live
should no longer live for themselves but for Him who
died for them and was raised again.... Therefore,
if anyone is in Christ, he is a new creation;
the old has gone, the new has come!

—2 *Corinthians* 5:15–17

Chapter One

West Texas, 1884

Camille Angelique Dupree stood on the boardwalk in San Angelo, watching the drunken stagecoach driver attempt to load the luggage. She winced as he dropped a valise for the third time, prompting an angry exclamation from the owner, Mrs. Watson. Unlike the other passengers and the ticket agent, Camille remained outwardly calm, projecting an image of serenity that came partly by nature and mostly by training.

Her dear departed mother's oft-repeated admonition echoed through her mind. Always remember that you are descended from two of the oldest and finest families in Louisiana. You are a lady, and a lady does not display her temper, particularly in front of her inferiors.

Not that Camille considered the stage driver or anyone else as inferior. Life had taught her the lesson her mother had never quite understood—that being born to wealth and privilege did not make one person better than another. Character mattered far more, especially when one was left with nothing else.

Sighing in resignation, she stepped down to the dusty street, intending to ask a young clerk standing nearby to have her luggage returned to the hotel where she had stayed the past few days. Though anxious to reach Willow Grove, risking her neck to do so was sheer foolishness. There would be another stage in a day or two, with a different driver, she hoped.

"Mama, he'll kill us all!" The shrill voice rose above the argument between the ticket agent and driver.

"Calm down, Joanna." Mrs. Watson rapped her teenage daughter's shoulder with a closed fan. "Going into hysterics will not help."

"But what can we do?"

Camille stopped beside them. "Wait for the next stage."

"Then we'll miss the box supper Saturday night." The girl turned to her with the anguish of a sixteen-year-old about to miss a major social event. "And Bobby's been saving up for a month to buy my supper."

"What's worse, Charlie is the only driver," said her mother.

A horse and rider came down the street at a quick trot, drawing Camille's attention. Slowing as he approached them, he stopped a few doors down from the stage office, and dismounted with the grace of a man accustomed to the saddle. He quickly looped the reins around the hitching post, his angry glare settling on the hapless driver. The cream felt Stetson did little to shadow his scowl as he stormed toward the stagecoach, the lapels of his black suit coat flapping in his self-made breeze. Tall, muscular and handsome, he practically had steam spewing out his ears.

"Charlie, you're fired!"

At his bellow, Joanna shrieked. Hiding a smile, Camille put her arm around the girl, drawing her out of the human locomotive's way. "I do believe one part of our dilemma has been solved."

"Oh, thank heavens. It's Mr. McKinnon. I didn't know he was here. He'll take care of everything." Mrs. Watson flipped open her fan and cooled her face.

It was unusually warm for the last day of January, but Camille wondered if her reaction was due to the weather or the gentleman towering over the driver. His type set most women's hearts aflutter. She glanced at the sign on the stagecoach door—McKinnon Stage Lines.

"Hi, boss." The stage driver wobbled a little as he tried to focus on his employer. "Just gettin' ready to leave."

"You aren't going anywhere." McKinnon settled his hands on his hips. Taking a deep breath, he made an obvious effort to control his temper. "You're drunk."

"Naw." Charlie shook his head, losing his balance. McKinnon caught his arm, righting him before he fell flat on his backside. "Just had a few drinks for Flo." Tears welled up in the older man's eyes and rolled down his cheeks. "Yesterday was her birthday. We always had a big to-do on her birthday."

"That was his wife," whispered Mrs. Watson behind her fan. "She died a year or so ago."

McKinnon's expression softened, and he clasped Charlie's shoulder, squeezing gently. "Go on over to the wagon yard and sleep it off. You can come home on the next run."

"I'm sorry, boss." The driver sniffed loudly, then wiped his eyes with the edge of his coat sleeve.

"It's all right, Charlie." The man's voice dropped a little deeper, grew quieter. "Next time, let me know if something special is coming up, and I'll find someone to fill in for you."

Mumbling, the driver shuffled off. McKinnon took off his hat, revealing wavy dark-brown hair, and turned to his passengers. "I apologize for the delay and anxiety, ladies. We'll be on our way as soon as everything is loaded."

"Are you going to drive the stage, Mr. McKinnon?" Joanna's expression shifted from youthful worship to wariness so quickly that Camille almost laughed.

McKinnon glanced at her, his brown eyes twinkling, before turning his attention to the girl. "Does that worry you, Miss Joanna?"

Her face turned red. "No, sir. It's just...well, you own a general store."

"It's a very big store." One corner of his lips twitched. "Takes a strong man to haul those crates around." When he smiled at the girl, Camille thought poor Joanna might faint. "Would it reassure you if I said I used to drive for the Ben Ficklin line?"

Joanna nodded, her eyes widening. "Yes, sir."

"Good. Now, if you'll excuse me, I'll take care of the bags." He turned to one of Camille's trunks.

She took a step toward him. "Careful, it's heavy."

Hoisting it to his shoulder with a soft *umph,* his gaze swept over her, a gleam of masculine appreciation lighting his eyes. With her strawberry-blond hair and light-hazel eyes, Camille had evoked a similar response in most men since she was barely more than a girl. Under her mother's careful tutelage, she had learned either to ignore it or use it to her advantage. At twenty-five, she considered herself immune to such admiration, so the little skip in her heartbeat caught her by surprise.

"I hope you're planning a long visit, ma'am." He lifted the trunk over the side railing onto the top of the coach, stepping up on the wheel hub to shove it into place. "Our social life probably isn't what you're used to. You might not have a chance to wear all these pretty dresses."

He stepped down and picked up her other trunk, hefting it to the top of the stage beside the first one. He strapped them in place, then hopped down. Picking up a smaller case, he carried it around to the back of the stagecoach.

"I'm not sure how long I'll stay, although there is a chance I'll settle in Willow Grove."

"Well, now, that's welcome news." He flashed her a grin, efficiently stowing away Mrs. Watson's luggage in the boot.

Mrs. Watson had said there was a shortage of eligible women in the new town, which had sprung up a few years back with the arrival of the railroad. Though Camille longed for a loving husband and family, she held no great hope of marriage, at least not to a respectable man.

Still, his apparent interest pleased her—more than it should have. She let his comment pass. "I've heard it's a nice place."

"It is, if you don't mind some rowdiness thrown in. We have a lot of fine folks living there, but when the cowboys come to town, it can get a bit wild, especially on payday."

"Then it shouldn't be boring."

"It seldom is." Taking a rope from a compartment, he deftly wrapped it around the boxes and cases in the boot. He tied a knot in the rope, testing it by pulling against it.

Camille glanced back at the Watsons, then moved to his side. "Have you really driven a stage before or were you just trying to calm Joanna?"

He slanted her a glance. "Nervous?"

"Should I be?"

He chuckled softly. "No, ma'am. I may be a little rusty, but it's not something you forget how to do. I drove the route from here to El Paso for two years."

"I've heard that was very dangerous due to the Indians."

"Yep." He straightened, rolling one shoulder. "And after driving this team all day, I'll remember just how dangerous. Took two arrows in the back on my last run. Decided I'd better do something safer for a living."

"Like running a store?"

The twinkle crept back into his eyes. "I became a Texas Ranger."

Camille laughed. "I'm not sure I should tell Joanna. She'll probably swoon."

"I'd be surprised if she doesn't already know. Better keep quiet, just in case," he said with a slightly lopsided grin. "Can't afford to lose any more time. By the way, I'm Ty McKinnon."

"Camille Dupree." She held out her hand, wondering why she hadn't given him the name she normally used. Perhaps for just a moment, she wanted to be Camille again, not Angelique. "I'm pleased to meet you, sir."

He took her hand in his large one, bowing slightly. "The pleasure is mine. You do realize you may cause a stampede in Willow Grove, don't you? Men, not longhorns."

"I believe you're flattering me, Mr. McKinnon." Camille gently pulled her hand from his.

"Merely speakin' the truth, Miss Dupree." He paused, a tiny frown creasing his brow. "It is *miss*, isn't it?"

"Yes."

"Good." He glanced up at the driver's seat. "Would you care to ride in the place of honor?"

Riding beside the driver was considered the best seat on the coach, a privilege given to the person of his choosing. Men had been known to beg for the opportunity, but if a young, single, and reasonably attractive female were present, they lost out. For a second, Camille almost accepted his invitation. Then caution wagged a finger in her mind's eye, warning her not to encourage the man too much. She had let down her guard once before, taking the words of a silver-tongued gentleman to heart, and paid a heavy price.

"Thank you, but I'd better not. I don't want Mrs. Watson to think I'm unsociable. Given that there are only the three of us making the trip, I'm afraid it would seem impolite if I abandoned them."

"True. She's a nice lady, but she still might get her feathers ruffled."

"I want to make friends, not enemies." At least for the duration of the trip.

"You'll do fine, Miss Dupree." He searched her eyes, and Camille had the impression that he was as surprised by their mutual attraction as she was.

Turning abruptly, he went back to the horse and retrieved his saddlebags, arranging with the ticket agent to have someone take the animal back to the livery for him. He tucked his gear away in the boot and fastened the leather cover.

Walking back to the side of the stagecoach, he opened the door and lowered the step. "Mrs. Watson, Miss Joanna, I think we're ready to leave."

"At last." Mrs. Watson smiled at McKinnon as he helped her up the step. "We will make it home tomorrow, won't we?"

Camille had been informed earlier that the stage currently didn't travel at night, due to road conditions and the lack of a second driver. They would spend the night as guests at one of the ranches along the route.

"We should. Haven't had any rain in a few weeks, so there won't be any swollen creeks or mud to contend with." He grinned at Joanna. "I'd hate to have to answer to Bobby if I don't get you home in time for a good night's rest before the party." McKinnon took the girl's hand, assisting her into the coach. "He's been working extra at the store while you've been gone. Doesn't want to take the chance of being outbid on your box supper."

Joanna giggled, her cheeks turning pink. "Nobody else wants to eat with me."

"Saturday's payday. There'll be more cowboys in town than minnows in the creek. Some of them are bound to be at the social instead of throwing away their money in the saloons. Anybody with a lick of sense will want to eat with you."

Joanna's eyes widened as she settled in the seat. "You really think so?"

"It's a guaranteed natural fact."

Leaving Joanna to discuss the possibilities with her mama, McKinnon turned to Camille, leaning slightly toward her and speaking quietly. "It will be a different story if you're there," he said with a tiny smile. "I might have to take out a bank loan."

Laughing softly, Camille shook her head. "You exaggerate, sir."

"A little." His expression sobered as he captured her gaze. "But I'll be competing with wealthy ranchers, Miss Dupree, not thirty-dollar-a-month cowboys."

She had the distinct impression he was talking about more than the upcoming supper. Mercy, how he set her heart to pounding! She smiled and tried to keep her voice light. "I'm afraid I won't be able to attend, Mr. McKinnon. I can't possibly move into a house by then, so I wouldn't be able to cook." Even if she knew how to.

"Then buy something at the restaurant and stick it in a box." His sudden grin held a great deal of mischief. "Because I intend to have supper with you Saturday night, Miss Dupree, and I expect to raise a pot full of money for the school in the process."

Torn between enjoying his attention and being annoyed at his arrogance, she said crisply, "I have other plans for that evening, Mr. McKinnon." She turned toward the stage door, then stopped, looking up at him. "Are you always this bold, sir?"

Shrugging, a hint of red crept across his tanned face. "Never."

He cupped her elbow, warming her skin through the blue calico sleeve, and guided her up the step. She had the sudden urge to bolt from the coach and run for the hills—except there weren't any close by big enough to hide in. She settled on the seat, and he shut the door, a frown creasing his brow.

"Well, I declare." Mrs. Watson laughed, glancing slyly at her daughter. The coach dipped as McKinnon climbed up to the driver's seat, and she turned her gaze to Camille. "He's quite the catch. The poor man lost his wife in childbirth three years ago. The baby, too."

No wonder he was so kind to the driver, thought Camille.

"He's one of our leading citizens. Filling in as mayor, in fact. He's a fine, God-fearing man who goes to church every Sunday. Besides the store and the stage line, he and his brother own a livery and a large ranch. The man is as wealthy as he is handsome."

Then he must be worth a fortune. "I'm not looking for a husband." She didn't say she didn't want one.

Mrs. Watson waved her hand. "Of course you are, my dear. Goodness, such exciting news. I can hardly wait to get home."

Camille barely stifled a groan. Well, this will put a new wrinkle in the usual gossip. The coach lurched as the horses sprang forward. When the motion smoothed out, she sank against the back of the seat, trying to relax.

The speculative whispers would change to scandalized murmurs when they learned that Angelique Dupree's stock in trade was a pack of cards, a deft hand and a keen mind. She had been seventeen when her sick father relinquished his seat at the card table to her. She had quickly proven to be an astute gambler.

After her father passed away, she stayed in New Orleans at the high-class gambling establishment. Eventually, restlessness took her to San Antonio, and now it had brought her out to the last vestige of the Wild West. For years, men had come from miles around to sit at the Angel's table and stare at her beauty while she took their money. She expected it would be no different in Willow Grove.

In the deepest, sheltered corner of her heart, she wished it could be. A sudden memory sprang to mind, one she hadn't known existed. She couldn't have been more than three or four at the time. Her mother, young and carefree, laughing as she slipped a lovely white camellia beneath the green ribbon on a hatbox wrapped in shimmering pink silk. She had winked at Camille. "Now, your father will know to bid on it, so we can eat together." After giving her daughter a kiss, she picked up the box containing their supper and glided down the wide steps of their beautiful plantation home to her husband and the carriage.

Tears misted Camille's eyes as she turned to the window, oblivious of the passing countryside. Her heart ached for what she had lost and for what she could never have...the simple pleasure of going to a box supper with a man like Ty McKinnon.

Chapter Two

Two days later, Ty stood on his back porch and took a sip of coffee, watching the first blush of dawn tint the sky above a distant mesa. He expected the cool morning to give way to another pleasant afternoon.

Business was thriving, both in the store and at the brand-new livery. Despite the fiasco with Charlie and the occasional interruption from ongoing road improvements, the stage line did a brisk business. The ranch was doing well, and most folks approved of Ty's performance as acting mayor.

By rights, he should have been a happy man. He supposed he was—when heartache and loneliness didn't close in on him like a suffocating fog.

He looked up toward the heavens, picturing his beloved Amanda's face, speaking softly. "You'd be proud of Willow Grove, honey. It's grown a lot in the last three years. We have four churches now." He smiled wryly. "And about twelve saloons. New one opened last week."

Ty figured if anybody heard him talking to his wife, they'd think he was plumb loco. Maybe he was, but he didn't care. He only hoped his voice floated up through the windows of heaven.

Normally, when the memories grew too painful, he would ride out on the range and spend a few days by himself. There, he could think out loud and talk to his sweet wife as much as he wanted to without worrying about somebody hearing him. But now he had too much to do. The things he used as a distraction had become a trap.

Leaning against a post, Ty set the cup down on the railing. Streaks of purple and gold spread across the sky. "Harvey Miller is running against me for mayor. He seems bent on slinging mud if he finds any. I sure could use your advice on how to deal with him." Tears stung his eyes. Amanda always had a knack for seeing right to the heart of a problem. More often than not, she worked out the solution, too.

But the night their baby was born, there had been problems no one could solve. Not the good doctor, who fought with every bit of his skill to save her. Not Ty, though he pleaded with God from the depths of his soul to spare his wife and child. Nor Amanda, though she held on as long as she could, promising to love him for all eternity.

"Why did you take her and little William, God?" Ty's voice broke as he whispered the words. "Was heaven so empty that you needed their love to fill it?"

He tried so hard not to blame God for the hollowness in his soul, going about his work with a cheerful attitude and ready smile. He attended church every Sunday, read a little from the Bible every day and prayed often. Then he wondered if God heard his prayers at all when there was such anger and bitterness in his heart.

He put on a good front, hiding his sorrow from everyone except his brother. Cade saw through the facade and knew that when he went off to be alone, the pain had become too great to bear. Ty suspected that Cade prayed for him even more when he was gone. Sometimes, he swore he could feel his brother's love wrapped around him. Or was it Jesus reaching out to him? Probably both.

"God, I'm grateful for the ways You've blessed me—the ranch, good businesses and being mayor. I know it's by Your grace that we've done so well. But, Lord, I'm so tired of being alone. There are times I'd just as soon burn this house down as spend another empty night here."

Ty stood there a few minutes longer, wiping away the tears as they rolled down his cheeks. Gradually the pain eased, and he took a deep breath. Thinking of the beautiful sunrise, a passage from Psalms came to mind, encouraging him.

> If I take the wings of the morning, and dwell in the uttermost parts of the sea; even there shall Thy hand lead me, and Thy right hand shall hold me.

"Help me to make wise decisions today, Lord. Hold me close to You."

His thoughts turned to the day ahead. Since it was Saturday, Cade and his family would be coming to town from the ranch. He glanced toward the house next door with a smile. Jessie had a grand time decorating it. The ranch house was comfortable. Their town home was fancy. Cade hadn't built her a mansion, but it was two stories with plenty of room in case the family grew bigger. He'd bought her fine furniture and carpets and drapes—basically anything that caught her eye. Now they stayed in their own place when they came to town instead of with him. He missed them taking over his house. At least they'd brought life to it.

He went inside and rinsed out the coffee cup, washed his face and slipped on his suit coat. Taking his Stetson from the rack by the front door, he glanced around the room. As usual, everything was neat and tidy, just as Mrs. Johnson had left it on Monday. It would have been the same even if he had been in town all week. Without Cade and his family scattering things a bit, his cleaning lady had started lecturing him about finding a wife.

For an instant, anger boiled to the surface, and he jammed his hat on his head. "I have a wife."

But you can't hold a memory.

The thought surprised him, but not nearly as much as the one that followed—Camille Dupree's lovely face and smile. His heart skipped a beat, and Ty drew a shaky breath.

He hadn't seen her since the previous evening when he'd stopped the stagecoach in front of the Barton Hotel and unloaded her trunks. Despite his attraction to the lovely Miss Dupree—or perhaps because of it—he had been careful on the trip from San Angelo not to pay any more attention to her than he did to Mrs. Watson or Joanna. At least when anyone was watching. When they weren't, he'd found himself staring at her time and again.

A sharp pang of guilt stabbed him. "I'll always love you, Amanda," he whispered. "Just like I promised."

But his precious wife had asked for something more. "Don't spend your life mourning me," she'd whispered as she'd lifted a feeble hand and laid it lightly against his chest. "You have a loving heart, Ty. Enough room for me and another. Find someone to share your life and to love little William, to care for him."

He could only bring himself to tell her that he would find someone to love their baby and to care for him. Within hours, William was gone, too.

In the years since, Ty could have had his pick of any eligible women in Willow Grove and a few other towns, too. Eventually, he'd grown to enjoy the attention, but no one had ever been interesting enough for him to do more than flirt a little. No one had ever lingered in his thoughts—except Camille Dupree.

The short walk downtown and the exchange of cheerful greetings with neighbors and other businessmen cleared his mind. He and Cade were partners in all their business ventures, but his brother ran the ranch while he handled things in town.

As the largest general merchandise store within a hundred miles, McKinnon Brothers supplied provisions to many of the ranches across several counties as well as the townspeople of Willow Grove. He took pride in carrying the best merchandise possible at a reasonable price. If a customer wanted something they didn't have—and he knew of no one else in town who had it—he would make every effort to order it for them. Ty and Cade were noted for their integrity, both personally and in business. They worked diligently to keep that reputation.

Four doors down from his store, Ty absently glanced through the window of the White Buffalo Saloon—and came to a dead stop. He turned slowly and looked again.

Standing at the bar with all the regal grace of a true Southern belle was none other than Camille Dupree. Ty shook his head, unable to believe his eyes. It was an unwritten rule that women did not enter the saloons in downtown Willow Grove. They did not come there to drink, nor to ply their trade. The dance halls and saloons where soiled doves catered to men's baser needs were just outside the city limits in the unofficial red light district. For the most part, those women stayed in that area, rarely venturing into the more respectable part of town.

Deep disappointment swept through him, followed by anger that he had been so easily duped. Two long strides took him through the open door and inside the saloon. Though he knew it wasn't officially open for business until ten o'clock, he was relieved to see that no one else had wandered in. He closed the door.

"Mornin', Mayor." Behind the bar, the Buffalo's owner, Nate Flynn, lazily dried a glass. "What brings you to my grand establishment?" A quick glance at Camille and the twinkle in his eyes told Ty that Flynn knew exactly why he was there. "You already have my vote in April."

Camille turned, resting her arm on the highly polished bar, and met Ty's gaze with a tiny, defiant lift of her chin. "Mr. McKinnon."

"Miss Dupree." Ty approached them slowly, his gaze flickering to the glass in her hand.

"Would you care to join me in a lemonade?" she asked, her lilting drawl slightly exaggerated.

"No." He stopped a few feet in front of her, resting his hands on his hips. "What are you doing in here?"

"Visiting with an old friend." She sent Nate an affectionate smile. "And discussing our business arrangement."

"What kind of business?" Ty worked to keep his voice steady. *Please God, don't let it be what I'm thinking.*

Camille set down the glass and picked up a deck of cards from the bar, shuffling them with lightning speed and the fancy style of a professional. She looked at him, a hint of sadness in her eyes. "Not what you have in mind, I assure you."

"That's a relief." He relaxed slightly, feeling ashamed that he'd instantly thought the worst. Though being a professional gambler was bad enough.

"Angelique is the finest little card dealer west of the Mississippi." Flynn winked at her. "Prettiest one, too."

Ty was tempted to remind Flynn that he had a wife at home. "Angelique?"

"Also known as the Angel," said the saloon owner. "Bonnie and I have known Angel since she was just a girl. Worked with her daddy when he was a dealer in New Orleans. Then I worked at her place in San Antonio for a while. We've been pesterin' her to move out here for over a year. I'm hoping to convince her to become my partner."

Camille laughed. "That's news to me. I might consider it, as long as you don't expect me to tend bar or drink with the customers."

"Know better than to ask. I'd want you to put that business savvy of yours to good use, doing the books and ordering supplies. And dealing cards, of course." Flynn flashed Ty a grin. "I figure just having her here will make the place the most popular one in town."

"With some people," Ty muttered. The women would have a different opinion.

"Will I see you at my table?" she asked, playing with the cards.

Ty had the feeling she knew exactly where each card was in the deck, though her attention seemingly was on him.

"No, you won't. I learned long ago not to throw away my money on gambling and card sharks."

Anger bristled in her eyes. "I do not cheat, sir."

"She doesn't have to," said Nate. "She uses skill."

"And distraction." Ty imagined her in a low-cut gown of pale green silk. The thought alone was enough to turn a saint into a sinner. "The men around here don't stand a chance."

Nate laughed heartily. "That's what I'm hoping for. But they have a few days to keep their money. She needs to rest up from the trip." His smile faded as he glanced out the window. "Maybe you could give her a tour of the town. The cowboys are riding in early today. I don't think she should venture out unescorted."

"I'll be fine, Nate." She stacked up the cards and handed them to him. "I'm not fresh out of the schoolroom."

Loud whoops and hollers sounded from the street. A second later, a bullet zinged past the window. Ty reacted instantly, grabbing her shoulders and pushing her to her knees at the bottom of the bar. Kneeling beside her, he shielded her body with his. Another bullet whizzed by, hitting the sign on the awning of the drugstore next door, making it swing. "Ransom, get out there," he growled.

"Who's Ransom?" While she kept her head down, her voice was slightly muffled.

"The sheriff." He realized she was hanging on to his coat. A bullet splintered a chunk of wood from the saloon doorframe, and she buried her face against his chest. He tightened his arms, holding her close, and silently, foolishly thanked the cowboy who was dumb enough to shoot off his pistol in town. The subtle scent of roses encompassed him, and he closed his eyes. *Lord, I'm in big trouble.*

Suddenly, the noise in the street hushed. "Sounds like the sheriff arrived," she said quietly. Ty loosened his hold but kept his arms around her. She raised her head, meeting his gaze. "Thank you."

He nodded, the brim of his hat coming close to the top of her hair. He should let her go, help her up. But he didn't want to. He noticed she was still clinging to his lapel. "Did I hurt you?"

"I bumped my knee. But it's much better to have a tiny bruise than a bullet through my heart."

"I don't want you hurt at all." But she would be once the women of the town heard what she was up to, even though they probably wouldn't shoot her.

She laughed softly. "I'm thick-skinned."

Nate leaned over the bar, wearing a big grin. "The sheriff has the boys corralled. Y'all can get up now."

Soft pink touched Camille's cheeks, and Ty's heart did a little two-step. He'd never seen a woman who worked in a saloon blush. He released her and grabbed hold of the edge of the bar, pulling himself up, then offered her a hand, helping her to stand. "Would you like that tour of the town?"

She shook her head. "I'm tired. I think I'll just go back to the hotel and take a nap."

Behind her, Ty caught Nate's frown. "Then I'll walk over there with you." When she started to protest, he interrupted. "No arguments. Nate is right. It wouldn't be safe for you to go alone. My brother doesn't let his wife stroll around unescorted on Saturday when the cowboys start coming into town. Most of them are fine, but there are always a few who like to cause trouble."

She crossed her arms, peering out the window. "I see two...make that three...ladies walking alone right now."

Ty turned, surveying the street. "Prune-faced matrons. Not a one of them would get a second glance from any of the men, and if they did, they could probably lay them out cold with one swing. But you'd be like the Pied Piper, with some of those boys following you right up to your room." An image of the meek hotel desk clerk popped into his mind. "Come to think of it, you shouldn't be staying at a hotel. Sam couldn't protect you even if he had the courage to try. None of the other hotel clerks could, either."

"I'll be fine. I've lived on my own for a long time."

When he turned back to face her, he saw kindness mingled with sadness in her eyes.

"Mr. McKinnon, I appreciate your concern. But being seen with me won't be good for your reputation."

Probably not. But right then his reputation was of less importance than her safety. "You being seen with me will make most of the men around here think twice about bothering you."

She lifted a delicate brow, even as a smile danced at the corner of her mouth. "Mighty sure of yourself, aren't you?"

"Pretty much. Besides, I have a big brother."

Nate chuckled and picked up her empty glass. "A very big brother."

"If I can't thrash 'em, Cade can." Ty motioned toward the door, relieved when she picked up her small purse and started toward it without further protest.

"That's an interesting philosophy for a God-fearing, churchgoing man."

"I don't go lookin' for a fight, but I don't back down if one comes looking for me." He opened the door, quickly checking the boardwalk and street outside.

He held the door open for her, and she walked out. "What about turning the other cheek?"

"Well, ma'am, to be real honest, I'm not very good at that. Never have quite understood the idea. I usually manage to talk my way out of trouble, but if I can't, I'll stand my ground. Out here, you have to. Especially when it comes to protecting someone else. I don't figure the good Lord would want me to allow someone to be harmed if it was in my power to stop it."

"Which is why you spent time as a Texas Ranger."

"That's right." He cupped her elbow as they went down the boardwalk steps, reluctantly releasing it as they walked across the dusty street. Every man on the block stopped what they were doing and turned to look at Camille. When they reached the boardwalk on the other side, he again gently took hold of her arm as they went up the steps. The action was not lost on the two cowboys standing in front of the hotel door. They quickly scrambled out of the way, hovering nearby, craning their necks for a better look at her. Ty opened the door, following her inside.

"Thank you for your trouble, Mr. McKinnon." Camille stopped in the middle of the lobby.

"I'll see you to your room."

A tiny frown marred her brow. "That really isn't necessary."

Ty slowly scanned the area. The Barton was popular with cattlemen, from men with modest ranches on up to the largest in the area. A good number of them were lounging in the lobby, and every last one of them was drooling. He took a step closer. "Most of the men staying here will treat you with respect, but there are some who might not."

"Which ones?"

"The one over there in the corner, and the big man leaning against the door to the hotel saloon."

She glanced surreptitiously toward both men. "Any others?"

"They aren't here right now, but I can think of a couple who might get a little pushy." The man leaning against the doorway straightened and started walking slowly toward them. "I need to see you to your room now."

She glanced toward the saloon and muttered something he didn't quite catch about men in general. Spinning on her heel, she marched to the hotel desk with Ty right behind her. "My key, please, Mr. Jones."

The clerk complied, surprising Ty by the way he shielded the row of keys with his body, making it difficult for anyone to see precisely which one he removed.

Camille thanked the clerk and headed for the wide staircase, barely glancing at Ty when he fell in beside her. When they reached the second floor and turned down the empty hall, she glared at him. "Now they'll think I'm under your protection. That's what you really wanted, isn't it?"

Ty frowned at the wording of her question, which implied that he wanted the others to think she was his mistress. "If they believe I'm interested in you, they're less likely to bother you."

She stopped at the door to her room and faced him, gripping the key tightly. "What do you want, Mr. McKinnon?"

"To be your friend."

"A friend?" Her tone indicated she didn't believe him.

"Yes." He wasn't sure if there could be anything else between them, but he didn't want to simply walk away from her. He wasn't sure he could.

Her expression turned icy. "I won't be any man's mistress. Not even yours."

Did that mean she was attracted to him? "I wouldn't ask you to be. As you said earlier, I'm a God-fearing man. But even more, I love the Lord and try my best to please Him by doing what's right. Sometimes things are a mite muddled, and I don't always succeed. But on this, the answer is clear. Having a mistress is a sin, and I'm not about to intentionally defy God by doing it. I like you, Miss Dupree. I want to keep you safe and hope to get better acquainted. It's as simple as that." Liar. The feelings she stirred in him weren't simple at all.

"That's not a good idea. I'm a professional gambler. I spend my time in saloons with men." A hint of pink touched her cheeks. "Only playing cards, but most so-called respectable people won't give me the time of day."

"Out here, even some of the most respected men enjoy their gambling. You'll likely find that they'll be as friendly to you on the street as they are at the table.

"Now the women are another matter. I can see why they would be jealous and resent every minute their men spend in your company. But they have other reasons to disapprove of gambling. The same ones I have. I've seen too many innocent people hurt when men lose money that should have gone to care for their families."

She looked away. "Then they had no business playing in the first place."

"Of course not, but some people can't help it."

"And you think I prey on them?" She met his gaze, defiance, anger and a touch of guilt in her frown.

Ty took a moment to answer, giving serious thought to the question. "I suppose I do."

"Then why on earth do you want anything to do with me?"

Ty shrugged, smiling wryly. "I haven't quite pegged that yet. Reckon that's why I want to get to know you, so I can figure it out." He felt a subtle prompting, one he knew came from the Lord. "I think you're a good, kind-hearted woman." He took a deep breath, wondering if he was sticking his foot in his mouth. "And that maybe you'd like a different life."

"A respectable one?" she asked irritably.

"One that gives you peace."

She blinked in surprise and quickly looked away. "Gambling is the only thing I know how to do."

"You could work at my store."

"And make less in a month than I do in one night?" Her eyes crinkled in amusement. "No thanks."

"If that's the case, you probably don't even have to work," said Ty with a grin. "Though, come to think of it, the newspaper publisher is looking for a partner. Mr. Hill has some health problems and is going to close up shop if he can't find someone to help him."

"I wouldn't know the first thing about running a newspaper."

"I expect he'd be willing to teach you. He has a good crew, so you wouldn't have to worry about setting type or the actual printing of the paper. Mainly, he's looking for someone to handle the business end of things such as bookkeeping and selling ads."

"Can a person make a living with a newspaper?"

"He has, though he's not rich by any means. Profits would probably increase about tenfold if you were the one talking to the businessmen. They'd buy an ad every week just to have you drop by. And if you collect the money, they'll be more likely to pay, too."

"They don't pay now?"

"Some have shamefully taken advantage of him. When his heart started acting up, he quit trying to get his money. Just refuses to do any more advertising for them." He noted a spark of interest in her eyes.

"What about writing articles? Would he expect that?"

"No, but if you're interested, he'd probably let you give it a try."

"I'll think about it. But I doubt if the good people of Willow Grove would patronize the paper once word gets out that I'm working at the White Buffalo."

"Then don't go to work there."

She shook her head. "I've already promised Nate that I would. He's depending on me to revive his business."

Ty laughed, leaning one hand on the wall beside her. "Miss Dupree, your old friend has been pulling the wool over your eyes. The White Buffalo is one of the most popular waterin' holes in town, catering mainly to the wealthiest ranchers." He paused, considering who her customers would be. "Maybe Nate has something else in mind."

"What?"

"A little matchmaking." Ty didn't like that idea one bit. He could think of any number of single men who were as well off as he was, and several who had a lot more money. At least half of them wouldn't think twice about asking Camille to marry them, probably the minute they laid eyes on her.

She considered it, then nodded slowly. "It wouldn't surprise me. But it won't do any good. I've never found men to be very trustworthy."

"Then I'll have to prove that all men don't come from the same mold." *With a lot of help from you, Lord.* "And that this is a place where people can start over, leave their past behind them. If you go to the box supper with me tonight, you'll meet some folks who likely have done just that."

Uncertainty flickered across her face. "I've never been to a box supper."

"It's the major event around here this month." Since her daddy was a gambling man, Ty doubted that she'd had a social life typical of the young ladies in Willow Grove. "I'll provide the supper if you'll go with me, though you may take some ribbin' about how well decorated it is. At least then, I'll know it's yours and to bid on it."

Her expression softened, wistfulness filling her eyes before she looked away. "A hatbox wrapped in shimmering pink silk, tied with green ribbon. And a white camellia tucked beneath the bow."

"I have the silk and the ribbon." Ty gently nudged her chin upward with his knuckle until she met his gaze. "But I'm fresh out of camellias."

She laughed quietly as he lowered his hand. "So is everyone else this time of year. You're a very persuasive man, Mr. McKinnon. No wonder you're the mayor."

"Acting mayor," he said with a grin. "Until April first. So will you go with me?"

She hesitated for a heartbeat. "Yes. What do I wear? I doubt my normal evening attire would be appropriate," she said dryly.

His imagination tormented him again with the thought of the kind of dress she probably wore to work in the saloon. "You'd raise a fortune for the school, but the ladies would tar and feather you." He lightly touched the sleeve of her golden-brown day dress. "This would be fine, or maybe something a little fancier. Something like you'd wear to church."

"The last time I went to church I had corkscrew curls and wore a pink taffeta dress over flounced pantaloons."

Ty chuckled at her mischievous smile, even as he felt a little twist in his heart at the description of a little girl dressed in her Sunday best. "Trying to start a new fashion?"

"Think it will catch on?"

"Probably not." He pulled out his pocket watch, checking the time. "I need to get to the store. I'll come by for you a few minutes after six."

Suddenly, Ty realized what he had just done. Camille would be the first woman he had escorted anywhere since Amanda died. An odd mixture of sadness and anticipation tightened his throat.

She took a deep breath. "I'll be ready."

Stepping back, he merely nodded and headed down the hall.

But was he?

Chapter Three

Camille waited by the window, watching McKinnon cross the street. When he disappeared into his store, she left her room, locking the door behind her. She tucked the key into her purse and went down the back stairs, slipping out the door into the empty alley. After walking along the alley for a couple of blocks, she turned up Pine Street toward Nate and Bonnie's house. Though she had eaten breakfast with her friend, she was anxious to talk to her about the newspaper.

Bonnie was sweeping off the front porch when she arrived. "That didn't take long. Of course, there isn't a lot to see in Willow Grove."

"I haven't looked around much. Nate didn't think I should go about by myself after some rowdy cowboys rode in trying to shoot up the town." Camille walked up the steps, shaking her head. "As if I haven't dealt with obnoxious men all my life."

"Still carry that Derringer in your purse?"

Camille grinned, opened the screen door and went into the parlor. "Yes, though I had to get a new purse. Shot a hole in the last one."

"You didn't!" Bonnie followed her inside, carrying the broom into the kitchen, setting it beside the back door. "Did you shoot someone?"

"No, I missed on purpose. But it scared him off." She laid her purse on the kitchen table and sat down. "That's the only time I've ever had to pull the trigger. I wouldn't have missed with the second shot."

"I doubt if you'll ever need it here. Despite what Nate said, most of the men are polite. And if one of them isn't, half a dozen others will come to your rescue quicker than a hot iron can scorch a cotton dress. Do you want some coffee?"

"No, thanks. I had some lemonade with Nate."

Bonnie poured herself a cup of coffee and joined her at the table. "I'm surprised Nate was concerned about it. He's never told me not to go downtown on Saturday. Of course, I'm not a young beauty like you."

"Don't give me that. You're only ten years older than me and still beautiful. Certainly not a prune-faced matron."

"Well, I hope not." Bonnie laughed and stirred a spoonful of sugar into her coffee. "Though I suppose we have a few in town."

"At least three according to Ty McKinnon. He agreed with Nate that I needed an escort, insisted on it, in fact. When I pointed out the ladies on the street, that's what he called them."

"Ty McKinnon?" Bonnie perked up. "Was he in the saloon?"

"He stormed in when he saw me through the window." She traced a flower on the tablecloth with her fingertip. "I'm sure he thought I was going to do something other than play cards."

"Nate doesn't have any cubicles in the back or an upstairs

for lewd women, and Ty knows it. I can't believe he jumped to that conclusion."

"He looked chagrined when he realized I was only a gambler. Though he didn't like that much, either."

Speculation gleamed in her friend's eyes. "It sounds to me as if our handsome mayor has taken a liking to you. Did he insist on being your escort?"

"Yes. Though I refused the tour of the town that he offered. I only let him walk me back to the hotel, where he also insisted on going to the door of my room. No doubt that caused all sorts of speculation with the gentlemen downstairs. But I couldn't dissuade him. He's a very stubborn man," she said irritably.

"And you're attracted to him."

"I shouldn't be. He says he wants to be my friend, and I expect he would be a good one. But when he held me, I felt as if I'd been standing too close to a lightning rod in a thunderstorm."

"Wait a minute. When he held you? I think you left out a big part of your story."

"When the cowboys started shooting at the store signs, McKinnon pushed me down beside the bar and knelt down, too, sheltering me. I guess it was natural for him to put his arms around me." She shook her head ruefully. "And just as natural for me duck my head against his chest and hide behind him like some ninny."

Bonnie sighed. "How romantic."

Camille shook her head. "I didn't come here for romance."

"But that's exactly what you need. Surely you don't want to spend the rest of your life playing cards in smoke-filled saloons with drunken men."

"They don't play as well when they're drunk. It's easier to win."

Her friend ignored her feeble attempt at humor. "Angel, you're young, beautiful and the most ladylike lady I've ever known. You don't belong in a saloon, but in a home with a family of your own."

Pushing back her chair, Camille strolled to the back screen door and gazed out at the remnants of the vegetable garden. Given her friend's green thumb, she had no doubt that the garden once had been beautiful and thriving. Now the few remaining plants were old and withered, soon to be uprooted and replaced with new ones in the spring.

How long would she still draw men to her gaming table? Another year? Five? Perhaps ten if she was lucky. Suddenly, the thought of another ten years at her profession filled her with dread and gloom. Be honest with yourself, she chided, silently acknowledging that she had no interest in spending one more evening gambling. The fever had never taken hold of her as it had her father. She could walk away and never miss it.

Camille looked back at her friend. "If I don't belong in a smoke-filled saloon, why did you and Nate persuade me to come to West Texas? Were you hoping to play matchmaker?"

"Yes." Bonnie pushed back from the table, walking across the room to join her.

"McKinnon thought so."

"I'm sure he also knew that you'd have a handful of marriage proposals the first night. Good, hardworking ranchers, many of them quite wealthy, and each one longing for a woman to warm his heart and home."

"A man so desperate that he would take someone like me for a mate?" Camille couldn't believe it, not after all the blatant propositions or subtle innuendos that had been thrown her way for years. "A plaything, perhaps, but not a wife."

"You forget that we have a major shortage of women. Generally, the men here are different than what you're used to. As long as a person is honest with current dealings, they don't ask questions about who you are or where you've been. No doubt there are plenty of folks here who left a distasteful past."

"McKinnon said the same thing." Camille expected that held true for men, but she doubted people had the same standards about women.

"I doubt there is much in his past he'd worry about. Even so, many of the men, such as Ty and his brother, started with nothing and have built empires."

Amused, Camille asked dryly, "McKinnon has an empire?"

"Well, I suppose that's an exaggeration but close to it." Bonnie slipped her arm around Camille's waist, giving her a loving hug. "I know you well enough to figure you have a nice tidy nest egg put away and that you don't need to worry about making a living for a while."

"A long while. I've made some good investments. But I'd go crazy with nothing to do."

"Believe me, dear, a husband and a home will give you plenty to do."

"I know you mean well." Camille's sigh was filled with regret. "But you forget that I loved a man once, and it only brought me heartache. Even if I find someone I can trust—and that is very doubtful—he won't want me once he learns about Anthony."

"Don't tell him."

"It wouldn't take him long to figure it out on our wedding night." She had only been with one man, but that had been enough for people to call her a harlot. And, she thought sadly, she supposed she had been, even though she'd been barely nineteen, suddenly left alone in the world, and terrified by it.

"By then it would be too late. You'd already be married."

Camille stared at her. "You honestly think I should do that?"

Bonnie shrugged. "Most men sow wild oats before they get married. They shouldn't be so judgmental toward a woman who's done the same."

"I'm not sure living with a man for six months would be considered wild oats."

"At least you showed commitment." Bonnie grinned and pushed open the back door. "Let's go sit out here on the porch." She took one rocking chair, and Camille took the other. "I love living here where there aren't so many people. It's building up, and I expect before long I won't have a clear view of the hills, so I enjoy them whenever I can. Even then, I don't think Willow Grove will ever become a big city."

"But it's big enough for a newspaper?"

Bonnie glanced at her with a puzzled expression. "Yes, and it's a good one, too, but I hear Mr. Hill is going to shut it down due to his health."

"Not if he can find someone to help him. McKinnon thinks I should become Hill's partner. Then I'd be respectable."

"He actually said that? So you'd be respectable?"

"No, not really. But that's what he meant." Partly, anyway. How could he have guessed that she secretly longed for a different life? She hadn't even realized what she was looking for until he'd said it. One that gives you peace.

"Angel, I think you should do it." Bonnie's voice rose in her excitement. "You've always had a way with words and a knack for writing. Your letters are so full of interesting stories that they're like reading a book or a newspaper."

"McKinnon said Mr. Hill wants someone to handle the business end of things, but that he might let me try my hand at writing something." Excitement raced through her. It would be a dream come true if she only dared take the chance.

"Nate won't care if you don't work in his saloon. We haven't told anyone about you. Figured if you changed your mind, it would be better that way. Besides, I've been trying to get him to sell it and do something else."

"Does he have anything in mind?"

"Nothing that he's mentioned. He says he's studying on it, but I'm not sure how seriously. I want him to have a business where he doesn't have to work every day. He does have more help now, so he's not gone all the time, but I'd love to have him home more."

"He said he wasn't working tonight. Are you going to the box supper?"

Bonnie nodded happily. "I finished decorating the box a few days ago. It turned out pretty nice." Her smile faded. "Oh, dear, I didn't even think about it being your first evening in town."

"Don't worry about it. It seems that I have an engagement as well."

"Doing what?" said Bonnie, clearly annoyed that she had been inconsiderate.

"I have an invitation to the social." Camille paused, waiting for Bonnie's reaction. She could practically see the wheels spinning in her friend's mind.

Bonnie's eyes widened, and she leaned toward her, whispering, "Ty?"

"He's even bringing the supper."

"Glory be!" Bonnie sat back in her chair and began to rock furiously. "He never takes a woman anywhere. He's friendly enough once he gets there...charms all the ladies... but it's a well-known fact that he has not called on a woman since his wife died. But he invited you." With a bemused smile, she slowed the rocking to a comfortable pace. "The Lord surely does work in mysterious ways."

At six o'clock, Camille checked her image in the mirror one last time. She had decided to wear a green silk dress, hoping it wasn't too fancy for Willow Grove. Though there were several ruffles edged in white lace draped across the front of the skirt and meeting at the bustle in back, it wasn't overly decorated. The high, rounded neckline was sedately modest, even adorned with her mother's strand of pearls. Touching the necklace, she whispered, "I wish you were here, Mama. I think you would approve of Mr. McKinnon."

She turned away from the mirror to keep herself from fiddling with her hair. It had taken her an hour to pin it up in soft curls. Now she wished she had just worn a chignon or braided it and pinned it up in a coil. "Stop fussing," she muttered to herself. "It's only supper."

Supper with a man who interested her as none other ever had. The attraction she felt for Ty was completely different than what she had experienced when she was nineteen. Anthony had been smooth and charming, his honeyed words soothing and exciting at the same time. He had filled the emptiness after her father's death with promises he'd never intended to keep. Even with her, he had been the consummate con man. He bragged that he could talk a preacher out of the Sunday offering, then proceeded to prove it.

Ty McKinnon was also charming and exciting, but he had a protectiveness and a goodness in him that was far more appealing than sweet, flattering words. He seemed to take his faith in God to heart, and if he had been honest with her, he attempted to live by it. He'd said he loved the Lord and tried his best to please Him. She had never met a man who talked like that, much less lived that way.

She had heard about the fear of the Lord, mainly from the fire-and-brimstone corner preacher who had shouted condemnation at her from time to time in New Orleans. She did believe in God, and in those rare moments when she let herself think about it, the thought of facing Him some day frightened her. But her parents hadn't had much use for God after they'd lost everything during the war. She suspected that they had mostly gone to church in the first place simply because it was expected of them. Certainly neither of them had ever mentioned loving the Lord or doing something because it would please Him.

A firm knock startled her. Taking a deep breath, she opened the door. Ty stood there, more handsome than ever in his crisp white shirt, black suit and tie. He held his hat in his hands, nervously tapping a couple of fingers against the brim as he glanced around the hall. She noticed a tiny mark on his cheek where he had nicked it with the razor.

"Good evening, Mr. McKinnon," she said quietly, afraid that if she spoke normally he might bolt.

He looked at her, and his fingers grew still. A soft glow warmed his eyes as his gaze slid over her, then back to her face, lingering there. "Good evening, Miss Dupree," he said with a smile. "You're even more lovely than I'd expected."

"Thank you. You look quite dashing—and nervous."

He grimaced and rubbed the edge of one ear. "Sorry. I was hoping it didn't show."

"Bonnie explained that you haven't taken a woman anywhere since your wife's passing. I don't have to go if this is too difficult for you."

"Well, ma'am, leavin' you here would be mighty rude of me." He frowned, tightening his fingers on the hat brim. "Unless you don't want to go with me."

"Do you want me to?"

"Yes." He paused, squaring his shoulders. "Very much."

"And that bothers you."

"I have some conflicting emotions."

"I do, too. Going to the social makes me as nervous as a cat in a room full of rocking chairs, but I truly would like to spend the evening with you."

"Good." He relaxed with a sigh and a sheepish smile. "Now that we have that out of the way, are you ready to leave?"

"Yes. I'll get my purse and coat." She didn't need the wrap now, but she would later after the sun went down.

He waited in the hall and put on his Stetson as she fetched her things.

When she returned to the doorway, she hesitated. "I forgot to ask if I should wear a hat."

"And hide that pretty hair? Nope. I doubt if very many ladies will wear one, unless they have something new they want to show off." He stepped aside. "Do you like fried chicken?"

"Who doesn't? I hope you brought extra napkins." She pulled the door closed and locked it.

"I did. And biscuits and potato salad. I picked all that up at the restaurant, then added a box of French chocolates."

"I think I should be the one bidding on the supper." She looked up at him as they walked down the hall. "It's very nice of you to go to so much trouble."

He smiled, offering her his arm as they started down the stairs. "Collecting the food wasn't a problem, but decorating that hatbox was a new experience. I never realized how difficult it is to wrap something round. I left it over at the store. Didn't want any of the cowboys following the smell of that chicken."

Camille laughed. "More likely, you didn't want them to spot you carrying a fancy box." When they reached the lobby, she was surprised to see that it and the saloon were almost empty.

Ty glanced around the room. "Most folks are already on their way to the party. Considering some of the ranchers I saw in here earlier, I'm glad I stopped by the bank."

"Took out that loan, did you?"

He looked down at her and winked. "Decided I didn't need to. We've had a good month."

When they stepped outside, she released Ty's arm and picked up her skirt so the hem wouldn't drag in the dirt. He gently gripped her elbow as they walked down the boardwalk steps and across the street. "Is the supper at the school?"

"No. It's not big enough. We're holding it at the K. P. Hall."

"Knights of Pythias?" It was a fraternal order, organized for benevolent purposes.

"Yes. They recently rented the floor above the furniture store for their hall." He chuckled quietly. "And pay for it by renting it out to everybody else. But it makes a good place for parties."

They waited to let a horse and rider trot past. Several couples strolled along the sidewalk toward the K. P. Hall, carrying decorated boxes and baskets. Perhaps a hundred cowboys wandered around downtown, catching up on the latest news, going in and out of the stores, saloons and billiard halls. Others, fresh from a visit to the barber's, were headed toward the social, along with a handful of well-dressed cattlemen.

Camille noted that many of the men turned to watch as they crossed the street. She caught the raised eyebrows, slight frowns and an occasional grin when their gazes shifted to Ty. Hoping he would not regret his impulsive invitation, she put on a bright smile when he opened the door to his store. "You weren't exaggerating when you told Joanna it was a very big store."

Ty laughed, though he seemed a bit tense again. "Largest one this side of Fort Worth. We supply most of the ranches to the west and north of here, as well as the folks here in town." A hint of amusement softened his expression as they walked past a case of musical instruments. "Carry everything from A to Z."

Camille stopped to study the case, which contained harmonicas, a guitar, a banjo, a fiddle—and a zither. She glanced around the store, spotted bins of fresh fruit and grinned. "Apples to zithers."

"Sharp as well as pretty." His pleased smile warmed her unwise heart. "Our supper is in my office at the back of the store." He touched the small of her back, gently urging her forward.

They walked past the main counter, where a clerk was pouring coffee beans into the large store grinder. Staring at Camille, he didn't notice the beans overflowing until a couple bounced off the counter onto the floor. Blushing furiously, he dropped the bag and swept the coffee beans on the counter into a pile with his hand.

Ty stopped, shoving a few that had fallen onto the floor out of the way. "Ed, this is Miss Camille Dupree. Miss Dupree, Ed Bennett."

"Good evening, Mr. Bennett."

"Evenin', ma'am. Welcome to Willow Grove."

"Thank you."

"Ed is my right-hand man here at the store. The place would fall apart without him."

Recovering from his embarrassment, Ed smiled at Camille. "Got him fooled."

"I doubt that."

"We'd better pick up the box and head over to the hall," said Ty. "Don't want to be late."

"Might save you some money," said Ed. "Sure would like to be a fly on the wall at that supper tonight." Chuckling, the clerk went back to his task. "Yes, sir, goin' to be an interesting evening."

"Too bad you have to work," Ty said dryly.

"Maybe you should give me a bonus for missing all the fun."

"Not a chance." Ty nodded toward the back of the store. "Let's get that chicken before Ed decides to eat it."

As they reached his office, Ty breathed a quiet sigh. "Good thing there's a lull in customers at the moment, or we'd never get to the party." He opened the office door, stepping back so she could go inside. The decorated hatbox sat in the middle of his desk.

"Think it will do?" he asked softly.

"It's beautiful." Sure enough, he had used shimmering pink silk to cover the box, then pulled all the edges up in the center of the top and tied them together with a big green bow. Nestled in the ruffle of material and tucked beneath the bow was a white silk camellia. Tenderness swept through her, both at the memory the image evoked and at his thoughtfulness. "It's almost like the one Mama made when I was a little girl, before folks quit having parties. Before we lost everything." She looked up to see understanding in his eyes. "Thank you."

"You're welcome. It was worth mangling three pieces of silk just to see your face right now."

Camille laughed, running her fingers over the silk. "Three?"

"I told you it took me a while to figure out how to do it."

"Where did you find the flower?"

"Pilfered it from a lady's hat I found on the shelf." He picked up the box. "Ready?"

Anticipation and sudden fear made her stomach churn. What if she saw someone who knew her, perhaps a man who had played cards with her? It wasn't likely, but not impossible. Plenty of people had moved west from San Antonio, even New Orleans. Simply being new in town would cause a stir. Being with Ty would attract even more attention.

Her mother had tried to teach her to be a true Southern lady, but what if she slipped and said or did something improper? Except for the first seven years of her life, she had been raised around saloons and gaming halls. A wave of panic rushed through her. I don't know how to behave with these people. She glanced up at Ty, aware that her face reflected her trepidation. *Please God, don't let me embarrass him or bring him shame.*

A frown creased his brow. "What's wrong?"

"I don't belong there."

He set the box down on the desk and took her hand, holding it with gentle firmness. She had come to expect honesty from him, and he didn't change now. "Folks might not think so next week, depending on what you decide to do. But even if you go to work at Nate's, I want to be your friend, and I'm honored by your company tonight."

In that moment, Camille knew she would never again earn her living with a deck of cards.

Chapter Four

Inside the hall, Ty handed the box to Mrs. Nickson, the school board chairman's wife, and introduced her to Camille.

"How nice that you could come tonight, Miss Dupree. I heard that you arrived on the stage with Mrs. Watson. You're every bit as lovely as she said you were." She glanced at Ty with a mischievous smile. "You're going to have plenty of competition tonight, Ty."

"I came prepared." He scanned the crowd, relieved to see there weren't as many single men present as he'd expected. Ty estimated the ratio of men to women at about ten to one, including Joanna and the other girls her age. Evidently, word about Camille hadn't reached the more distant ranches and their affluent owners. "I hope you have some extra suppers for all these gents who are going to lose out."

"We do. But they still have to pay for them. It is a fundraiser, after all. Miss Dupree, if you'd like, Kathy will hang up your coat."

"Thank you." Camille handed her coat to the girl standing beside Mrs. Nickson.

"You'd better find a seat. The bidding has already started."

Ty offered Camille his arm, keenly aware of the light touch of her fingers as she rested them on his forearm. "My brother and sister-in-law are over there in the corner. They're saving us a place."

"Too bad he didn't claim a table closer to the door," she murmured.

"He planned to, but I think they were running late, too."

If he hadn't been so tied in knots, the others' reactions to their arrival might have been amusing. People stretched this way and that, some even standing on tiptoe for a better look. Jaws dropped, conversations stopped, and a predatory gleam lit the eyes of men he normally called friends. He wondered how many were plotting his rapid demise.

"Ready to run the gauntlet?" he whispered.

Her fingers tightened on his arm, and she looked up, meeting his gaze. He caught a flicker of fear in her eyes, and without thinking, covered her hand with his.

Her eyes widened slightly, and she smiled. "Ready."

A young woman nearby muttered an unladylike curse. Recognizing her voice, Ty didn't bother to look in her direction.

Camille's lips twitched as they stepped away. "An admirer?"

Ty nodded. "And she knows the feeling is not mutual."

"I don't think she had given up hope."

"Don't know why not. I told her point-blank that I wasn't interested in anything beyond friendship."

"Are you always so blunt?"

He ducked his head, speaking quietly near her ear. "Only when a woman decides to crawl through my bedroom window in the middle of the night."

"Oh, my." Camille laughed, the light, musical sound dancing around him. "I expect to hear the rest of that story sometime."

Breathing in her rose perfume, he was suddenly aware of how intimate the exchange appeared. And felt. He straightened and tried to make his voice light. He didn't quite succeed. "I can arrange that."

She glanced up at him, a hint of concern replacing her smile.

He took advantage of the ongoing auction to head straight for Cade and Jessie. When they reached their table, he breathed a sigh of relief.

Though his brother gave Camille his friendliest smile, Ty knew he was sizing her up. He hadn't told Cade much about her, other than that he'd met her on the trip from San Angelo and that she was beautiful. He figured he didn't have to say anything about being attracted to her. Bringing her to the social said that plain enough. They exchanged introductions, then took their seats at the table. Camille smiled and mouthed a greeting to Nate and Bonnie Flynn, who were seated two tables over. Ty nodded a greeting to her friends.

The school board chairman held up a basket trimmed in pink lace. Nickson lifted one corner of the fancy print cloth covering the food and smacked his lips. "We have hard-boiled eggs, some cheese and fruit, a loaf of bread and a whole apple pie. That pie looks so good, a man could make a full meal just with it. Who'll start us off?"

"One dollar." Bobby smiled at Joanna, who blushed furiously as she smiled back.

"I assume that's Bobby?" whispered Camille.

Ty nodded.

"A dollar-fifty," called out Mr. Watson.

Joanna frowned at her father.

"She eats supper with you every night," called one of his friends, prompting a ripple of laughter.

"Yep, and I know how good that pie is," replied her father with an affectionate smile.

"A dollar seventy-five," said Bobby.

"Two dollars." A young cowboy stepped forward from the line of men along the wall, his gaze focused on Joanna. She stared at him in shock.

"Two-fifty."

The cowboy glanced at Bobby, then looked back at Joanna. "Three-fifty."

"Five."

"Seven."

Joanna blinked at the cowboy's last bid. Her expression slowly changed from shock to interest as she studied him. A faint smile touched her lips before she shyly lowered her eyes.

"Uh-oh," murmured Ty.

Cade chuckled. "This could get interesting."

"It doesn't seem fair," said Camille. "That man is probably five years older than Bobby."

Ty leaned a little closer to her. "If you weren't here, half the men along the wall would be bidding on her supper. Even the ones older than her father."

Bobby squared his shoulders, his expression resolute. "Ten dollars."

The cowboy glanced around the room and caught the eye of another pretty young miss who gave him an encouraging smile. He looked back at Joanna, winked, and stepped back against the wall.

"Ten dollars going once, twice...three times. That's it. Determination won the day." Nickson handed the basket to Bobby. "Enjoy your dinner."

The lad nodded and walked to Joanna's side. But he didn't appear particularly happy.

"The trials of young love," said Jessie. She straightened and nudged Cade in the side as Nickson picked up another box. "That's our supper."

"Don't you go smiling at anybody who bids against me."

"We're supposed to be raising money." Jessie sent her husband a teasing look. "I see a couple of gentlemen who called on me before we got married. They might be interested in a home-cooked meal."

Nickson lifted the lid on the box. "Fried catfish, coleslaw, potato salad, biscuits and chocolate cake. May I eat with whoever buys this?"

"Nope." Cade stood. "Fifteen dollars."

"Twenty." Ty grinned at his brother.

"Twenty-five."

The sheriff, Ransom Starr, lifted his hand. "Twenty-seven." When Cade frowned at him, he shrugged. "I like catfish."

"So do I," said Cade. He glared at his old friend, and everyone laughed. "And I don't intend to let you to eat supper with my beautiful wife. Thirty-five dollars."

"Now I know why the county commissioners didn't give me that raise," said Ransom with a good-natured grin.

"Thirty-five dollars. Going once…going twice…sold to Mr. Cade McKinnon."

Cade went to the makeshift stage and picked up the box. He took a detour by Ransom on the way back to the table. Lifting the lid, he waved it under the lawman's nose as he passed by.

Ransom made a great show of smelling the contents. "Careful or I'll throw you in jail for disturbing the peace."

"Yours?"

"Yep." Ransom pretended to reach for some fish.

Cade slammed the lid down and headed back to their table amid laughter and applause.

Ty turned to Camille, glad to see her laughing and clapping. "Having fun?"

"Yes. I assume your brother is a good friend of the sheriff's?"

"Both of us are. We rode together when we were Texas Rangers. Ransom showed up last summer and kidnapped Jessie."

"He what?" Camille stared at him.

"He was a private detective tracking a killer, a man named Wyman. Turned out that Wyman was head of a cattle-rustling operation, only we all thought a local attorney, Doolin, was the man in charge. Jessie's brother had infiltrated the gang, leading to the lawyer's arrest. Wyman was afraid Doolin would spill the beans if he was convicted, so he wanted Jessie kidnapped to keep her brother from testifying."

"But how did Sheriff Starr become involved in the kidnapping?"

"He had followed Wyman to a saloon on the outskirts of town and overheard him trying to get a couple of men to do the job. One man refused, and the other wasn't capable of doing it on his own. When Ransom realized that the woman they were talking about was Cade's fiancée, he volunteered."

"He actually took her somewhere?"

"Miles from town. But he left little signs along the way. Made it pretty easy to track him once we spotted the first one. When we found them, he explained that Wyman was actually the ringleader and had hired him to help take Jessie. The man with him had been tricked into becoming part of the rustlers, then kept in the gang because he feared for his mother's safety. That was the same ploy Wyman used to get him to kidnap Jessie. He was more than happy to throw in with us and testify against them.

"We returned to town the next day right before the trial. Wyman panicked and pulled a gun he had hidden in the courtroom. Ransom shot and killed him before anyone else could even clear leather."

"So he became your sheriff."

"The sheriff we had at the time was moving up to the U.S. Marshal post. He suggested Ransom for the job. After the way he'd handled Wyman, he was quite a hero. We're fortunate to have him."

"Given how quickly things settled down this morning, he must be keeping the peace."

"That he is. Cade and I had known for a long time that he was a good man, but he made his reputation in this country that day in the courtroom. He doesn't put up with any foolishness."

Cade returned to the table and sat down. "Whew! What a battle. Now, I'm really starving."

Jessie rolled her eyes. "I don't know how you could be." She leaned forward to talk to Ty and Camille. "He ate half the chocolate cake before we came."

"Just a quarter of it. The kids had some, too."

"How many children do you have?" asked Camille.

"Brad is ten, and Ellie is five." Jessie smiled at Cade, love shining in her face. "She has her daddy and her uncle wrapped around her little finger. They act tough, but they're really big softies."

"She is a sweetheart." Cade squeezed Jessie's shoulder. "Like her mama. I'm proud as can be of Brad. When I married Jessie, I got myself a ready-made family."

"And he's been happy as a pig in slop ever since." Ty hadn't paid much attention to the last two meals that had been auctioned off. They went quickly, with the husbands outbidding a few of their neighbors who were only hiking up the price.

The young cowboy who had bid against Bobby managed to buy supper with the other young woman who caught his eye. A few more single girls' boxes caused a flurry of bids until two more spit-and-polished cowboys won the pleasure of sharing a meal with a young lady.

Then Nickson picked up a hatbox wrapped in pink silk.

Ty tensed, praying that he had enough money in his pockets. As soon as he made his second bid, people would realize whose company he was vying for.

"Well, now, this is a pretty one."

Camille glanced at Ty, a twinkle in her eyes.

"But I can't see what is in it. No way to open it without ruining the decoration." The chairman lifted it up and took a deep sniff. "Fried chicken. Don't know what else, but it sure enough smells like fried chicken. Who'll open the bidding?"

"Two dollars."

Ty couldn't see who had spoken up.

"Two-fifty," called one of the cowboys along the wall.

"Five dollars," said Ty.

"Ten dollars," called one of the ranchers who had seen him with Camille in the hotel that morning.

Ty noticed Ransom studying him and Camille.

"Fifteen." Ty held his breath, waiting for the reaction. He didn't have to wait long.

"Twenty." Another rancher jumped to his feet, his gaze fixed on Camille.

"Twenty-five." Ty tried to not appear anxious as he stood.

"Thirty-five."

"Forty," yelled the second rancher.

Ty glanced at Camille. Though she appeared completely composed, her cheeks were pink and her hands were clasped tightly on her lap. "Fifty."

"Fifty-five."

Ty opened his mouth but the other man cut him off.

"Sixty."

The two ranchers were getting too caught up in the excitement. He had to raise the stakes.

"One hundred dollars," Ty said calmly. He heard a few murmurs, but most conversation had stopped.

"One hundred-twenty-five." The man joining the bidding was the one Ty had warned Camille about.

Ty took a deep breath, looking at Camille again. If he didn't throw a rope around her right now, he might lose any chance with her. "Three hundred."

A collective gasp mingled with his brother's low whistle.

Ty stood his ground, staring down the last man who had bid.

The rancher held up his hands and shook his head. "Past my limit." He nodded to Camille. "Maybe another time, ma'am."

Nickson cleared his throat. "We have three hundred once...three hundred twice...sold to the mayor." He smiled at Camille. "On behalf of our school, thank you for coming tonight, ma'am."

That broke the silence. Furious clapping and excited conversation erupted as Ty made his way up to the stage for the box. He hurried back to the table, troubled by Camille's bright red face. Her beauty had triggered the bidding war, but he had made a spectacle of her.

He sat down, putting the box on the table in front of them, wishing it could shield them from curious eyes. The auction was finished. Cade and Jessie busied themselves with digging into their box and setting out their supper. Ty figured he'd get a grilling from his brother later, but Cade would never question him in front of Camille.

Ty pulled the flower from the bow and laid it on the table. "I'm sorry I embarrassed you," he said quietly. "I had to try to stop it before they went beyond what I had."

"You spent so much. Now, people truly will think the worst."

"They will think that I'm captivated by a beautiful, charming lady. And they're right." He untied the bow and lifted the box away from the silk. She pulled the material out of his way, folding it. "Folks know I'm not a tightwad. Raising money for the school is a worthy cause. Enjoying the evening with you is, too."

And he did enjoy it, more than he'd thought he could. Once she relaxed, she was delightful company. Witty, charming, intelligent and cordial to Cade and Jessie. The food was good, too, though he didn't pay much attention to it—except when she bit into a piece of chocolate and sighed. He mentally did an inventory of how many boxes of French chocolates he had in the store and decided he'd better order another carton right away.

"I never did hear what brings you to Willow Grove, Miss Dupree," said Jessie.

Ty held his breath. If Camille were completely honest about her history, he didn't know how his sister-in-law would react. Jessie's first husband had been a worthless scoundrel who'd spent his time drinking, gambling and running around with other women. He had seldom bothered to work. Instead, he had taken the money Jessie earned as a housekeeper, leaving her with barely enough to feed their children. Getting himself killed by an irate husband was the only good thing the man had ever done for his family. Though Jessie was as kind as the day was long, she didn't cotton much to people who ran saloons or worked in them.

"I wanted to see the last of the Wild West before it disappeared. Everyone assures me that Willow Grove is rapidly becoming civilized, but I'm happy to see that it isn't completely tame yet."

"One of the new boys at the Lazy R decided to announce his arrival this morning with a little gunplay," said Ty.

"Which didn't sit well with Ransom, I expect. That's one cowboy who is spending his first night in town in the calaboose." Cade laughed and rested his hand on Jessie's shoulder, caressing the back of her neck with his thumb.

Sadness crept into Ty's heart. How many times had he touched Amanda in the same tender way? He was used to the loving, comfortable affection between Cade and his wife. Normally, he rejoiced to see his brother so happy and content. Tonight, their closeness reminded him that his hands were empty, that he had no one to touch, no one to love.

Camille glanced at Ty as if trying to decide how much she should say. She turned back to Jessie. "I have friends here. Nate and Bonnie Flynn. I've known them since I was a girl. At the time, my father worked with Nate in New Orleans. They've been begging me for over a year to come for a visit."

"I've talked to Mrs. Flynn a bit at church," said Jessie. "She seems very nice."

"She is. They've been kind to me, especially after my father's death several years ago."

"You should have Ty bring you out to the ranch," said Cade.

"I'd like that. I've never been to a ranch."

"I'll give you a grand tour." Ty rested his hand on the back of her chair, being careful not to touch her. "Otherwise, Cade's liable to put you to work."

A twinkle lit his brother's eyes. "Have you ropin' cows in no time."

They chatted with Cade and Jessie for a few more minutes. Nate and Bonnie came over, and they visited with them until others began stopping by the table to meet Camille. Ty noted that her friends said nothing about Camille's profession or that she would be working at the White Buffalo. He decided that he would never have any time alone with her if they didn't leave soon. "Shall we try to make our escape?"

Camille glanced toward Mrs. Watson, who was bearing down on them. "It may take a while."

"We can work our way toward the door." He stood and pulled out Camille's chair. Earlier, she had rolled up the silk and tied the ribbon around it, tucking the flower beneath it. She picked up the bundle along with her purse as she stood.

"How lovely to see you again, Miss Dupree. And especially in the company of our handsome mayor." Mrs. Watson was practically busting her buttons. "I told Joanna...and a few others…that I thought we had a romance in the making. How exciting to see I was right."

"You're getting ahead of things, Mrs. Watson." Ty plastered on the most charming smile he could muster considering how much he wanted to wring her neck. "I simply thought this would be a good opportunity for Miss Dupree to meet people."

"Meet, perhaps. But you certainly weren't inclined to have her eat with anyone else." Mrs. Watson laughed.

"A generous donation to the school fund," he said tightly.

"I expect everyone knows how generous Mr. McKinnon is." Camille smiled at Mrs. Watson. "I noticed that Joanna had two young men vying for her company this evening." She slid her arm around the other woman's waist. "I really should go speak to her. I wanted a closer look at her pretty dress. Was it specially made for her?"

"Yes. We found the pattern in *The Delineator* and had the local dressmaker stitch it up. She did an excellent job."

"I'll have to pay her a visit. I could use some new dresses."

Ty was annoyed when she walked away without him, until he realized that Joanna was standing right by the doorway. Chuckling, he retrieved the hatbox containing the remnants of their supper.

"Will we see y'all at the house?" Cade stood also, waiting while Jessie finished a conversation with a friend who had stopped by the table.

"Maybe." Ty shrugged, mindful of his brother's scrutiny. "It's a nice evening. I thought she might like to go for a walk down by the creek."

Cade nodded. "It's good to see you with someone."

"Don't know if it will lead to anything, but I like her."

"I noticed." His brother grinned and squeezed his shoulder. "I'd say you like her a lot." His expression sobered. "I'm glad. The Lord was right when He said it isn't good for a man to be alone. I never knew what true happiness was until I found Jessie. Now, go on before some other ornery cuss decides to escort her home."

When Ty caught up to Camille, he smiled at Joanna. "I told you someone besides Bobby would want to eat with you."

"I was so surprised. I don't even know that cowboy."

"Did Bobby leave already?"

"No. He went after more punch. I think he's still mad."

"Try to cheer him up. It will be bad for business if he mopes around the store all day on Monday."

Joanna giggled. "I will. Mama said I could invite him over for dinner tomorrow."

Ty touched Camille's elbow. "Shall we go?"

She nodded, bidding Joanna and Mrs. Watson a good evening while Ty fetched her coat. He helped her put it on, being careful not to touch her in any way that Mrs. Watson and her cronies might consider intimate. Ty followed her out the door and down the stairs. When they reached the sidewalk, he moved to her side.

Boisterous laughter poured out the open door of a saloon as they walked past. She barely spared the room a glance. He wondered if she could size up the competition in such a short time, then decided she probably could. After all, there wasn't a saloon or gambling hall in town that could hold a candle to one with an angel.

Angelique. The name evoked a sense of mystery, a hint of the exotic. It was a beautiful name, but somehow it fit the gambler more than the genteel woman walking beside him. He preferred Camille, both the name and the lady.

"Would you care to take a stroll down by the creek? It's only a few blocks away, at the end of town. There will probably be other folks taking the evening air, too."

"It is pleasant out, but we probably shouldn't."

Disappointment swept through him. "Why?"

"We've provided enough grist for the rumor mill for one evening."

"By morning, everyone in town will be talking about us anyway." Ty paused in front of his store. "Let me throw this box inside." He opened the door and tossed the hatbox on a counter. "Ed, would you put that it my office?"

"Sure thing, boss."

He moved back to her side and held out his arm. "Walk with me a while." As if on cue, the full moon rose above the grove of willows at the edge of town.

Camille slipped her hand around his arm, laughing softly. "You're a very persuasive man, McKinnon."

They strolled down the street in companionable silence, broken only by an occasional greeting when they met someone. When they reached the willow grove, Ty led her to a two-person wooden bench beside the creek. He decided that adding a half-dozen benches and declaring the area a park had been his brightest idea since becoming mayor. "Welcome to Willow Grove City Park."

"It's lovely. My goodness, look at all those stars." She sat down, smoothing her coat out of the way so he would have room to join her. "But you were mistaken. There isn't anyone else here."

"God is kind."

"So you asked Him to keep everyone else away?"

"No, but I'm sure He knew I wanted a little time alone with you. Seems like we've hardly been able to say two words to each other without an audience. What do you think of Willow Grove?"

"It's a good town, with good people."

"They like you."

"They seemed to, didn't they?" Wonder shaded her voice. Ty was taken aback by the emotion shimmering in her eyes. "I will always thank you for that, Mr. McKinnon."

"I'm afraid their attitudes will change if you start working at the White Buffalo. Even Jessie's. Her first husband was a drinking, gambling womanizer."

"She would hate me." Camille took a deep breath and looked away. "I don't want that. I don't want to meet Mrs. Watson or the other women on the street and have them turn away in disgust. Tonight I had a taste of how different life could be. It's a nice feeling."

Ty caught his breath. "You're not going to work for Nate?"

"No." She looked up at him. "I've decided not to. If I ask Nate and Bonnie to keep quiet about my past, they will."

"So will I. I haven't said anything to anyone, not even Cade."

"Do you honestly think the newspaper editor would consider having me as his partner?"

"He'd miss a good opportunity if he didn't. He's a very bright man, so I expect he'll see the wisdom of it."

"I've thought about the possibility all day. Bonnie's excited about it. You were right. They encouraged me to come out here so they could play matchmaker, not because Nate needed my help." Camille looked up at the moon. "But I didn't make up my mind until tonight."

"When you discovered how much people like you."

She shook her head. "No, it was when you said you were honored by my company, even though you thought I might still go to work at the White Buffalo."

Ty felt the wall around his heart crumble a little more. "I meant it."

"I know." She met his gaze. "No one has ever treated me with that kind of respect."

> To every thing there is a season, and a time to every purpose under the heaven: A time to weep, and a time to laugh; a time to mourn, and a time to dance....

And a time to heal. He figured they both needed that.

Chapter Five

Ty and Camille stayed at the park for a little while talking. When it began to grow colder, he decided he'd better take her back to the hotel.

"Would you mind walking me over to Bonnie and Nate's instead?" asked Camille.

"Not at all. I assume he'll see you back to your room?"

"Yes. I'm sure you'd be welcome to stay and visit."

"Another time. I've taken up enough of your first day in town. I expect they want you to themselves."

They didn't talk much on the way, simply enjoying the moonlit evening and each other's company. Ty had forgotten how pleasant silence could be when it was shared with someone.

Nate opened the front door of his house as they strolled up to the porch. "I was wondering if you'd show up." He grinned at Ty. "Thought maybe you had better things to do than come by here."

"We've been to the park," said Camille. "Did you enjoy the supper?"

Nate stepped back, motioning them inside. "If I'd known those things were that entertaining, I'd have gone to one sooner."

"It did get a bit interesting." Ty followed Camille inside.

Nate chuckled, slipping his arm around Bonnie's waist when she stepped up beside him. "You could say that. But we don't need to stand here. Let's go sit down."

"Y'all go ahead," said Ty. "I'd like to come back another time, but tonight I expect you have a lot of catching up to do."

"That we do." Bonnie glanced at Camille with an impish grin.

Ty turned to his lovely companion. "Thank you for a very nice evening."

Her smile warmed his heart. "It was my pleasure. Thank you for taking me and for providing the supper."

"I'll talk to Cade about going out to the ranch next week. Is any particular day better for you?"

"No. I don't have anything else planned."

Ty shook hands with Nate, then nodded politely to the women. "Good evening, ladies."

When he stepped out the door and turned to pull it closed, Camille was the only one standing there.

"It's been quite a day," she said softly, her hand curled around the doorknob.

Images of the day flashed through his mind—seeing her in the White Buffalo, holding her close during the shooting spree, nervously waiting in front of her hotel-room door, then having his breath taken away when she opened it. The tenderness, mingled with a hint of sadness that had filled her face when she saw the hatbox. He suspected he would be reliving this day all night long. "Yes, it has. I wouldn't trade a minute of it."

"Not even when you stormed into the White Buffalo ready to run me out of town?"

Ty grimaced. "I wouldn't have gone that far. Reckon maybe I overreacted."

"It wasn't what you expected," she said gently. "I should have told you why I was coming here when we first met."

"Why didn't you?"

"It was nice simply being Camille. I could be myself, not play a role. I haven't done that since before I started working." She frowned thoughtfully. "That's been over eight years now. I knew you'd find out about the gambling soon enough. I suppose I wanted to put it off as long as I could."

"You're a mighty fine lady, Miss Dupree," he said, resting his hand on the doorjamb. "I expect you are even as the Angel."

"It's the way my mama taught me to be. Daddy said it was part of what drew men to my table."

Ty laughed quietly. "Men are attracted to you because you're the most beautiful woman they've ever seen. But they stayed at your table—even though they were probably losing money—because you're a true lady. Charming, graceful, soft-spoken, polite. You bring out the best in men."

"Not always."

Without realizing it, he had shifted toward her. All he had to do was lean down, tip his head slightly, and they would be lined up perfectly for a kiss. A kiss he wanted very much. Surprised and embarrassed, he straightened quickly. "Sorry."

"I wasn't talking about you." She glanced at his mouth. Was that longing he saw in her eyes? "Thank you again for a lovely evening."

"You're welcome. I'll see if Saturday will be all right for us to go out to the ranch." Ty didn't want to wait that long to see her again. Though he probably should. He had the feeling he was tiptoeing around the edge of quicksand. "Good night."

"Good night." Her voice and smile were just a little too bright. She had pulled back, too.

He wanted to kick himself.

But as he turned away, she spoke again. Her voice had returned to normal. "Saturday would be good."

He stopped and looked back at her. "Yes, it would. Dress comfortably. We'll need to leave early, about eight o'clock."

She laughed, her hands resting on the door. "It's a good thing I've been traveling lately and am used to early mornings. Before this trip, I rarely got up before noon."

"I'll let you know if it doesn't work out. Then you can sleep as late as you want."

"Thanks." Giving him a smile to take with him, she closed the door.

Ty caught himself whistling as he walked down the street and turned the corner, heading for his house about five blocks away. He quit making noise, not wanting to disturb the neighbors any more than their barking dogs already were. Besides, after seeing him at the supper with Camille, they would put too much into the fact that he seemed so happy.

Once at the house, he had just enough time to light a lamp and take off his jacket and tie before Cade tapped on his back door.

"Come on in." He filled a glass from the kitchen hand pump, taking a drink as Cade walked through the door.

"Did you go down to the park?"

"Yep." Ty took another long drink and set the glass on the counter. "We sat there a while and talked. Then she asked me to walk her over to the Flynns'."

"You're right. She's one pretty lady." Cade wandered into the living room, sprawling in one corner of the sofa, propping one bare foot on the cushion. It was a good thing they had a nicely worn path between their back doors. Otherwise, he would be picking grass burrs out of his feet. "Tell me about her."

"She's originally from Louisiana." Ty settled across from him in his favorite chair, a big overstuffed one with a footstool. "Her parents owned a plantation when she was little, but they lost everything in the war. I think that's when they moved to New Orleans."

"Where her father worked for Nate. In a saloon?"

Ty hesitated, wondering how much he could tell his brother without him guessing the rest. He hadn't promised to keep her father's profession a secret. "Yes. As a gambler."

"Well, Miss Dupree seemed to turn out all right anyway." Cade grinned. "Must have been her mother's influence."

Ty relaxed. "Camille said her mama taught her to be a lady."

"It shows. Camille is it? On a first-name basis already?"

"In my mind anyway. If I've slipped up and called her that, she didn't protest. I thought I might bring her out to the ranch on Saturday."

"Fine with us." Cade studied him for a minute or two. "Three hundred dollars?"

"I didn't want Peasley near her."

"Don't blame you, but you might have tried two hundred first."

"It's my money."

"I didn't think you pilfered it from the store."

Ty glanced away. "I wanted to make a point."

"That she's your woman."

"That I'm interested in her."

Cade laughed and shifted his position. "Little brother, anybody with eyes in their head could see that the minute you two walked in the door. In case you haven't noticed, she's interested in you, too."

"I noticed." He got up and walked over to his bedroom. Inside the door, he hooked first one boot in the bootjack and tugged it off, then the other. Going back to his chair, he sat down and wiggled his sock-covered toes. "I can't decide whether I'm caught in a whirlwind or about to fall into quicksand."

"Either one could be tricky." Cade's expression grew serious. "There's nothing wrong with having feelings for her."

Ty leaned his head back on the chair and stared up at the ceiling. "Amanda was perfect. Sweet, gentle, kind, loving and smart. Not to mention beautiful. Nobody can take her place. How can I be so attracted to someone else?" *Enchanted* described it better.

"Well, in the first place, Amanda wasn't perfect. Almost, but not quite. Nobody is. And you're not looking for Camille to replace Amanda in your heart. If she expects you to, then she's not the woman you want. God gives us the ability to love. I don't think He puts restrictions on how many people we can care for."

"True." Ty looked over at his brother. "Do you like her?"

"She seems nice. We enjoyed talking to her. Reckon I'll need to get to know her better before I can give you a real answer." Cade pushed himself up off the sofa. "I'll leave you to your daydreaming. Try to get a little sleep. Don't want you snoring through the preacher's sermon."

"You could always poke me with your elbow and keep me awake."

"Nope. More fun to watch everybody laughing at you."

"Go back to your wife."

"Best advice I've heard all day. Did you invite Camille to go to church with you?"

"No. I thought about it, but I was afraid I'd seem too pushy. Maybe she'll come to church tomorrow with Mrs. Flynn."

"That'd be good. See you in the morning."

"'Night." Ty didn't bother to get up. He and Cade didn't stand on formality. He stayed in the chair for about fifteen minutes, then decided the bed would be more comfortable. His shoulder was still sore from driving the stage.

Carrying the lamp into the bedroom, he sat down on the bed and pulled off his socks, tossing them into a basket in the corner. He unbuttoned his shirt and wondered if Camille would go to church the next morning, or any time. She had indicated that she hadn't attended a service since she was a girl. Did she believe in Jesus? Or even in God?

"Reckon that's something I'd better find out."

Chapter Six

"You two are the talk of the town." Bonnie curled her bare feet up on the couch and tucked them beneath her skirt. "I don't think there's been this much excitement since Sheriff Starr shot that murderer, Wyman."

"I'm used to gossip." Camille propped her elbow on the back of the couch, resting her head against her hand. "Though this isn't the normal kind." She looked first at Bonnie, then Nate. "I'm not going to work for you."

"I figured you might not." The tenderness of a long friendship softened his eyes. "I don't really need you there. I'd much rather see you test your wings with something else, whether it be with Ty or taking on the newspaper business."

"Thanks. I'm going to talk to Mr. Hill at the paper tomorrow. If he isn't interested in working with me, I guess I'll twiddle my thumbs for a while."

"Not if Ty is around, which I think he will be," said Bonnie. "The man is taken with you."

"Which isn't unusual." Nate took a sip of whiskey. "Most men are."

"But this is different. Ty isn't the kind of man she would meet in a saloon."

Nate's eyebrows shot up. "I think I've just been insulted."

Bonnie frowned and threw a small pillow at him. "I didn't mean it that way."

Camille knew the story well. Wanting a job as a singer, Bonnie had walked into the saloon in New Orleans where Nate was working. He knew the owner would insist on her entertaining the men in other ways, so he hustled her back outside and explained just what would be expected of her there and most other similar places in town. She never did go to work as a singer, but she married Nate six months later.

"Though I wish you would close the place and do something else." Bonnie toyed with the fringe on another pillow, avoiding her husband's gaze.

"Like what?"

"I don't know. Open a furniture store. Or a lumberyard. We could use more of both."

"Here it comes."

"What?" asked Camille, uncomfortable with the sudden tenseness between her dear friends.

"She'll start pesterin' me about church. Ever since she got religion, she's been after me to go to church with her and sell the saloon."

"I just think you should do something better. Something that helps people."

"Selling whiskey helps people." Nate set his glass down hard on the table and stood, heading for the front door. "It helps them forget about nagging wives." He jerked his hat from the hall tree and jammed it on his head.

"Nate!" Bonnie jumped and ran after him, but he slammed the door. She leaned her forehead against it, tears streaming down her face.

Camille hurried to her side and put her arm around Bonnie's shoulders. "He'll be back once he calms down."

"I know." Bonnie wiped her eyes with her fingertips and sighed heavily.

Camille urged her back to the sofa. "That wasn't like the arguments I've seen between you two before." Not that there had been all that many.

"You mean the ones where I shrieked and threw whatever was handy at him?" She slumped down on the sofa. "After I broke that beautiful vase Nate gave me for my thirtieth birthday, I quit throwing things. I try hard not to shriek anymore. He's right. I have been harping at him about selling the saloon."

"Because you want him home in the evenings."

"Yes. And because liquor harms people, not helps them. And the fights! It seems like every week or so, some of them get into fistfights and smash up half the place." She fished a handkerchief out of her pocket and blew her nose.

"There have even been a couple of gunfights. I'm so afraid that one night Sheriff Starr is going to knock on my door and tell me that Nate's been shot because some idiot was too drunk to point his pistol at the right person."

"I thought the men were supposed to check their guns in at the sheriff's when they came to town."

"They are, but a lot of them manage to hide a second one. Or else they don't bother at all if the sheriff is out of town."

"But Bonnie, all saloons have that problem. Nate has dealt with it for years." So have I. She hadn't bothered to keep track of how many times she'd ducked under a table to keep from being hit by a stray bullet.

"I know. That's what scares me. It's happened so much that one of these days, he's bound to be killed."

"Yet, you wanted me to come work for him?"

Bonnie's expression grew sheepish. "The men were usually nicer when you were around. Besides, I didn't think you'd be there more than a week before some rich rancher persuaded you to marry him."

"Have you told Nate the real reason you want him to quit?"

"No. He'd think I'm featherbrained."

"He might think you love him and are worried about him."

"Maybe. But it's not the only reason. It does bother me for him to be selling beer and whiskey. Ever since I started going to church and reading the Bible and learning how we're supposed to live, I've felt differently about it." She threw up her hands. "I don't know how to explain it. It just feels wrong."

"Could that be because church people frown on it so much?"

"It's part of it. I've thought about it a lot. What they think of him or me isn't all of it. You know as well as I do the sorry state some men leave in. They go home drunk and beat up their wives. Or get robbed because they're too drunk to stop it. Or they get to where they can't live without it." Fresh tears filled Bonnie's eyes. "I'm ashamed of Nate and what he does for a living, and I don't want to be. I love him so much."

"How does him going to church fit in?"

"I thought if he went with me, he'd realize it was wrong, too." She wiped her eyes again and grimaced. "But even if he went, it would probably take a lightning bolt to get anything through his thick skull."

Until they'd moved to Willow Grove, Bonnie hadn't attended church. She'd never mentioned even being interested in it. "Why did you start going to church?" asked Camille.

"I was lonesome. Here, just about all the women go to church. The girls down in the district don't, of course. There are a few others who don't have any use for it. For some, it's strictly a social thing. That's what it was for me when I started. Then I bought a Bible so I could follow along when the preacher read the scripture during the service. I started reading it in the evenings when Nate was gone. I had a great big hole inside, an emptiness that nothing I seemed to do could fill.

"Then one night I realized that Jesus loves me. Me. Not just those women at church who went because they had a tender heart for God. He loved me. All of a sudden I didn't feel so empty, so alone anymore. I can't explain it very well. I guess it's something you have to find out for yourself."

Camille knew all about loneliness, emptiness. Though she certainly hadn't been as lonely since she met Ty. Could he fill that hollowness in her soul? Or did it take God to do that? "I'd like to go to church with you tomorrow."

"You would?" Bonnie stared at her.

Camille nodded. "And it's not just because Ty will be there."

"But you'll look for him anyway," said Bonnie with a smile.

"Of course. Perhaps if Nate sees that I can go to church with you and not become a fanatic overnight, he won't be so afraid to try it."

"You're a good friend."

"So are you and Nate. I don't like to see you two at odds." Camille picked up her purse and the decorations from the supper box. "I'll see you in the morning. What time?"

"Church starts at eleven. I'll come by the hotel about fifteen minutes earlier and we can go together. Oh, dear! I'm sure Nate forgot about escorting you back tonight."

"I'll be fine. I often walked home alone in New Orleans or San Antonio."

Bonnie followed her to the door. "I'll pray for your safety, ask God to send His angels to watch over you."

"Thanks." True angels to watch over a false one. It was an interesting thought. Camille gave Bonnie a hug. "Make peace with your husband."

"I will, as soon as he comes home. You be careful."

"Always am."

Even though Camille kept a watchful eye on her surroundings, she felt an unusual peace all the way back downtown. As she turned the corner at Pine Street, she met Sheriff Starr.

"Miss Dupree, did McKinnon abandon you?"

"No, he left me with my friends, Nate and Bonnie Flynn. Nate was supposed to walk me back to the hotel, but he had to go down to the saloon for a while." She shrugged lightly. "I didn't want to wait for him."

"Then I'll go with you the rest of the way. Some of the boys get a mite wild on occasion." He walked with her, escorting her past three saloons along the way and numerous men milling about the street.

Without his presence, she very well might have run into trouble. "This morning I heard the shooting. It didn't take you long to calm things down."

"That one didn't know the rules. I expect his amigos didn't bother to tell him so they could have a little fun at his expense. Happens pretty often when somebody new hires on at one of the ranches, unless the rancher fills him in."

He stopped in front of the Barton. "Here you go."

"Thank you, Sheriff."

"Good thing there was a little scuffle down at the Dugout. Otherwise I would have been on the other end of town making my regular rounds."

"I'm grateful you weren't there or hauling someone off to jail."

"The two fellows who were about to shoot each other decided they were the best of friends by the time I got there. Reckon they decided they didn't want to spend the night in the calaboose." He studied her for a second, then glanced upward at the stars. "Or maybe the Almighty figured you needed some help." With a slight nod, he touched the brim of his hat. "Good night, ma'am."

"Good night."

A few heads turned as she walked across the lobby, but the men merely nodded. No one followed her up to her room. She supposed she had Ty to thank for that.

Closing and locking the door behind her, she set her things on the table and went over to the window. Starr had crossed the street and was strolling toward the other end of town. Had God answered Bonnie's prayer in the form of a handsome sheriff?

Shaking her head at the thought, she turned away from the window. Why would God care about protecting someone like her?

Chapter Seven

Camille tried to quell her nervousness as she and Bonnie walked into the church building Sunday morning. It was foolish to think that simply by being there, people would look at her and know all about her. She had dressed carefully and was relieved to see that her attire fell somewhere in between the elaborate silk dress of the banker's wife and the simple calico worn by the schoolteacher.

They arrived a couple of minutes before the service began and took seats three rows from the back. There was no one behind them, which suited Camille fine. Maybe that way, only the people on either side of them would notice that she didn't know what to do. She quickly spotted Ty sitting with Cade and Jessie and their children near the front.

A man walked up the two steps to the pulpit.

"That's Reverend Brownfield," whispered Bonnie.

The preacher greeted everyone, then told them to turn to page twenty in the hymnal.

Bonnie picked up the book from the pew beside her and glanced at Camille. "We stand up to sing," she whispered.

Camille nodded, wondering how she could fake it since she didn't know any of the tunes. She vaguely remembered the congregation singing when she was a little girl, but she'd never paid much attention to it. Church had been a time to look at pictures in a book, make faces at her friend, Jimmy, or watch an ant crawl along the windowsill. The singing and preaching had only been adult noise.

Bonnie opened the hymnal to the correct page, holding it so Camille could see, too. Camille gripped the edge of the book and took a deep breath as Bonnie and the others began to sing.

O for a thousand tongues to sing my great Redeemer's praise,
The glories of my God and King, the triumphs of His grace.

After the first verse, she quit trying to mouth the words and simply listened. It seemed that Bonnie's lovely singing voice was even more beautiful than it had been in years past. Slanting a glance at her friend, she noted the happiness on her face. Surreptitiously looking around, she saw some with the same joyful expression. Others frowned in concentration and a few seemed to be singing merely out of duty. She wished she could see Ty's face instead of the back of his head.

Jesus the name that charms our fears...

The words brought her gaze back to the hymn book, but she didn't find where they were until the beginning of the next verse.

He breaks the pow'r of canceled sin, He sets the pris'ner free;
His blood can make the foulest clean, His blood avails for me.

How can sin be canceled? And His blood make someone clean?

"You're all in fine voice this morning," the preacher praised his flock.

Camille thought he must not have been able to hear the man across the aisle from them. Though he couldn't carry a tune in a bucket, he made up for it with enthusiasm. Maybe that counted.

"Page one hundred one, 'I Love to Tell the Story.'"

Camille released her side of the hymnal so Bonnie could turn the pages.

"Let's sing it out so everyone in town can hear it," proclaimed the minister.

I love to tell the story of unseen things above,
Of Jesus and His glory, of Jesus and His love;
I love to tell the story because I know 'tis true;
It satisfies my longings as nothing else can do.

Camille again watched those around her. They sang louder this time. Especially Mr. Off-key. He was an attractive man, probably in his early forties. He obviously doted on the younger woman next to him, and she on him. When he hit a particularly sour note and winced, she merely beamed him a loving smile.

Camille's mind drifted back to the song. How did the ones who seemed to truly believe what they were singing reach that point? How did they know it was true and not just some grand deception someone had made up centuries ago?

I love to tell the story, for some have never heard
The message of salvation from God's own holy word.

The Bible. Bonnie had said that she realized Jesus loved her when she had read the scripture. But it was only a book. How could mere words convince someone of that?

"Wonderful singing. Please be seated." The reverend paused a few seconds, checking something on the lectern in front of him. "John Woods hurt his back yesterday and is laid up. So we need to remember him in prayer." He scanned the room. "I'm sure he and Mrs. Woods would appreciate it if you ladies took some meals over to them this week. She's already mighty busy with her little ones. Tending to John puts an extra load on her. My wife will coordinate it if y'all want to help out. We wouldn't want to take everything over there on the same day."

He nodded to a young lady in the front row. "Kathy Perkins will play for us while we take the offering."

Miss Perkins nervously stepped to the front, tucking a violin beneath her chin as people began to fish in their pockets and purses. When she began to play, Ty and another man stood, each carrying a small basket. They started at the front row, handing the baskets to the people next to the aisle. Ty took the side Camille and Bonnie were sitting on. The baskets were passed down the row to the end, then handed over the pew to the people behind them. When they reached the aisle again, Ty and the other man took them and gave them to the next in line. She noted that Ty always had a smile or a kind word when he passed on the basket.

She barely heard the sweet violin music. Her heart began to pound. How would he react to seeing her there? If he seemed too shocked, people would wonder why. *Please God, don't let him drop the basket. Why did I come? Why am I pretending to be something I'm not?*

He was three rows ahead of them when he spotted her. Surprise flashed across his face, but it was quickly replaced by a smile. A very pleased smile.

It warmed her clear to her toes. Camille was certain that the thoughts racing through her head weren't even close to what she should be contemplating during church. He looked away, speaking to someone else. She caught her breath and dug a dollar from her purse. Keeping her face forward, she watched him out of the corner of her eye.

When he reached their row, she took the basket carefully, making sure her fingers didn't brush against his. She dropped her money into it and handed it to Bonnie who held it over to the man next to her. Only then did Camille look up at Ty, her heart melting at the tenderness in his eyes.

He leaned over to take the basket as Bonnie handed it back to him. "Wait for me after church?" he whispered.

Camille nodded. When did the day turn so warm? They really should open the windows. A quick peek told her the windows were partially open. She'd have to remember to bring a fan with her. Oh, dear, I'm getting as bad as Mrs. Watson.

The man across the aisle must have seen their exchange. When Ty turned to go back down to the front, he gave him a big grin.

She had a difficult time paying attention to the sermon. Judging by the minister's soft voice, she expected he was a kindly man. Though perhaps livelier oration would have kept her gaze, and her mind, from drifting to Ty McKinnon.

Had she noticed his broad shoulders before? They weren't as wide as his brother Cade's, but she liked Ty's better. He might not be able to carry quite as heavy a load as Cade, but he could pull his weight. There was plenty of room for a lady to rest her head if she were so inclined. He had a nice neck, too, strong and straight. And those pretty waves in his hair. Her fingers positively itched to touch them. She definitely would have to bring a fan if she sat behind him again.

She felt guilty for not listening more closely to the preacher. A lot of what she heard didn't make sense anyway. Phrases like *washed in the blood, the Lamb of God,* and the *Alpha and Omega.* She supposed she needed to buy a Bible and do some reading, as Bonnie had done. Maybe things would be clearer then.

The minister finished his sermon and everyone stood for the final hymn. On the last verse, Reverend Brownfield moved to the back of the church by the door.

When the song ended, Camille stepped out of the pew. The man across from her did the same, waiting for the woman with him. Camille noticed that she wore a wedding ring.

"You must be Miss Dupree." The young woman smiled at her, and the man nodded with a friendly grin. "I'm Lydia Noble and this is my husband, Asa. We live out at the McKinnon Ranch. Asa is Ty and Cade's wagon boss."

"It's nice to meet you."

"You, too. I hope we see you out at the ranch soon." Mrs. Noble glanced behind her. "But I guess we'd better not clog up the aisle."

Bonnie and Camille followed them to the door, where Bonnie introduced her to the minister. "It's a pleasure to have you with us, Miss Dupree. Are you visiting for a while?" He glanced somewhere behind her, speculation in his eyes. "Or do you plan to make Willow Grove your home?"

"I'm just visiting at the moment. But it seems like a nice town. I might decide to stay."

"Good. I hope you're here long enough to come have dinner with the wife and me."

They moved on down the church steps and out of the way. Several of Bonnie's friends came over to meet Camille, but she'd barely made the introductions before Ty was by her side.

"Good morning, ladies." His smile briefly covered them all before his gaze settled on Camille.

She almost laughed at the chorus of greetings, hers included. The man did have a way of charming the ladies, even with a simple good morning.

"Wasn't the sermon excellent?" asked one of the women. Camille couldn't remember her name.

"Yes, it was, as usual," said Ty. "How is Sam, Mrs. Tucker?"

"He's almost over his cold. Would have been better days ago if he hadn't insisted on going to the feed store every day."

"It's not easy to stay home when you have a business to run. Give him my best."

"I will. I suppose I'd better get on home and make certain he's resting right and proper. It's nice to meet you, Miss Dupree."

"And you, Mrs. Tucker." Camille silently thanked Ty for calling the woman by name.

The others all decided they needed to go, too. Bonnie spied someone she needed to speak to, leaving Ty and Camille standing there alone.

He grinned at her. "Thought they'd never leave."

She laughed quietly. "So, *was* it an excellent sermon?"

"Couldn't prove it by me. I barely heard a word once I spotted you. But he usually does a good job. What did you think of it?"

Camille felt her cheeks grow lightly warm. "I had trouble concentrating, too. I didn't understand much of what I heard." How did this man prompt such honesty from her? She doubted she would ever have admitted such a thing to anyone else, except Bonnie.

His expression softened. "I remember when I first started going to church, it seemed like the preacher and everybody else talked another language."

"How did you figure it out?"

"I started reading the Bible. That helped." He hesitated for a heartbeat. "Amanda explained what I couldn't sort out on my own."

"So she's the one who got you to attend church?"

"Yes."

"You were trying to impress her." Camille put a teasing lilt to the statement, hoping that he would realize that she understood his love for his wife. She also wondered if she wasn't trying to impress him, at least a little bit.

"Yes, ma'am." He brushed one side of his jacket back and tucked his thumb into his pants pocket. "Even went out and bought my first Sunday-go-to-meetin' suit the week before."

"And now you wear a suit all the time."

He slipped one finger beneath his collar, tugging on it. "Which isn't necessarily a good thing. When I go out to the ranch I don't usually wear one. Unfortunately, I don't get out there often enough."

Bonnie joined them again. "Would you like to come to dinner, Mr. McKinnon? We're having pot roast."

"I wish I could, but I promised Miss Nola I'd take her out to eat and for a buggy ride."

Disappointment jabbed Camille. Don't be silly, she silently chided. You have no claim on him. But she couldn't quell an unexpectedly strong spurt of jealousy.

"I'm sure she's delighted," said Bonnie.

Camille glanced at her, hiding her irritation. Of course she is. What woman wouldn't be?

"I always enjoy her company, too." Ty scanned the crowded church yard. His gaze came back to Camille. "I'd like for you to meet her. I think you two will hit it off."

She certainly felt like hitting something. Smacking him over the head with her parasol came to mind. Except her parasol was in her trunk. And it wouldn't be ladylike.

Sometimes acting like a lady was such a bother.

"There she is talking to Cade and Jessie."

Since Cade was taller than most of the men present, it only took a few seconds to find him and Jessie—and the petite, gray-haired lady smiling affectionately at him.

Bonnie giggled. She knew Camille too well. "Just wave when you're ready to leave. I'll visit with Annie."

"All right."

His expression puzzled, Ty watched Bonnie walk away. "Did I miss something?"

"Nothing much." Thank heavens. "Shall we go meet your friend?"

He smiled and offered her his arm. Camille slipped her fingers around it, glad he hadn't picked up on her annoyance. Perhaps Mama was right after all with her admonishments not to display her temper.

"Good morning, Miss Dupree," said Cade with a friendly smile. "Nice to see you again."

Ty made the introductions. "Miss Nola, this is Camille Dupree. Miss Dupree, may I introduce Mrs. Nola Simpson, affectionately called Miss Nola by just about everyone. She is a dear, longtime friend."

"Good thing you didn't say *old* friend, boy." The elderly lady laughed merrily, turning her keen eyes on Camille. "The gossips were right. You are a beauty. Welcome to Willow Grove, Miss Dupree."

"Thank you, ma'am."

"You drop by for a visit sometime this week, and I'll bend your ear about this rascal here." Mrs. Simpson shifted, leaning more fully on her cane.

"Uh-oh, I'm in trouble now," said Ty. "She's known me since I was a kid."

"It should be interesting." Camille welcomed any insight she could get about Ty. Maybe it would help her understand why she was so drawn to him. She also took an instant liking to the older woman. "Would two o'clock on Tuesday be a good time?"

"Perfect. I suppose if I were nice, I'd let Ty take you out to dinner and for a buggy ride."

"Oh, no ma'am. That isn't necessary." Camille glanced up at him to gauge his reaction. For once, the man had a poker face. "He's looking forward to spending the afternoon with you."

"Child, no matter how nice a man is, he doesn't prefer an old woman's company to a young one's."

"Sometimes a man enjoys both." The gentle smile Ty gave Miss Nola was filled with love. "And I think Miss Dupree already has plans for today."

"I do. The Flynns have asked me to dinner. I haven't even begun to bring them up to date with news of their former neighbors in San Antonio."

A boy and a little girl ran up to them. The boy stopped beside Jessie, studying Camille quietly. Cade scooped the girl up in his arms, giving her a hug. They were beautiful children.

Camille smiled at them. "You must be Brad and Ellie. Your uncle has told me a lot about you."

"You must be the lady Uncle Ty spent all that money on last night," said Ellie, giving her the once over.

"Ellie!" Jessie's face turned red.

"I heard you and Daddy talking after you came home." With childish innocence, Ellie ignored her mother. "Daddy said Uncle Ty must have it bad to spend so much money just to eat supper with you. What does *it* mean?"

It was Ty's turn for a red face. Camille felt hers heat, too.

"That's something you'll learn about when you're older." Cade sent them an apologetic look.

Ellie sighed heavily, meeting Camille's gaze. "That's what he says about everything."

Camille laughed and wished she could hug the delightful child. Everyone except Ellie joined in the laughter. "Your daddy is right, honey. Though I expect you'll learn that lesson much sooner than he'd like."

"Don't remind me." Cade ran his fingers through his dark hair. "I'm gettin' gray just thinking about it." He glanced at the thinning crowd. "We'd better head on over to the restaurant. Otherwise, we won't get a table."

"I'll bring the buggy over, Nola," said Ty.

"I'll see you Tuesday afternoon." Camille smiled at Miss Nola, then turned to Cade and Jessie. "I hope to see you again soon as well."

"We're looking forward to Ty bringing you out to the ranch."

"I am, too."

"Ty suggested Saturday. That would be a good day for us if you can make it," said Jessie. "The children and I will be staying in town during the week now that the new school term is starting."

"Are you coming to see us?" Ellie's face perked up.

"Yes." Camille glanced at Ty. "On Saturday." He nodded his agreement.

"Brad and me can show you the new kittens. They're down in the barn. We have a lot of cats."

"Good. I like kittens. Now, I'd better let you go to dinner."

"I'll walk you over to Mrs. Flynn. The buggy is in that direction." When they were out of hearing of the others, Ty said quietly, "Thank you."

"For what?"

"For graciously deflecting Nola's half-hearted offer to let me spend the afternoon with you. She's been looking forward to that drive since before I went to San Angelo."

"It would have been very discourteous of me to try to interrupt your plans. Your kindness to her speaks highly of your character, Mr. McKinnon."

He shrugged. "She's been like a mother to me. I try to treat her the way she deserves."

When Ty found out about Anthony, would he treat her the way she deserved?

A chill shrouded her heart and seeped into her soul.

Chapter Eight

On Monday morning, Camille walked into the *Willow Grove Gazette* office with a twinge of fear and a great deal of anticipation.

The young man setting type looked up from his work and froze in place.

"Good morning." Camille gave him a pleasant but not dazzling smile. She glanced around the room, spotting an open door leading into another office. "I would like to speak to Mr. Hill, please."

The typesetter hopped up from his chair, bumping a tray of lead type in the process. "Yes, ma'am. I'll get him." He hurried across the room and knocked on the door sill. "There's a lady here to see you, sir."

A tall, thin man quickly appeared in the doorway. Camille estimated his age to be late fifties or early sixties. He smiled cordially as he approached. "I'm Ralph Hill. How can I help you?"

"I'm Camille Dupree." Judging from the glint of recognition in his eyes, he had heard about her. "I understand you're looking for a business partner."

"I am." Curiosity shaded his voice.

"I'm looking for a business."

He broke into a broad grin. "Well, Miss Dupree, I think we have some talking to do. Come into my office."

Hill motioned for her to precede him into the other room. He left the door partially open, waiting until she had taken a chair in front of his desk before he sat down behind it. "Do you know anything about running a newspaper?"

"No. But I owned a store in San Antonio." She didn't like shading the truth, but she was certain that if she told him she'd owned a saloon, he would show her the door. "I am experienced at bookkeeping, handling employees and generally running a business. I'm sure you could teach me what else I need to know. I'm impressed with the quality of your paper. There seem to be plenty of things to write about in Willow Grove, but you have good coverage of news from other parts of the country, even the world. That's important."

"I agree, though sometimes I just use that to fill up the paper when there isn't enough going on around here." He grimaced. "Or when there isn't much advertising. Did Ty suggest you see me?"

"Yes, he did."

"I thought he might have had something to do with it. Mrs. Nickson dropped off a little article about the box supper for this week's issue. It doesn't mention you or the mayor's high bid, but she took great delight in telling me the story."

"I'm surprised you hadn't already heard about it," Camille said dryly.

"Actually, I had. But as a newspaperman, it always pays to listen to someone else's version." Chuckling, he swiveled around in his chair and took a ledger from a shelf behind him.

Laying it on the desk, he shoved it across to Camille. "As you can see, I'm still in the black, but barely. If I hadn't done some extra printing—flyers and such—I would have closed shop a month ago. Several accounts are long past due, but my old ticker can't handle the hassle of trying to collect the money." He sighed heavily. "Actually, I haven't had the energy to go around and solicit business. There are regular paying customers like Ty, but we have new businesses starting up almost every week. I just haven't felt well enough to go talk to them about advertising."

Camille opened the ledger and scanned the figures with a frown. "Some of these people owe you for months of advertising."

"Which is why I no longer do business with them."

"Are they so certain of their customers that they don't need to seek more?"

"Some are. There's only one ice house in town. Same for the photographer. There are three boardinghouses, but they're full up. If someone vacates a room, word spreads so fast that half a dozen people will be lined up at the door before it shuts behind him. For now, the carpenters have more business than they can handle. I don't think it's even worth talking to any of those folks. But the others all have competition."

"How long ago did you quit taking their ads?"

"Two months for some. Three for the rest."

Camille tapped her fingertips on the page. "By now they may have noticed a drop in customers." Studying the names of the businesses, a plan began to form, along with the excitement of a new challenge. "Shall we see how persuasive I am, Mr. Hill?"

"Be my guest, Miss Dupree."

"I'd like to establish our business arrangement before I go talk to them, so I can officially represent the paper." She studied the ledger again. "I'm willing to invest enough today to cover all expenses for the next three months, including a salary for you. Then we can see how things are going at that point."

He considered her offer for a few minutes. When excitement lit his eyes, she knew her money, and perhaps her enthusiasm, compensated for any lack of qualifications.

"Sounds fair to me. If you can round up more business, you won't have to put in any more money and will start getting a return on your investment. How do you see splitting up the ownership?"

"Seventy-thirty for now. This is your paper. I'm just a beginner. We can renegotiate in three months." If I'm still here.

"You have an itch to do some writing?"

"I'd like give it a try later. I'll trust you not to let me embarrass myself by publishing something awful."

"I'll make certain you don't." He stood and leaned across the desk, holding out his hand. "Welcome to the *Willow Grove Gazette,* Miss Dupree."

She stood also and shook his hand. "Thank you, Mr. Hill. What bank do you use?"

"First National."

"Good. I opened an account there this morning. I'll have them transfer the money into the *Gazette* account right away."

"I appreciate it."

"Now, I need to make a list of who owes you and how much. Anything you can tell me about them would be helpful, too."

He stepped aside. "Take my chair. Here's a notepad and pencil. Would you like some coffee?"

"No thanks." Camille moved around the desk as Mr. Hill walked over to a corner cabinet and poured himself a cup of coffee. After she sat down, he took the chair across from her. "I assume that these other businesses are all doing well enough to pay their bills?"

"Should be. Town's booming."

They spent almost an hour compiling the list and discussing the various owners. By the time she was ready to leave, Camille had a good idea of who might pleasantly tell her to go away and who might be belligerent. "Now, I need a copy of the paper. I left mine in the hotel room."

"Sure thing." Mr. Hill rose and walked out into the front office. He returned a minute later with Friday's paper. He handed it to her, watching as she read over the ads. "How do you intend to proceed?"

She smiled, folded the paper, and tucked one end of it into her deep, drawstring purse. She added the notepad and pencil to her bag. Taking out a small bottle of perfume, she dabbed a drop of the rose scent beneath each ear. "I'm going to size up the competition of our errant customers. Then I'll try to convince the folks on this list how much better off they'd be to pay their bills so they can advertise." She batted her eyelashes. "If that doesn't work, I'll try to charm them into doing it."

Mr. Hill laughed as she stood. "Miss Dupree, I like your style. Don't be surprised if you catch me eavesdropping."

"Just stand clear if anybody starts throwing things."

Camille stopped by the bank first and asked them to deposit the money into the newspaper's account. She visited several of the stores which had ads in the paper and inspected the merchandise, particularly any sales items highlighted in the ads.

When she came out of Siler's Grocery, she spotted Ty standing in the doorway of his store. He crossed the street and walked down the boardwalk to meet her.

"You're a busy lady this morning. I can understand your interest in the grocer's and apothecary's, but why the hardware store?" They walked down the sidewalk together.

"Have you been following me?"

"Nope. Just standing in my doorway, watching the goings-on in town. I can't help it if you're the prettiest thing around to look at."

"My, my, flattery so early in the morning."

"It's easy." His voice dropped a little lower. "Especially when I've been thinking about you most of the time since Saturday night."

She'd been thinking about him, too. Far more than was wise. Camille glanced up at his face. If he just wasn't so handsome, so nice to be around.

"Did you go see Hill?"

"I did. I am now part owner of the newspaper."

"Congratulations. I figured he'd jump at having you for a partner. Have you been calling on customers?"

"In a way. I'm about to call on the people who owe us money. So I thought it would be wise to check their competitors' stores, see if there is a way to compare the businesses."

"Good idea. Sounds like you may have a knack for this business."

Camille laughed, stopping in front of the Willow Grove City Bank. "We'll see how successful I am."

"You'll have them eating out of your hand. Come see me later and tell me all about it."

"I will. You'll be at the store?"

"Should be. I haven't done a lick of work all day." He leaned a tiny bit closer and took a deep breath. "Mercy, woman, you smell good."

"Part of the strategy. Befuddle their brains with perfume and a smile and before they know it, they've paid their bills."

"They won't know what hit 'em." He smiled briefly, but it quickly faded. "Be careful."

"Always." Except around you, she thought. He had an uncanny way of slipping inside her defenses before she even realized it. "Go make some money."

He chuckled. "You, too."

She walked into the bank with a happy smile and asked to speak with the bank president.

A minute later, a heavyset man, strutting with self-importance, came out to meet her. "Good morning, Miss Dupree. I'm Edgar Montworth. How can I help you?"

"I'd like to speak to you about your account at the newspaper."

The man blinked, then hastily showed her into his office and offered her a seat. Taking his chair behind the desk after she sat down, he rested his clasped hands on his expansive stomach. "It isn't time to renew my subscription."

"I'm talking about the twelve dollars you owe for past advertising, Mr. Montworth. I am now Mr. Hill's partner in the *Gazette*. My first task is to collect past due accounts so that we will be able to keep the paper solvent." She flashed him a smile. "I'm sure you understand solvency better than anyone else in town. That's why I feel certain that this is simply something that has been overlooked accidentally."

"I...uh...perhaps that is the case."

"Being new to Willow Grove, I can tell you that advertising in the local newspaper is very important. Why just this morning I opened an account at First National. Their ad is what brought them to my attention. Now, if Willow Grove City Bank had also advertised, I would have considered your bank, too." At least until she talked to Nate and he recommended First National, saying he didn't trust Montworth as far as he could throw him.

"Well, that is something to consider. The town is growing."

"By supporting your local paper, you'll show all the residents, both new and old, how civic-minded you are. Seems to me that's a small price to pay for the goodwill of the community."

"You are as persuasive as you are beautiful, Miss Dupree."

"Thank you. Once your account is caught up, you will be billed on the fifteenth of the month. If your payment isn't made by the thirtieth of that month, we will not accept your business until the bill is paid in full. After that, advance payment will be required."

"You're also a tough businesswoman," said the banker, his good humor fading.

"No more than a man would be if he wanted to succeed." She stood. "Mr. Hill publishes an excellent paper. I intend to see that it continues. If you'll drop your payment off at the office by Wednesday, I'll stop by on Thursday or Friday to discuss what you want in your ad for next week."

He waved his hands in surrender. "A small price to pay for the goodwill of the community and the pleasure of your company for a few minutes." Montworth came around the end of his desk as Camille turned to leave.

She wasn't surprised to feel his hand rest against her back as they walked toward the doorway.

"Lovely perfume, my dear," he murmured.

Camille made a mental note to go easy with the fragrance next time. "It's called Summer Rose. I expect you could order a bottle for Mrs. Montworth at McKinnon's or one of the other stores in town. It's a bit pricy, but I doubt you spare expense when it comes to your dear wife."

"Of course not."

The pressure of his hand vanished.

"I look forward to seeing you later in the week, Mr. Montworth," she lied through a fake smile. "Thank you for taking care of the misunderstanding."

"Of course. That's all it was. I'll see that it's rectified right away."

Camille nodded her appreciation and escaped. At two of the grocery stores and the butcher shop, she used similar tactics—pointing out that their specials were only evident if someone walked by and saw the signs in the windows. She mentioned how new people in town were apt to turn to the paper for information rather than simply wander up and down the street comparing prices. It took a little talking, but they were finally convinced to pay their bills and run ads again the following week.

She took a slightly different route with the druggist, advising him to emphasize his twenty years of experience as an apothecary as well as playing up how he needed to attract those new to the area. It amazed her how they all seemed to discount that necessity. Willow Grove was not a large town, but there were many businesses vying for the same customers. The druggist eventually agreed to pay his bill and take out a small ad the following week.

The man who owned the hardware store was a cranky old grump. She soon discovered that he had a personal dislike for the newspaper editor. She suspected he might have taken out the ads with the intention of never paying for them. She didn't waste more than a few minutes with him.

Mr. Hill had told her not to bother with the harness maker since he only owed for two weeks. Hill also said he was on the distasteful side. Camille had dealt with distasteful men most of her life, so she disregarded the editor's advice—and quickly regretted it.

Sam Cline glared at Camille when she explained her reason for being there, then his lip turned up in a sneer. "You just trot your fancy backside right out that door and don't bother to come back. I ain't goin' to pay you or old man Hill nuthin'."

Camille narrowed her gaze, her temper rising. "I assume that you expect your customers to pay for the goods you provide them?"

"Dang right, I do. Cash money when they pick up their order."

"But you don't have the courtesy to do the same. Not even to pay something that is two weeks past due."

"Those ads didn't do one bit of good. Didn't bring in no customers."

Camille checked some reins draped over a hook, noting the prices. "I expect people compared your prices to the ones down the street." She pulled the newspaper out of her bag and laid it down on the counter, turning it around so he could read it. "You're charging twice as much as your competition."

"Those are on sale. And they ain't as good as mine."

"Are yours so much better that you expect someone to pay double the price? Perhaps you not only need to consider how you pay your bills, you need to take a fresh look at how you price your merchandise."

"Who are you to question how I run my business? You ain't got no call to be paradin' around town trying to do a man's job. You go back to your kitchen where you belong and stay there. That's the only place for a woman." He leered at her. "Or maybe down in the district at Calico Sue's."

"You're disgusting." Camille grabbed the newspaper and stuffed it into her bag. Turning on her heel, she started for the open door.

"A gal like you would earn a pretty penny down there."

She stopped, looking back at him. As her icy gaze skimmed over his greasy hair and dirty clothes, she curled her fingers around the Derringer in her skirt pocket.

He spat tobacco juice in the general direction of a spittoon on the floor near the wall.

"Do you consider yourself an expert on the ladies in the district?"

He took a deep breath, his chest puffing out. "Reckon you could say that."

"Then it should be quite obvious that you wouldn't be able to afford thirty seconds of my time." She headed for the doorway.

"Why you—"

Cline's footsteps thudded on the floor behind her. Camille quickened her pace.

"You can't talk to me like that."

Jerking open the door and stepping onto the boardwalk, she practically ran into Sheriff Starr.

He looked behind her. "Is there a problem, Miss Dupree?"

She released the gun and withdrew her hand from her pocket. "Not now."

"Arrest her, Sheriff. She was trying to rob me."

Starr glanced at Cline, then focused on Camille, his expression vaguely amused. "Seems to me you could pick a better place to rob, ma'am."

"I only came by to collect the two dollars he owes the *Gazette*." Moving beside the sheriff, she looked at Cline with contempt. "But he had other things in mind."

"Knowing his propensity for trouble with the ladies, I expect he did."

Cline frowned. "What's propensity mean?"

"Ability."

For a second Cline looked pleased, then he realized what the sheriff meant. "Ain't done nuthin' lately," he muttered.

"Shall I throw him in the calaboose, Miss Dupree?"

"I don't think you can arrest people for being insulting. But I would like the two dollars he owes the newspaper."

"Hand it over, Cline." When the harness maker hesitated, Starr shook his head. "Stubborn as a mule. Either pay the lady what you owe her or go to jail for attempted assault."

"I didn't do nothing to her," Cline shouted.

"But you were about to." Starr had clearly run out of patience.

Grumbling, Cline went behind his counter and took the two dollars out of the cash box. He came back to the sidewalk and handed it to Camille with a scowl.

She took the money and dropped it into her bag. Murmuring her thanks to the sheriff, she walked away.

"She insulted me."

"Quit whining and go back to work." The sheriff caught up with Camille. "I think you hurt his feelings."

"That oaf doesn't have any feelings. Besides, he insulted me first." She glanced at Starr, smiling wryly at his uplifted brow. "I know it sounds childish."

"Yep. But that's the way most fights start. Do you have a pocket pistol?"

"Yes, a Derringer. I suppose now you'll want it."

"We allow women to carry a gun for protection. Though most of them don't use it," he added with a stern note in his voice.

"I wouldn't have unless he tried to grab me."

A frown darkened Starr's brow. "You aren't the delicate Southern belle you seem to be, are you, Miss Dupree?"

"Few women of the South are delicate, sir. Hardship forges a strong heart and a backbone of steel. I've been on my own for a long time. I can take care of myself."

The sheriff scratched his temple with one finger, his expression rueful. "Well, ma'am, I don't rightly think that's the way things are going to be. Looking after folks in general is my job. And judging from the way Ty has been acting since you came to town, he's decided that lookin' after you is his."

Chapter Nine

"She what?" Ty stared at Ransom as the sheriff shut his office door.

"She had a run-in with Sam Cline." Ransom sat down and leaned back in the chair, balancing on the rear legs. "She said she stopped by because he owed the *Gazette* some money, but he had other things in mind."

"Did he hurt her?" Ty jumped up and started toward the door.

"No, he didn't. There's no need to go off half-cocked. He didn't touch her, but he followed her out the door, clearly intending to do something."

"I'll talk to Cline. Make sure he knows he'll have to answer to both you and me if he tries anything." Fear gnawed at his belly. He figured Camille was used to handling obnoxious men, but he didn't want her thinking that she had to do it entirely on her own. He didn't want anyone else thinking that, either.

Ransom leaned forward, the front legs on the chair hitting the floor with a thud. "Good." He stood and walked to the door, pausing with his hand on the door handle. "Should I worry about her causing trouble?"

"No more than what happens when any beautiful woman comes to town."

"All right. If you decide you need to enlighten me on the lady's history, you know where I am. In the meantime, I have other things to worry about."

"Such as?"

"The city council hiring a town marshal. When are y'all going to figure out you have to pay a decent salary to get a good lawman?"

"I keep telling them that, but they don't think they need to pay much for somebody to enforce the dog license ordinance."

"Well, you don't. But a marshal worth his salt would take care of the drunks and a lot of other problems here in town. Leave me and my deputy to handle things in the rest of my territory."

"You don't have a deputy." It was something that concerned Cade and Ty both. Ransom's jurisdiction included two other counties besides their own.

"That's another problem. Tell Cade to get those commissioners off their duffs and hire somebody. I can't be on duty twenty-four hours a day. Can't be two places at the same time, either."

"Not that you've had to be. Your reputation is keeping the outlaws in line."

"That won't last much longer. Folks will forget about Wyman." Ransom frowned. "I'm not just griping, Ty. What if I have to go off chasing a horse thief or something? I know you and Cade will back me if I need it, but Cade has a family now. And you're so moonstruck, you probably wouldn't be much help, either."

Ty laughed. "I think you're just jealous. I saw you giving Camille the eye at the box supper."

"Me and every other man in the room. But you know I won't infringe on your territory. Now, if you decide you aren't interested, let me know."

"I'll keep that in mind," Ty said dryly.

Ransom opened the door and scanned the store. "Looks like you'll have a chance to hear the whole story." He left the office, meeting Camille about ten feet away.

Ty stood in the doorway watching them, relieved when he didn't see a spark of interest in Camille's face as she talked to the lawman.

"Telling tales, Sheriff?"

"A few. Doin' a little fishin', too."

She paused, glancing at Ty, then looked back at Ransom. "Did you catch anything?"

"Nothin' bigger than a minnow." With a nod, he continued down the store aisle. He stopped at the main counter and bought some hard candy.

Ire lit her eyes as she approached Ty. He stepped back so she could come into the office. Then he quietly shut the door.

"What did you tell him?"

"Nothing. He asked me if he needed to worry about you causing trouble."

"And?"

"I told him no more than any other beautiful woman would. But he had some interesting things to tell me." Ty moved in front of her, standing close in an effort to intimidate her. Not that it seemed to work. Blast that perfume! He forced himself to ignore it—and how pretty she looked, even with the flush of irritation in her cheeks. "What happened at Cline's?"

She stepped over to the desk, absently toying with a horse statue paperweight. "He thought I should go to work at Calico Sue's. Figured I'd make lots of money there."

Ty barely stifled a curse, a word he hadn't said in years. "I'm going to turn him inside out."

A smile teased her mouth. "Though that would be interesting to see, it wouldn't be wise. I appreciate your willingness to defend me, but it isn't necessary."

"I'll talk to him," he said stubbornly. "Cline has a mean streak. He hurt a girl at the parlor house last year. Watch yourself around him."

"I don't plan to go near him. If no one mentions this to him or anyone else, the incident will pass. If you threaten him, he'll think it's all over town. Then I'd have a big problem."

"You have a point." If he caused a scene, it might rile the man up even more. "I don't like it, but I won't say anything to him unless he threatens you or mouths off about you." Ty moved closer, leaning back against the desk right beside her and crossed his arms. "I gather Cline didn't pay up?"

"Actually, he did. But only after the sheriff gave him the choice of paying or spending some time in jail. I didn't have to recruit any help with the others." She shrugged. "Well, I wasn't successful at the hardware store, but I didn't waste much time there. What a grump. But everyone else saw the error of their ways."

"Too bad I'm all paid up." He shifted a little closer and relaxed his arms, resting one hand on the desk. "It might be interesting to see how you'd convince me."

Her gaze darted to his lips, then back up to his eyes. "I'd probably change tactics to persuade you."

Ty settled his hand at her waist, his gaze dropping to her mouth. It was too soon to kiss her, but he wanted to in the worst way. He didn't stop to sort out his feelings, except to acknowledge that he felt more alive than he had in a long time. Surely, that was a good thing. "So your perfume and smile worked."

She rested her hand on his shoulder. "Yes, though I should probably skip the perfume next time or go lighter with it."

"Until you come here." He edged her closer, thinking about her comment. "Did someone else fall under its spell?"

"Montworth."

Ty frowned, his fingers tightening minutely at her waist. "Did he try anything?"

"No, but his tone implied plenty when he complimented me on the fragrance. I suggested he buy a bottle for his wife."

Ty laughed softly, slipping his other hand around her waist, and drawing her even closer. "You're good, lady."

"I've had a lot of experience deflecting men's attentions."

"Do you want to deflect mine?" He knew the answer—he could see it in her face, feel it in her touch—but he felt honor bound to give her the option.

"No," she whispered, closing her eyes and lifting her face toward his.

He kissed her gently, half expecting guilt to swamp him, but he felt only a twinge. When she sighed softly, he tightened his embrace, cradling her head with one hand. He pulled back just long enough for a breath, then kissed her again. When he raised his head, she gave him a dreamy little smile and rested her forehead against his chin.

"Nice," she murmured.

"Yes, it was." That didn't come close to describing it. He held her loosely, not wanting to let her go.

"Now you'll think I'm fast."

He leaned back and tipped her chin up with his fingertip so she looked at him. "Because you let me kiss you so soon after we met?"

She nodded. "I don't normally do this."

"I didn't think so. A man can usually pick up on that kind of thing by the way a woman flirts."

"Like the woman who crawled through your bedroom window?"

Ty rolled his eyes. "Prissy was so obvious that everyone in town knew she was after me. Or after my money, more likely."

"Don't be so sure of that."

He figured he grew a foot taller in that instant. "You sayin' you'd like me even if I wasn't well off?"

"Probably." A smile hovered around her mouth.

Now he knew he'd have to duck to go through the doorway.

"Well, I doubt Prissy would feel the same. I've been very careful never to be alone with her, never given her one bit of encouragement. Reckon that's why she got so desperate and came calling in her nightgown."

"My goodness." Camille smoothed the edge of his coat lapel. "You weren't tempted at all?"

A flush warmed his cheeks. "I can't say that. She's a desirable woman, and I'm a normal man. For a minute all I could do was stare. But it would have been wrong to act on it."

"God wouldn't have approved."

"Definitely not. The Bible has a heap of scriptures on the evils and dangers of lust. I hustled her back out that window faster than a whirlwind can snuff out a match."

She eased away from him, her expression bemused. "Most men would have taken advantage of the opportunity."

"Depends on their beliefs, I guess. But even if I wasn't a Christian, I wouldn't have done anything different. She's not a woman I'd want to be tied to. I'd never be able to trust her." He straightened, moving away from the desk. "Now, enough talk about Prissy. Will you let me buy your supper?"

"Do I look presentable?"

"Yes, ma'am. I didn't even mess up your hair." But someday he would. He knew it and so did she. "Your hat's still on straight, too."

"Then I accept your invitation. I had a good breakfast, but only ate an apple around noon." Camille opened the door, pausing while he put on his hat. "Do you know of a house I could rent? Now that I'm sure I won't be leaving soon, I'd rather not stay at the hotel."

They walked out the office and down the aisle. Ty was mindful of the curious glances from the clerks and several customers. He nodded a greeting to a couple of them but kept on walking. "I can't think of a single house for rent. Right this minute, there isn't even one you could buy."

"Mr. Hill said all the boardinghouses are full."

"They are." He opened the front door of the store, following her outside. "But Miss Nola might like to have you live at her house. She's a widow and doesn't get around as well as she used to. Jessie and the kids stayed with her a little while before she and Cade got married. Jessie worked as her housekeeper. She has someone else doing that job now, but Hester is only there during the day. I think Nola would like to have someone there at night."

"I don't know. I've lived by myself for a long time."

"Nola's easy to get along with." She was also a woman who loved Jesus. He couldn't think of a better place for Camille to stay. "Cade and I went to work for her husband on their ranch when we first came west. She used to be a schoolteacher, so she talked him into letting her teach us a couple of days a week. I owe her a lot. Besides the usual schoolwork, she instructed us in manners and behaving like gentlemen."

"She taught you well."

"She thinks so," he said with a laugh. "If you want, I can stop by her place later and see if she's interested."

"It would be good to know before I call on her tomorrow. I don't want her to think I'm being pushy."

"She wouldn't think that. There would be another advantage to you moving in with her."

"What?"

"You'd have a ready-made chaperone."

Camille stopped, bringing him to an abrupt halt, too, as she searched his face. "Do I need a chaperone?"

"In this small a town—yes. Probably would even in a city."

"I understand the social requirement. But why do I need one?"

Her expression was leery, but he saw longing in her eyes. The same longing he felt in his heart. He figured Amanda was sitting up in heaven smiling in approval. "Because, Miss Dupree, I would like very much to come calling."

Chapter Ten

That night, Camille sat at the small table in her room and shuffled a deck of cards. Piano music from a saloon a few buildings down from the hotel drifted on the breeze through the open window. If she had not met Ty McKinnon, she would be sitting across the street in the White Buffalo, dealing a poker hand instead of solitaire. She laid the cards out one by one, playing the game more by habit than concentration.

The day had been enjoyable for the most part, except for the confrontation with Cline. Persuading those tight-fisted shopkeepers to pay up had brought her more satisfaction than a hundred-dollar night at the card table. She should have been focusing on the newspaper and ways to improve it, but her thoughts lingered on Ty.

And that kiss. It had been six years since she'd let a man kiss her, but she didn't think she had ever experienced anything quite like it. Thoughts of the past and the future had vanished in the sheer pleasure of the moment. There had been desire in his touch, but tenderness and respect had overshadowed it.

He wanted her to live with Mrs. Simpson so he could come calling in a proper way.

He just wants to protect his reputation, she thought. Any politician worth his salt avoids a scandal, especially close to an election. She laid a nine of spades down on a ten of hearts. But he had taken her to the social even when he knew she might work at Nate's.

"So he wants to protect my reputation, too," she whispered, "now that people think I have a good one."

She had known men who went to church on Sunday morning after spending half the night in the saloon, drinking and playing cards. Some had offered her a small fortune to play other games. She supposed it could be counted to her credit that she had always refused.

Ty wasn't like them. He was an honest, decent man. A noble man who took his faith to heart and tried to live the way the scriptures told him to.

She had never read the Good Book, not one word. She remembered looking at the family Bible when she was a young child and tracing her fingers over the scrolling letters. By the time she could read, the Bible, like their home, was a pile of ashes.

"Nothing can undo those months I lived with Anthony," she said out loud, throwing down the cards and feeling sick at heart. "Nothing can make me good enough for him." No matter how much she wished for it.

Blowing out the lamp, she walked over to the window, pushing aside the curtain in the darkened room. The cool air felt good. She stood in the shadows to avoid giving anyone a glimpse of her in a nightgown and wrapper.

It was almost nine, but the saloons in the main part of town wouldn't close until two. Those down in the district stayed open twenty-four hours a day. A drunken cowboy, singing off-key to imaginary cattle, staggered down the sidewalk. There weren't as many people in town as on the weekend, but the saloons and some of the stores still had customers.

The lamps burned in McKinnon's across the street. She saw two men inside the store approach the front door, followed a minute later by Ty. He joined them for a brief conversation. They shook hands and the other men left as Ty held the door open for them. He paused, surveying the street, then looked up toward the second floor of the hotel—right toward her window. He was too far away for her to read his expression, but the fact that he looked in her direction made her heart skip a beat.

He turned and walked back inside. One by one the lights went out, until there was only a soft glow from the back of the store. In a few minutes, it, too, disappeared. She waited until he came back out. He locked the front door and turned down the lantern hanging beside it, blowing out the last flicker of light.

He walked past the White Buffalo, glancing inside, but not slowing his pace. As he crossed the alley, she lost sight of him for a few minutes in the shadows of the next block, then spotted him again as he walked through the light shining from the windows of another saloon. At the end of that block, he turned the corner, disappearing from sight.

He hadn't looked up at her window again.

Camille wondered why she felt both relieved and disappointed. Shaking her head, she took off her wrapper, climbed into bed and wound up tossing and turning for hours.

It's just because I haven't gone to bed before three in the morning for years. It has nothing to do with Ty.

"And it snows in Texas in July," she murmured on a tired yawn.

* * *

The next afternoon Camille sat in Mrs. Simpson's parlor, chatting sociably and drinking tea as if it were an everyday occurrence. She had double-checked with Mr. Hill, confirming that there wasn't any other place in town for her to stay.

"How my husband loved working with cattle," said Mrs. Simpson with a nostalgic smile. "Even after we had a place of our own, he always called himself a cowboy, not a rancher. Said it sounded too self-important. Of course, I never agreed with him. I liked the sound of it." She laughed and set her empty cup on the table by her red velvet chair. "But enough about my man, let's talk about yours."

"I don't have one." Camille took her last sip, hoping she didn't choke on it.

"Not officially I suppose. But I think Ty would like to be."

"You're making too much of his kindness."

Her hostess smiled, her eyes sparkling in delight. "Kindness didn't pay three hundred dollars to have supper with you Saturday night."

"He was raising money for the school." Camille resisted the urge to shift in her chair, her mother's voice whispering in her mind. Angelique, sit still. Squirming is not ladylike.

"From what I hear, he didn't give a hoot and a holler about how much he raised for the school. He usually spends about fifty dollars, and that's considered generous. Ty didn't want anybody else keeping company with you and that's a fact."

"I don't suppose it would do any good to argue that point."

"Not a bit." Mrs. Simpson's expression softened. "I love Ty and Cade like they were my own sons. It's been heartbreaking to watch Ty since Amanda died. There for a while, I was afraid he'd work himself into the ground, too. I can't tell you how good it is to see him interested in someone again."

"He loves his wife very much."

Mrs. Simpson's eyes narrowed. "Not loved?"

"No, ma'am. He still loves her. I'm sure he always will. As he should."

"You're right, but that doesn't mean he can't love someone else, too."

Camille laughed, trying to lighten the conversation. "He's only taken me out to eat a couple of times."

"Which is two more times than he's taken anyone else out. And he suggested you stay here with me."

"Because I want to move out of the hotel, and there is no room at any of the boardinghouses."

The older lady shrugged. "That's part of it. But he also knows I won't toss him on his ear when he comes courtin'. Won't watch you like a hawk, either."

Camille felt her face grow warm. "He did say something about coming by."

"That scalawag. He already comes to dinner about once a week anyway." Mrs. Simpson laughed as her housekeeper took away the tea tray. "I expect we'll see him more often now."

Hester joined in the laughter, glancing at Camille. "Yes, ma'am. No doubt we will. And he won't be sitting in the parlor shooting the breeze with you. He'll put that porch swing to good use."

"About time somebody did." Mrs. Simpson practically wiggled with merriment. "It's been sitting idle pert' near every evening since Cade and Jessie married."

Camille had noted the white wooden swing when she arrived. It was tucked into one corner of the porch, perfect for watching sunsets or waiting expectantly for a beau.

"What you're asking for room and board is more than reasonable. I'd like to add some for Hester since I'll be causing more work for her."

"That's fair." Mrs. Simpson nodded her approval and glanced toward the kitchen. "She'll appreciate it. When can you move in?"

"Would tomorrow be too soon?"

"Not at all. That's Ty's regular night to come to dinner anyway."

"No wonder he made sure I was still coming to see you when he stopped by the newspaper this morning. I'll have my things sent over from the hotel tomorrow." She stood, picking up her purse. "I should be getting back to the office. Mr. Hill is going to try to teach me about advertising."

Mrs. Simpson picked up the cane propped against her chair and stood also. "It should be interesting work. You're fortunate to be able to do something other than the typical women's jobs."

I've never had a typical woman's job, thought Camille. She supposed she should thank her father for that. "I wouldn't be any good at teaching, and I can't sew a straight seam. I'm not a very good cook, either."

"Never you mind, dear. That's why I have Hester. When she's not here, I'm still able to cook fine." Mrs. Simpson accompanied her to the door, the cane tapping on the wooden floor. "I'll enjoy your company." She smiled slyly. "And Ty's when he comes around."

"If he—we become a bother, please tell me," said Camille.

"A bother? Land sakes, child, I can hardly wait for the fun. It's been boring around here since Jessie left."

Camille wasn't sure she wanted to provide the old lady with entertainment. She opened the door and pushed open the screen door. Stepping out onto the porch, she looked around. It was a nice home, with gingerbread trim, a honeysuckle vine trailing along the white picket fence, and a shady, inviting porch that wrapped around the house. It was bigger than the one she had rented in San Antonio, and in a much better neighborhood.

She turned back to Mrs. Simpson. "I'll see you tomorrow, probably in the afternoon."

"Anytime is fine with us. Tell Mr. Hill that y'all could

do with some social news in that paper of yours. Keep us up to date on who's visiting and what's going on in the town."

"But if we printed all that in the paper, what would folks have to talk about?" teased Camille.

"All the things you can't put in print—such as what lady has caught the mayor's eye."

Camille listened intently as Mr. Hill explained the various types of ads, showing her examples. Pointing to one for the railroad listing schedules and potential destinations in very fine print, she asked, "Do you ever have complaints because the print is so small?" She practically had to squint to make out some of the words, and she had excellent vision.

"Used to, until folks figured out it wasn't going to change. That's the way the Texas & Pacific sends it. I tried to convince them to increase it to two columns and enlarge the type, but they refused. Guess they figure since they're the only railroad in these parts folks will find somebody who can read it for them." He picked up another page for that week's paper and laid it on the work table. "A lot of businesses want to put in plenty of information, but don't want to pay for a larger ad."

"So they miss all the customers who can't read it."

"Ty tells me he does a good business in magnifying glasses."

Camille laughed, studying the page, particularly the large advertisement for McKinnon's. It was easy to read due to the variations in size and style of type and plenty of white space.

"The mayor not only knows how to run our town, he knows his business," said Mr. Hill. "Though I suppose that's obvious by his success. He pretty much laid this one out by himself, including the size of the type. The only changes we made were the style differences."

Camille silently read it, admiring Ty's ability to get his message across in a concise, orderly manner. Each line was centered in the two column width.

MCKINNON BROTHERS
WILLOW GROVE, TEXAS.
Receiving and Forwarding Merchants.
Cattle Drovers and Contractors.

—DEALERS IN—
GENERAL MERCHANDISE.
HAVE THE LARGEST STOCK OF
DRY GOODS AND GROCERIES
ON THE FRONTIER.

Ready Made Clothing.
BOOTS, SHOES, HATS, CAPS.
CANNED GOODS, HARDWARE,
GLASSWARE, CROCKERY, WOOD
AND WILLOWARE, ETC.
At Lowest Living Prices
ARMS, AMMUNITIONS, ETC.
Always kept in stock.
Wool, Hides and Cattle will be taken
at Market Prices.

An examination of our goods and prices is
earnestly solicited.
MCKINNON BROTHERS

"It is impressive. Is this the one he runs every week?"

"Yes, it's his standard ad."

"We'll have to see if we can persuade him to change it."

"We?" Mr. Hill gave her a skeptical look. "You, maybe. What do you have in mind?"

"Include things that are on sale. That's what I harped on to the other customers. Mr. McKinnon shouldn't be treated any differently."

"Whatever you say," Mr. Hill murmured dryly.

She felt her cheeks grow warm and quickly turned her attention to the ad next to Ty's. "This one is different." It was one column in width and four inches long, but the words were printed so that you had to turn the paper sideways to read it. It, too, was for a general merchandise store. "Is this effective?"

"What do you think?"

"The novelty of it attracts attention. But it doesn't say very much. Only that they have a well-selected stock of goods that they propose to sell cheaply." Camille thought about it, trying to imagine how it would affect the reader. She looked at Mr. Hill. "Some people would go there at least once to see what he has to offer, especially if they're frugal."

"So it works to bring in customers."

"Yes. But it won't lure some people away from McKinnon's. Not the ones who are more interested in the prestige of shopping at the largest store in town."

"Not to mention the one owned by the mayor. He's very well thought of."

"So I've discovered." She hoped things stayed that way.

Chapter Eleven

On Tuesday evening, Ty called the city council meeting to order. "It's good to see we have enough aldermen here to get started on time."

"Yeah, Nichols. Where were you the last meeting?" Tom Carmichael was clearly teasing his friend.

"Out of town. You know that. I mentioned it the previous week."

"I think you should fine him, Mayor," said Carmichael with a big grin.

"The fines are for being late. Not for missing a meeting. Not yet anyway. Though if y'all start skipping too many, we may need to reconsider it. Now, let's get down to business. Cade says the county commissioner's court has finalized the purchase of the Woodard Block for the courthouse."

"It's about time." Jim Talbot, the city clerk, readied his pen. "Did you ask him about giving us a couple of lots for a city hall and new calaboose?"

"Yes. He said he'd take it up with the commissioners at their next meeting. He figures they'll go along with it."

"We need to do something about the Tripoli." Roger Smith leaned forward, resting his forearms on the desk. He owned a furniture store next door to the saloon that had turned into a variety theater unexpectedly. "I've gotten five complaints since Mulhany brought that theatrical troupe in on Saturday. The music's too loud and the theatrics too bawdy. Yesterday, they were acting out scenes on the side-walk. Things that would make a decent woman blush. Once in the afternoon and once earlier in the evening. The sher-iff sent them back inside, but it didn't help the noise much."

"I've had some complaints, too." Ty had gone by the Tripoli earlier in the day to speak to the owner, but he hadn't been there. Ty had spotted an actress lounging in the corner. If her attire was typical of what she wore during the performances, she could have been thrown in jail for inde-cent exposure. "It isn't the type of thing we want going on downtown."

"Miller will be all over this if we don't take care of it quick." Frank Nichols spun his pencil around on the table. "All of our opponents will be, too."

"We can't just tell Mulhany to quit," said Smith. "It wouldn't do any good. But we could pass a special ordinance about dis-turbing the peace with a theatrical or musical performance."

"That could cause a problem with some of the church so-cials," said Ty. "I think our ladies are planning a lawn and archery party in May. There will probably be music and lots of whoops and hollers during the archery contest."

"That kind of noise doesn't really bother folks." Carmichael tapped his fingers on the arm of the chair. "Es-pecially if they don't go too late. But the music and dramas at the Tripoli are immodest at best. I hear some of them are downright indecent. I walked by this afternoon and heard a loud joke that made me blush."

"Whew! It must have been a bad one." Nichols chuckled at the chance to get back at his friend.

"Then we need to be specific." Ty scribbled some thoughts on a notepad. "What about the fine?"

"It needs to be big enough to do some good." George White leaned against the back of his chair. "Say not less than twenty-five dollars and not more than two hundred."

"That should do it. How should we word it?" asked Ty.

They discussed various options, finally settling on one that seemed to cover all the necessary points. Ty read it back to them:

> Any person operating within the corporate limits of the city, who helps or in any way is concerned in keeping a house or business where indecent, loud, or immodest musical, dramatic or theatrical performances are given, in a manner calculated to disturb the inhabitants of the city, shall be determined guilty of a misdemeanor if found guilty in the Recorder's court and shall pay a fine of not less than twenty-five dollars nor more than two hundred dollars for each offense.

"I think that covers it," said Carmichael. "Especially if he's cited every time they have a performance."

"All in favor of this ordinance, say aye." Ty scanned the group, noting that all were in agreement. But to make it official, he needed to ask, "All opposed?" None of them were. "The ordinance is passed and the city clerk will post it in the next edition of the paper and have the sheriff put up fliers. I'll also have Sheriff Starr advise Red Mulhany about it so he has a chance to settle things down on his own. If I get the chance, I'll talk to Red, too.

"That brings up another concern." Ty set the pencil on the table. "We have to hire a town marshal. We have to approve a salary large enough to hire someone good and keep him."

"Why should we spend the money?" asked Smith. "The sheriff is doing a good job."

"We're overworking him. If we aren't careful, he'll leave. He can't handle everything in town and two counties by himself. You know what happens when he's out of town."

"Yeah, you fill in for him."

"Well, I'm not going to anymore." Ty knew he was issuing an ultimatum, but the council had to fulfill their responsibilities.

"What's the matter, Ty? Too busy with your new lady friend?" asked Nichols.

"If I was steppin' out with a lady like her, I wouldn't want to be spending my time playing marshal, either," said Carmichael. "Besides, Ty is right. The sheriff doesn't even have a deputy right now. He's busy just keeping the peace. One man can't do that twenty-four hours a day. We don't have anybody to follow up on collecting fines or making sure people comply with the ordinances."

"Like cleaning up their privies," added Talbot. "Some parts of town are starting to stink now that the weather is warming up."

"Or making sure the taxes are paid." Ty was encouraged that they at least saw the need.

"I recommend we set a salary of fifty dollars a month," said Nichols.

"That's only ten dollars more than the last one. We have to pay a salary comparable to what other towns are paying, enough to hire and keep a good marshal. I've lost track of how many we've had."

"Think it's around five or six," said Smith.

"How much do you think we should pay him?" Carmichael was more generous with the funds than some of the others. "I'm thinking it will take at least eighty a month to get someone good."

Nichols shook his head. "That's too much money."

"We pay Thompson forty a month to keep up the streets. Seems to me that eighty isn't too much for a marshal. Probably not enough. Talking to people about their outhouses and dogs isn't all he'll do. I sure wouldn't walk into a saloon and break up a fight for less than that."

"I agree," said Smith. He pulled out his pocket watch. "I think we should bring it to a vote. Eighty a month for a marshal. Advertise in the paper. We need folks to be assured that our town is safe. Otherwise new people won't move in, and some of the ones already here will move out."

"I second the motion," said Carmichael.

"I'm not sure advertising is such a good idea," said Ty. "We've tried that before and didn't have much luck. What if we make up a list of men we believe would do a good job and then talk to them to see if anyone is interested?"

"I can think of a couple of men who would be good," said Carmichael. "And who might take on the job for the right pay."

They discussed several possibilities and made a list.

"Ty, I think you should be the one to talk to them. Since you've helped the sheriff numerous times, you have a better idea what's involved." White glanced around at the others. "Having been a Texas Ranger doesn't hurt, either." He grinned at Ty. "In fact, I think we should put your name at the top of the list."

When the others laughed, Ty joined in. "Sorry, George. You'd have to up the ante about ten times to get me to play that game again."

He waited a minute or two before calling for the vote. Everyone but Nichols voted for it. "Motion passed. I'll start at the top of the list, since we put them in order of preference. Is there anything else?"

"We have people driving too fast across the creek bridge," said Nichols. "My brother Henry said they're going to shake it apart if they don't slow down. He should know. He's a bridge engineer in St. Louis."

"How fast can they go?"

"He said nobody should ride or drive faster than a walk across it. We'd have to put up a sign on both sides of the bridge advising people of it."

"What about a fine?" asked Ty.

"Five dollars. That should make people slow down."

"All right. Frank, do you want to put all that into the proper motion?"

"Yep. I move that no person be allowed to ride or drive faster than a walk across the creek bridge subject to a fine of five dollars if they break the law. And that a sign be posted on both sides of the bridge stating the ordinance."

"I second it," said Carmichael.

"All in favor?" Ty noted that everyone agreed.

"All opposed? Let the records show that the ordinance passed with a unanimous vote."

"Frank, will you see that the signs are posted?" When the alderman nodded, Ty continued, "Be sure and bring us the bill for your expenses."

Ty looked at Talbot. "Do we have anything that needs to be paid?"

"Only one item. Sheriff Starr has turned in a bill for thirty-six dollars and seventy-five cents for board for the city prisoners at the county jail."

"They're feedin' those boys too good," muttered Nichols.

"Have to if you want them to work on the streets to pay off their fines." Ty was getting tired of Nichols's stingy streak.

"I move we pay it." White yawned. "There was plenty in the treasury at the last meeting, even after we approved bills."

"I second it." Carmichael stifled a yawn. "Let's vote before we all fall asleep."

Ty called for the vote, which passed. Even Nichols approved of it. "Anything else?"

One by one, they shook their heads.

"Good. Talbot, I trust you'll see that there is a write-up of the meeting in the paper as well as the ordinances posted for the next couple of weeks?"

The city clerk nodded as he penned the details of the bill for Ransom.

"Meeting adjourned. I'll see you in two weeks unless something urgent comes up." Ty stood and stretched his back as the aldermen left. He pulled his watch out of the vest pocket. Nine-thirty. They'd done pretty well with the time. His concentration hadn't wavered a bit. Which was more than he could say for the rest of the day. He waited until Talbot wrote out the check for the sheriff, then added his signature along with the clerk's.

"You want to give that to Sheriff Starr?" asked Talbot.

"I'll drop it by on my way home. If he's not in the office, I'll give it to him in the morning." Ty stood by as the clerk packed up his things, then blew out the lamp. They walked out together, with Ty locking the door behind them.

"How soon will they start building the new courthouse?" asked Talbot.

"They've been working with an architect for the last couple of months. Cade said they would advertise in the Dallas and Fort Worth papers, as well as the *Gazette.* He's hoping that one of the local builders will win the job, but they have to seek bids from several places to make sure they get the best one."

"Do we have to wait for the courthouse to be finished before we start on city hall?"

"Nope. As soon as they transfer the land over to us, we can start selling bonds or whatever we decide to do to raise the money."

"Exciting times, Mr. Mayor."

"Yes, they are. Good night, Jim."

"Evenin'." Talbot went in the opposite direction, shaking his head when he walked past the Tripoli.

Ty stopped by the sheriff's office, but evidently Ransom was out making his rounds, so he headed on home. When he was across from the Barton Hotel, he automatically looked up at Camille's window. A dim light shone through the curtain, and he wondered what she was doing. Probably getting ready for bed.

That was not a good direction for his thoughts. He forced himself to think about some of the goods he needed to order for the store. That lasted maybe all of a minute.

Lord, it sure felt good to kiss her yesterday. I know I shouldn't have. But I don't think she minded. He laughed quietly. "No, she didn't mind at all." He absently turned up his street, barely noticing who was still up and who wasn't until he reached Cade and Jessie's.

He could see Jessie sitting on their front porch in a rocking chair, lamplight shining through the window. When she waved, he walked quietly across the yard, taking the chair next to hers. "Kids asleep?"

"Yes. Brad is tired from school. It takes him about a week to get used to the routine again. Thank goodness Ellie has a couple of friends her age or I'd be worn out from trying to keep her busy. She can't wait until next fall to start school. I hope she likes it as much as she thinks she will. Did you have a council meeting tonight?"

"Yes. They finally voted to pay a decent salary for a marshal, so maybe we can get some help for Ransom. You think Quint might be interested?"

"I don't think so, but you can ask." Jessie's brother, Quintin, had been the one to infiltrate the gang of cattle rustlers the year before. If it hadn't been for him, they might not have caught them. He normally worked for Cade at the ranch and had hightailed it back there as soon as he could after the trial. Being considered a hero made him uneasy. "Did you see Miss Dupree today?"

"No. But I saw her yesterday." He wasn't about to tell his sweet sister-in-law too much about what happened. "In fact, I took her out to dinner."

"My, my. Is this becoming a real courtship?"

"Maybe."

"Well, she certainly seems nice. Though I expect it's not easy for you. After I met Cade and was so drawn to him, I felt guilty sometimes because I hadn't cared that way for my first husband. I know it's not the same with you because you loved Amanda so much."

"It's a little different, but the guilt is the same. I wonder how I can be so attracted to Camille when I loved Amanda with all my heart."

"I didn't have the privilege of knowing your wife, but from what you've said and what Cade has told me about her, I don't think she would want you to go through life alone."

"No, she didn't. She told me so the night she died." Sadness and pain lay heavy on his heart. "Even at the end, she was thinking about me and my happiness."

"Because she knew she would soon have peace and happiness, while you would be left with the pain and sorrow. I've known both, Ty, and like your Amanda, I wish you happiness and love." She sighed heavily. "Sorry. After I put the kids to bed, I get melancholy without Cade. I've been trying to figure out how we could have a school close to the ranch, so we wouldn't have to stay in town."

"There aren't enough young 'uns out that way to make it worthwhile. Maybe you could hire a tutor. We could build him—or her—a little house at the ranch."

"I thought about that. But Brad and Ellie need to be with other children. Cade will be here tomorrow night."

"He doesn't like to be alone any more than you do."

Jessie laughed softly. "And he's not shy about telling me."

"Nor me. Gripes about it all the time." Ty laughed with her. "Miss Dupree talked to Mr. Hill at the paper yesterday. She is now his business partner."

"Well, that's exciting. Has she worked in the newspaper business before?"

"No. But she has experience with accounting and such. She went around and collected most of the paper's back advertising debts." Ty grinned, relieved that they had shifted the conversation to a more cheerful subject. "Charmed those tightwads right out of their money. Most of them, anyway. Now, she's going to concentrate on bringing in more advertising." He yawned loudly. "Sorry. I think I'd better hit the bedroll. Morning comes early."

"Yes, it does. Thanks for stopping by. Even a few minutes chat helps."

"I'll keep that in mind. Try to do it more often. 'Night."

"Good night. Sleep well."

He merely nodded. He hadn't slept well since he met Camille Dupree. He doubted tonight would be any different.

Chapter Twelve

Ty stopped by the sheriff's office early Wednesday morning and asked him to tell the Tripoli's owner about the new ordinance.

"The council finally agreed to a decent salary for a marshal, so maybe we can hire a good one." Ty handed him the check for the prisoner's board.

"Who do you have in mind?" asked Ransom, tucking the check in a drawer. He leaned back in the chair and propped his feet up on his desk.

"Quint is at the top of the list."

"Figured as much, but I'm hoping he'll turn you down. I've already talked to him about becoming my deputy. He's still studying on it."

"Just between you and me, I'd rather have him helping you," said Ty. "We have a list of some others who would probably be fine as marshal. But I can't think of anyone else I'd rather have as deputy sheriff."

"But you still have to offer him the marshal's job."

"Told the council that I would. Quint will make up his own mind anyway. We also passed an ordinance to keep the bridge from being jarred apart. No one can go over it faster than a walk."

"You mean I'm supposed to arrest the kids if they run across it? What if somebody's late for school?" Ransom almost managed to keep a straight face.

"Not kids—horses."

"How am I going to arrest a horse?" He was grinning outright now.

"Point your six-shooter between his eyes and haul him off to jail. Or let him haul you. Frank's putting up signs at the bridge."

"English?"

"Yes."

"We'll have a problem if it's a Spanish pony."

Laughing, Ty shook his head. "You've had too much coffee this morning."

"Just starting on my third cup." Ransom picked up the coffee, watching him over the rim of the cup. "What's Miss Dupree's connection to Nate Flynn?"

Ty wasn't fooled by his friend's casual demeanor. "Her father used to work with him." The half-truth came far too easily. That bothered him. "She's known Nate and Bonnie since she was a kid."

"Well, next time you leave her over at their place at night, you might want to hang around to walk her back to the hotel. She came back by herself Saturday night. It wasn't a problem because I ran into her when she reached downtown, but next time it might not work out that way."

"I assumed Nate would walk her back."

"She said he intended to, but he had to go to the saloon for a while and didn't get back before she was ready to leave."

"She's moving in with Mrs. Simpson today, so that should take care of it for the most part. I'll keep an eye on her anyway."

Ransom laughed and shifted his feet to the floor. "I have no doubt about that. Given the way she handled Cline, I expect she can protect herself, but I don't like to take chances."

"Neither do I."

Ransom's smile faded. "She's not the fragile lady she appears to be. I expect having her daddy working in a saloon might have something to do with it. Was he a bartender?"

"No. Professional gambler." Ty waited for Ransom to pounce on that, his friend's thoughtful expression troubling him. "They owned a Louisiana plantation but lost everything in the war."

"So her father turned to gambling. He certainly wasn't the only Southern gentlemen to earn his living that way."

"Nor is she the only Southern lady to have plenty of backbone."

"True." Ransom grinned as he stood. "You and Cade seem to take a likin' to that type of woman. Reckon I would, too."

"Can't see you with a simpering, clinging vine."

"Me, either. I've mastered spotting them. They swoon, and I make my getaway when they hit the floor."

Ty knew better. Ransom would catch them, set them in a chair, then hightail it. "I'd better get on over to the store."

Nothing went right for the next couple of hours.

Mrs. Newsom's new shoes were the wrong size. It didn't matter that they were the size she always ordered or that she had worn them three times before deciding the company had made them too small. She demanded a refund, which Ty gave her. The customer was always right—even when they weren't.

Mr. MacCorkle, the male version of the town busybody, came by to complain about his neighbor's cat. "Caterwauled all night long. Didn't sleep a wink. Not a wink. We need a law against cats. Disturb the peace, that's all they're good for."

He was followed a short time later by Mrs. Jordan, who complained about Mr. MacCorkle's dog barking all night. "I barely slept for all the racket."

"He was probably barking at your cat," murmured Ty, trying to keep from yawning. He hadn't slept much, either, but it had nothing to do with barking dogs or yowling cats. "Be a good neighbor, Mrs. Jordan, and keep your cat inside at night. Ask Mr. MacCorkle to do the same with Rover."

"His dog's name is Wilbur. The beast. And my Petunia shouldn't have to stay in at night. Cats are nocturnal animals."

"Then let her knock things off your dressing table. If she's roaming around outside at night, the coyotes are liable to get her. I know you don't want that."

"Coyotes in town? Whoever heard of such a thing?"

"Spotted one just a few nights ago." Ty didn't bother to tell her that the critter was on the very edge of town, not in her neighborhood. That didn't mean it couldn't wander closer to civilization. She left the store grumbling, but Ty figured she'd be back, at least to shop. He might not get her vote for mayor, though.

Then the produce shipment arrived from Dallas, complete with a box of smashed oranges. The carton of expensive French chocolates was squashed, too.

Ty decided then and there that he needed a change of scenery. Grabbing his hat, he headed for the front door. "Hold down the fort, Ed. I'm going out to the ranch. If anybody else comes by to complain, tell them they'll have to talk to me tomorrow."

"Sure thing, boss." Ed, the unflappable, kept stacking apples neatly in a pile.

Ty went to the livery, the one with McKinnon Brothers painted across the front. After greeting Joe Smith, who ran the place, he saddled his horse. Joe stopped cleaning out stalls and came over to talk.

"Where you headed, Mr. McKinnon?"

"Out to the ranch. Did the stage leave on time this morning?"

"Yes, sir. Right on schedule. Had three passengers, too. Pete Eden and his boy, and a perfume drummer out to make the ladies of San Angelo smell purty."

"He stopped by the store yesterday. Some of it wasn't bad." Ty mounted the horse. "See you this afternoon."

"Give my best to your brother."

"Will do. I expect you'll see him later today, too." Ty leaned forward and patted the horse on the neck. "Ready for a good ride, Dusty?" The animal answered him with a toss of his head and a few prancing steps. "Easy boy. We have to walk through town, then I'll let you go.

"Joe, if anybody comes in, tell them they have to keep the horses to a walk across the bridge. We passed an ordinance last night. They'll get fined if they go faster. Nichols's brother is a bridge engineer, and he said we'd eventually shake it apart if we keep going over it too fast."

"I'll tell them."

"It'll be in this week's paper, and we'll put some notices up. Some signs by the bridge, too."

Ty was glad nobody stopped him on the way out of town. He looked for Camille, but didn't see her. Would have stopped for her, he thought wistfully. Once he was clear of town, he gradually let Dusty build up to a smooth canter. As they covered the miles, he felt the tension unwind. He relaxed, riding easily and comfortably, enjoying the scenery.

His mind drifted and wandered all over the place. Thoughts of Amanda brought both sweetness and pain. How she'd loved this country. She'd been so proud of Willow Grove, even though it was mostly made up of tents and a few stores when she went to Glory. He was so thankful he'd built her that house right away. She'd been the first woman in town to have a real house.

"Guess I did some things right, sweetheart. But you did more for me than I did for you," he said out loud. Despite all his faults, she'd loved him fiercely. She had tamed the man who craved adventure and danger. The man who sometimes drank too much and fought at the least provocation. She'd taught him that patience and tact achieved better results than flying off the handle. You can catch more flies with honey than vinegar. She'd said it so sweetly, with so much conviction that he knew she had to be right. Yet she also understood that some circumstances required a show of force and a steady gun hand.

But her greatest gift had been leading him to Jesus. He hated to think what would have happened to him when she'd died if he hadn't had the Lord's comfort. He doubted that he'd still be around. Not that he would ever commit suicide, but he could imagine recklessly going into a gun battle and not coming out of it.

He saw some cattle up ahead and took a little detour to check the brand. Sure enough, they belonged to the McKinnon Ranch. Looked in good shape, too, for the time of year. There were a couple of others from a nearby ranch mixed in, but that happened often since few ranchers in the area had put up barbed wire yet.

He and Cade had fenced in a big pasture near headquarters for the horses and another for their prized Hereford bull, but otherwise they took advantage of the open range like most everyone else. But times were changing. They had been buying as many sections of land in their territory as they could, and they leased others. He figured by next spring they would start enclosing the ranch.

In Tom Green County, ranchers had been fencing their land for a couple of years, as much as twenty thousand acres in some cases. Some up in the Panhandle were doing likewise. It was the only way to improve herds with Durhams and Herefords.

But it caused plenty of problems with the ranchers who were advocates of free range. Ever since those first strings of barbed wire went up, fence cutting had led to great frustration and violence. The state legislature was working on a law to put a stop to it by making fence-cutting a felony. He hoped it worked. There were two sides to the issue. Some ranchers fenced in public land or land that belonged to someone else. That wasn't right, either.

He thought about Camille and wondered if anyone had bent her ear yet about fencing versus free grass. So far, Hill had kept a neutral position, but other newspapers across the state had taken sides and loved to editorialize about it. The *Fort Worth Gazette,* one of the most popular out-of-town papers, was staunchly free grass, though they did not support fence cutting.

As he rode into ranch headquarters, he spotted Cade at the corrals. He slowed Dusty to a walk as they approached his brother. One of the cowboys was attempting to ride a bucking bronc inside the pen. He didn't stay in the saddle very long.

Cade walked over to meet him. "You're just in time to show 'em how it's done."

"Not me." Ty dismounted, leading Dusty to the water trough. "I'm smarter than that these days."

Cade chuckled and looked back at the corral. Two men had roped the untamed horse and were holding it steady while the younger man gingerly approached it. "You and me, both. He's had enough for today, boys. Let Cyclone loose in the pasture for a while."

"Looks like you named him right. You think anybody will ever ride him?"

"I'm beginning to wonder. Nobody around here has managed it. What brings you out today?"

"Cranky customers and griping citizens." Ty loosened his tie. "I'm not in the mood to listen to complaints about barking dogs and howling cats."

"Tough job being mayor. Come on up to the house. I'm not working hard today, so I can head into town early."

"Let me take Dusty in to where he can visit with his friends."

Cade gave instructions to a couple of the men while Ty unsaddled his horse then opened a gate and led Dusty into a corral containing two other horses. The animals greeted each other as if they were catching up on all the news.

When they started toward the house, Cade rested his hand on Ty's shoulder. "So what really brings you out here?"

"I needed some country peace." Ty soaked up the scenery while they walked. "Sometimes I envy you living and working out here."

"Sell the businesses or turn them over to somebody else. You know I'd like having you around all the time. I miss you."

"You have a family now. I don't want to barge in. It's one thing to spend the night occasionally, but y'all would get sick and tired of me if I moved in."

"Then build another house. I'm serious. If you want to move out here and help run the ranch, it won't bother me a bit."

"Until I start ordering you around."

"You know you can't boss me. I'm the oldest."

"There you are. It wouldn't work. I'd probably be bored in a week." They walked up the porch steps, with Ty leading the way into the house. "I don't want to give up the businesses—or being mayor. I just needed a break today." He hung his hat on the hat rack by the back door. "Mostly I came out to see if I could persuade Quint to take the marshal's job. The city council finally upped the salary to eighty dollars a month."

"Can't have him." Cade hung his hat up and walked over to the dry sink. "Want some water?"

Ty nodded. "Don't you think that's up to him? That's twice what he's making here."

"But it's twenty dollars less than what he's going to make as deputy sheriff."

Ty sat down on the sofa. "Ransom said he talked to him yesterday. Quint's agreed to do it?"

"Yep." Cade handed him a glass of water, then sat down across from him. "The county commissioners had already settled on paying him a hundred a month if he took the job. He wanted to sleep on it. Gave me his answer this morning. He's at the bunkhouse packing his belongings right now."

"He's the best man for the job. It will suit him better than marshal. Even if he was at the top of our list, I can't really see him going around and telling people to pay their taxes or clean up their outhouses. I know he wouldn't shoot a dog if it doesn't have a license. I wish the city council had never passed that ordinance."

"How many licenses have you paid for now?"

"Ten." Ty rubbed his forehead. "Molly Peterson's dog had four pups a couple of weeks ago. Cute as can be, too. She couldn't shell out four dollars for licenses." He took a long drink, thinking about the elderly woman. "Seein' how happy she is with those puppies is worth every cent." *Especially since the pups and their mama were the only companionship she had. I don't want to grow old alone.*

"I'm glad you're looking out for her."

"I don't do much. Her neighbors are mighty good to her. They take care of her."

"So how's Camille?"

"Industrious. She's now part owner of the *Gazette*. Talked to Hill Monday morning and by Monday afternoon she had collected most of the delinquent accounts."

Cade laughed. "Hill's no fool. He took one look at that lady and figured his prayers were answered."

"She's moving in with Nola today."

"That will be good for both of them."

"Yes, it will."

"And make it easy for you to go courtin' if you're so inclined."

"I already thought of that." Ty shrugged. "I'm supposed to have dinner with them tonight."

"That doesn't count. You have dinner there every Wednesday night."

"But I don't sit on the porch swing with an enchanting lady every Wednesday night."

"I take that to mean you don't sit on the porch swing. Nola would have your hide if you didn't say she was enchanting."

Ty laughed and set down his empty glass. "She'd scold me from here to Sunday. I can hear her now—"

"Us sitting there in her parlor, a couple of green cowboys who didn't know the first thing about charming the ladies, young or old," said Cade with a nostalgic smile.

Ty sat up very straight, folding his hands in his lap and spoke in a falsetto voice, "A gentleman always makes a lady think she's the belle of the ball, whether she's young or ancient or so ugly she'd scare a drunk man sober."

"I thought I was goin' to bust out laughing when she said that."

"Me, too. But she was so sincere, I couldn't. Later when I realized how scarce womenfolk were in ranching country, I saw the wisdom of it."

"Not to mention that she wanted us to learn to be kind," said Cade.

"It was a while before that lesson took."

"Kindness is the last thing on a man's mind when he's busy chasing desperados, even the female kind."

"Like Sagebrush Rose." Ty absently touched the six-inch scar on his side left by the woman's knife.

"You learned the hard way that time. Can't trust saloon women. It doesn't matter whether they work there or own the place. I never met one who didn't lie through her teeth whenever it suited her."

Uneasiness tickled the back of Ty's neck. Was that what Cade would think of Camille if he ever found out about her past? "That's a little harsh. Rose was rougher than most."

"That kind of life hardens them, more than men I think. But you're right. Rose was worse than usual. Most gals don't shoot a man in the back."

"We'd need a lot more lawmen if they did." Ty decided it was past time to change the subject. His brother knew him too well. If he wasn't careful, Cade would sense Ty's discomfort and want to know the reason for it. "Do you have any food around here?"

"Some cheese and crackers." Cade glanced at the mantel clock. "It is about time for some chow. There's some canned stuff in the cupboard."

"Let's see what we can rustle up. I'm starving." That was stretching it a bit, but food was always a good distraction. Ty took his glass to the kitchen table, then walked over to the cabinet where Jessie kept her canned goods. "Want some stewed tomatoes?"

"Suits me. You could make a ham sandwich if you want one."

Ty shook his head as he rummaged through a drawer for the can opener. "Cheese and crackers are fine. Got anything for dessert?"

"There's some peach cobbler in the pie safe."

"That alone is worth the trip out here." Ty carried a couple of plates, bowls and spoons over to the table. He opened the tomatoes and divided them into the bowls while Cade sliced some cheese. "We should finish it off since Jessie probably has something else for you to bring back. I talked to her for a few minutes last night after the council meeting. She was sitting out on the front porch when I got home."

Cade set the cheese and tin of crackers on the table. "Was she all right?"

"Lonesome. Otherwise she was fine." Ty sat down, watching Cade pour them some more water.

"I hate being out here and her in town. But there's no help for it. Brad has to go to school."

"Maybe I should run the ranch and you take over the store and livery. I could live out here, and you could stay in town." Ty knew it would never happen. Cade's eyes glazed over if he stayed in the store more than a couple of hours.

"Don't tempt me. I'd probably bankrupt us in a month."

"And go loco."

"I'm going loco without her here. But I'll ride it out. It's not quite so bad as long as I get to town every couple of days to see them. Besides, if I moved to town, you'd expect me to play mayor, too."

"The thought alone would scare fleas off a dog."

While they ate, they chatted about the ranch and discussed the latest news article about the wrangling legislature. They talked about the new courthouse and possible men for the position of marshal.

Ty considered once again how fortunate he was to get along so well with his brother. Not all men were on good terms with their kin. Since Cade was the only kin he had, he was mighty thankful that they loved and respected each other.

Boot steps and the jingle of spurs announced Quintin's arrival at the back screen door before he even knocked. When he came in, Ty stood and shook his hand. "I hear you're our new deputy sheriff."

"Ransom and Cade finally talked me into it."

"At least this way, you won't have to hook up with any rustlers. Everybody will know you're the law. You need a place to stay? I've got a spare bedroom."

"I wouldn't mind bunking there until the end of the week. Ransom said Mrs. Franklin has a room coming open on Friday. He's already arranged for me to have it."

"You're lucky. I hear the food there is the best in town. I came out here to ask you to be town marshal, but I'm glad you're taking the other job. That's where we need you."

"I wish I had as much confidence in me as y'all do."

"You'll do fine. Ransom will teach you anything you haven't figured out on your own. Are you ready to go?" asked Ty. "I need to head back to town."

"He has to get back in time to go courtin'." Cade winked at his brother-in-law.

"It's that serious?" Quint looked at Ty in surprise.

"Maybe. We'll see. I've only known her six days."

"Sometimes you don't even need that long. I fell for Jessie the minute I laid eyes on her," said Cade.

"You always were the impulsive one." Ty took his hat from the peg and eased it on his head.

"I just know my own mind. And my heart."

That was the trouble. Ty wasn't sure he still had a heart. How could he when it had been shattered into a thousand pieces?

Chapter Thirteen

When Ty and Quint got to town, they dropped by the house for a few minutes so Quint could leave his belongings. Then the new deputy headed for the sheriff's office while Ty went to the store. He worked on the accounts for a while and filled out an order to send off the next day. A little before five, he decided to try once more to talk to Red Mulhany.

Approaching the Tripoli, Ty heard piano music, but no loud or boisterous singing or theatrics. Even the music was quieter than the usual saloon tune. He paused at the door, barely hiding a grin as he scanned the small, dejected crowd. The visiting performers were packing up their props and carrying them out the back door, grumbling as they did so.

Ty walked through the double swinging doors, nodding to Mulhany who leaned against the shelves behind the bar.

"Come to gloat, Mayor?" Surprisingly, the Tripoli's owner didn't seem too angry.

"No. I just came by to see how things were goin'."

"Well, they're goin' all right." Mulhany stared at the theatrical troupe. "Headin' off toward El Paso or somewhere in between. I can't pay a fine every time they do a show, even if it's only twenty-five dollars a hit."

"It would have been at the higher end of the range."

"That's what I figured." Mulhany poured himself some whiskey. "Want some?"

"No, thanks."

"Didn't think so."

"You're taking this better than I thought you would."

Mulhany downed the rest of his drink and leaned on the bar, speaking quietly. "Well, just between you and me, y'all did me a favor. This bunch is a lot raunchier than I'd expected."

"Better suited to the district than here on Main Street."

Mulhany nodded. "I ain't interested in movin' my business down there. An acquaintance in Fort Worth recommended them. The way he bragged on them I thought they were a high-class outfit. Turns out he has some monetary interest in the company, but I didn't know that at the time. Signed 'em up for a week."

"So you couldn't break the contract without losing money."

"Right. But since y'all passed that ordinance, it gave me legal cause to finagle my way out of it. The way the sheriff read the law to them helped."

"How's that?"

"Well, I don't know if you meant it this way, but he implied that the performers might be fined, too, since they're involved."

Ty laughed. "I doubt that interpretation would hold up in court, but we won't mention it to those folks."

"In a way, I wish they could stay through Saturday. Business has never been so good. But I'd lose money with that fine every day, and drive all my neighbors loco. You know,

I think there were plenty of cowboys who came in here to see the show just because it was entertainment, not because it was bawdy. Several of them walked out after the first act or sooner."

"Maybe you should build an opera house."

"I'd like to, but even if I sold this place, I wouldn't have nearly enough money for a building and starting the business, too. You have to guarantee the performers a certain amount or they won't come. It don't matter whether you bring in enough money or not, you still have to pay them."

"What if you had some partners? I've toyed with the idea for over a year now, but haven't had the time to do more than think about it. I bet we could find a few other folks who would be interested enough in having good-quality entertainment to join us."

Mulhany's eyes lit up. "Do you think we could? We wouldn't be able to get out-of-town entertainment here all the time, but local people could use it, too."

Ty had a knack for judging people, and he knew that Red Mulhany was honest and a hard worker. He also knew that Red's kind of enthusiasm for a dream went a long way to making it happen. "You been thinking about this for a while?"

The saloon keeper shrugged. "Yeah, over a year now for me, too. But I knew I couldn't do it on my own."

"Let me talk to a few people, see what I come up with."

"I've drawn up some sketches, ideas for the stage and seating. The wife likes to go to Fort Worth and Dallas every so often to visit her kinfolks. We usually try to take in a play or musical, too. I've tried to make mental notes of how the theaters are set up."

"You're way ahead of me," said Ty with a grin. "That's good information to pass on to would-be investors." He pulled his pocket watch from his vest pocket and flipped it open. "I need to get moving. Got a dinner date."

"With Miss Dupree?"

"Yes, and Miss Nola. Miss Dupree is going to stay at her place."

Mulhany grinned. "That'll make it convenient to go callin'. Especially since you go over there on Wednesday nights anyway."

Ty wondered if everyone in town knew he ate dinner with Nola on Wednesday, then decided they did. Chances were the saloon keeper already knew that Camille had moved in with Nola. Most folks in town knew just about everything about everybody else. "That it will."

As he turned to leave, he heard a commotion outside, like someone was pounding on the boardwalk.

"Close down the Tripoli! Close this den of iniquity!" Harvey Miller's strident voice was unmistakable. "Ride 'em out of town on a rail! And Red Mulhany with them."

Other voices joined in, shouting their disapproval and condemnation. Looking through the windows, Ty counted about ten men and women. He didn't blame them for voicing their displeasure and trying to protect the integrity of the town. He just wished Miller wasn't heading up the group.

"He's in fine form this evening," muttered Ty. He glanced at the traveling troupe as they each grabbed a handful of belongings and hurried toward the back door. "No need to panic, folks. I'm sure Sheriff Starr will be along directly." He looked back at Red. "I'll go talk to them. I don't expect any trouble, but if I were you, I'd lay that shotgun of yours up on the bar in clear view and easy reach."

Grimacing, Mulhany pulled his gun from beneath the counter and checked to make sure it was loaded.

As Ty walked to the door, he heard the dull thump as Mulhany set it on the bar. Pushing the door open slowly, Ty almost ran into Miller. Naturally, he was on the steps so everyone could see him. A hush fell over the crowd as Ty stepped outside. Miller slowly turned around, holding a baseball bat in both hands.

"The ball field is at the end of town." Ty scanned the crowd, then pinned his opponent with his gaze. "Or did you come down here planning to bust a few heads?"

"We're here to drive these disreputable elements out of our fine city," shouted Miller. "Looks like we need to start with you." He turned back toward the group that had come with him and the dozen or so others who had wandered over to see what was going on. "See what a fine mayor you have? You saw him walk out of there bold as brass. Is this the kind of mayor you want? Someone who spends his afternoons cavorting with indecent women and disreputable men?"

"No!" The lone voice belonged to Mrs. Miller.

Ty noted that Camille had crossed the street and stood at the back of the crowd. She met his gaze, her tiny smile telling him she had a good idea why he had been in the Tripoli.

The minister of Miller's church—a man who had already quietly told Ty that he would be voting for him—cleared his throat. "Mayor McKinnon, what were you doing in there?"

Quintin walked down the sidewalk, the deputy sheriff's badge shining brightly on his chest. Ransom was with him, the sound of their boots echoing in the silence after the reverend's question. They joined Ty, standing on each side of him.

"I came by to talk to Mr. Mulhany about the ordinance the city council passed last night." Ty pointed to the notice tacked up on the post a foot from Miller's head. "Sheriff Starr, would you care to read the new ordinance to these good folks?"

Ransom took a step forward, elbowing Miller out of the way, and loudly read the ordinance.

"Thank you, Sheriff." Ty made eye contact with a couple of people in the crowd who had arrived with Miller. "Mr. Thomas, why don't you come up here and peek in the window and tell us what you see."

The man hesitated, then bolted up the steps and peered in the window, framing each side of his face with his hands. He turned back around toward the street. "They're leaving. The last one is going out the back door right now."

"We drove them out of town," shouted Miller.

A few people cheered, their voices trailing off as Ty shook his head. "You didn't have anything to do with it, Miller. They were already packing up when I got here." He tapped the ordinance flier with his fingertip. "Your city council had already taken care of the problem. This ordinance and a threat of a fine is what sent them packing. It also enabled Mr. Mulhany to get out of his contract with the theatrical troupe. A contract he made, by the way, because he had been led to believe that their entertainment was of the highest decency and caliber. Their performances took him completely by surprise."

"So there won't be any more loud singing and indecent play acting?" asked the minister.

"No, sir." Red Mulhany stepped out of the saloon. He'd left his shotgun behind. "Your womenfolk and children can walk down the street without being scandalized or embarrassed. I apologize for what has transpired the last few days. I only wanted to provide the cowboys with some entertainment, but I never intended for it to be that kind."

"You folks go on home and have your supper," said Ransom. "The problem has been resolved." He glanced at the bat in Miller's hands. "Without me having to arrest anyone for assault and battery."

Ty wondered how his friend kept a straight face. A couple of people snickered. The crowd slowly dispersed, much to Ty's relief and Miller's obvious disgust. Ty's political opponent didn't have anything else to say. He just glared at Ty and stomped down the steps to where his wife waited. Mumbling under his breath he stormed right past her. She spun on her heel, racing after him.

"Thanks for backing me up." Ty spoke to both Ransom and Quint. He paused, studying the shiny tin star on Quint's shirt pocket. "Looks like it belongs there."

Quint made a face and rubbed the back of his ear. "Couldn't you have waited a day or two before you raised a ruckus?"

Ty laughed, his gaze shifting briefly to Camille as she approached. "Don't blame me. It was Miller's idea. Good way to initiate you, especially with Ransom here."

"Good way to make me go back to the ranch," grumbled Quint, smiling as he said it. His gaze moved to Camille, his eyes widening slightly.

As she stepped up onto the boardwalk, Ty felt an unexpected swell of pride. "Miss Dupree, this is Quintin Webb, Jessie's brother and our new deputy sheriff. Quint, may I present Miss Camille Dupree."

"Ma'am." Quint nodded, touching the brim of his hat. "It's a pleasure to meet you."

"The pleasure is mine, Mr. Webb. Between Ty and Mr. Hill, I've heard all about how you helped capture the rustlers last year. We're very fortunate to have you as our deputy."

"Thank you." Quint took a deep breath. "I sure hope I can live up to everyone's expectations."

"Bein' a hero does have a few drawbacks," said Ransom.

"Like half the unmarried ladies in town inviting you to dinner or baking you pies." Ty slapped his friend on the back. "I think you're puttin' on a little weight."

"From the pies maybe. I never have time to accept the dinner invites. Might now though since I have help. 'Course they may turn their sights on Quint and leave me out in the cold."

Camille laughed and moved into the waning sunshine. "Judging by all the ladies who stopped to watch when you two walked down the street, neither of you will be lacking for meals or desserts. You garnered as much attention as Mr. McKinnon."

Quint looked at Ty. "Observant, isn't she?"

"You've been hiding out at the ranch too long," said Ty. "Women have an innate ability to know what other women are thinking."

"Especially when it comes to men." A gust of wind stirred up the dust in the street. Camille shivered and buttoned her coat. "Is it just me or is it turning colder?"

"It's getting colder." Ty glanced at the wide, gray cloud lying across the northern horizon. "We have a blue norther blowing in. You'd better dig your heavy coat out of the trunk tonight."

"I don't have a heavier coat. This was all I ever needed in San Antonio."

"Then we'll take care of that right now." He cupped her elbow, pointing her in the direction of the store.

"It was nice to meet you, Mr. Webb."

"You, too, Miss Dupree. Don't you let Ty run roughshod over you."

"Not a chance," murmured Ransom, smiling at Camille.

Ty and Camille walked briskly toward his store. The temperature was dropping by the minute.

"I suppose now he'll tell Mr. Webb all about my run-in with the harness maker."

"Probably. But he'll do it because he wants Quint to know there might be a problem with Cline, not because he's telling tales on you." Ty opened the door to McKinnon Brothers, holding it for her to go inside. "Do you have a rubber coat in case it rains?"

"Yes. Overshoes, too. We had plenty of rain in San Antonio. Even more in New Orleans." She shivered again. "But not this biting cold. Do you stock gloves and warm hats?"

"Right this way, miss." Ty rested his hand at the small of her back. "We'll fix you right up. I have a nice heavy wool coat that has your name on it."

He guided her down the main aisle, then another until they were standing in front of the ladies' coats. Pulling a golden-brown one off the rack, he held it up in front of her. "Good color for you. I think it might be the right size."

Camille raised an eyebrow and checked the tag. "Exactly the right size. The color *is* nice."

He helped her put it on, smiling in satisfaction when she faced him again. "The color is perfect. So is the fit. It could be an inch or two shorter, but I don't think it will drag in the mud if we have rain. There's a mirror on the other side of those dresses. See what you think."

"I think it's warm and feels good." She walked around the rack of dresses, stopping in front of the mirror. "It should be all right. If it bothers me, I can always have it shortened after the cold spell."

"The alterations are free." At her questioning expression, he added, "For all our customers."

"Do you sew, too?" Mischief played across her face, making Ty smile.

"No. We use the local seamstress." He pointed to some shelves nearby. "Here's what's left of our winter hats and gloves. Do you see any you like?"

Camille perused the shelves, picking out dark-brown gloves and a matching wool hat. She pulled the hatpin from the flowery hat she had on and lifted it from her head, handing it to Ty. Putting on the new one, she tugged it down to cover her ears and smiled happily. "Now my ears don't feel like icicles." She tried on the gloves, too. "Perfect. I'll take them all."

"They're on sale for half price."

"I don't see a sign."

"That's because I just put them on sale."

"And will the sale end when I walk up to the cash register?"

Ty had the notion she wouldn't like that. "Nope. I need to clear out the stock to make room for the order of spring coats and hats coming in next week."

"Good answer, McKinnon." She led the way to the counter, removing her gloves only to write him a check.

Then she put them back on, watching as Ty put her other hat in a hat box. "Do you think it will get much colder?"

"Probably, considering the way the wind is picking up and the temperature is dropping." Ty picked up some scissors lying on the counter and cut the tags from her new purchases, then handed her the hat box. He stopped by a display of men's coats, taking one for himself and removed the tag on it, too. "Ed, you and John grab coats before you head home."

"Thanks, boss." The wind rattled the window. Ed frowned, walking over to peek out. "Think we'll need 'em. You two better get on over to Mrs. Simpson's before it starts raining."

"We're goin'." Ty grabbed an umbrella as they walked toward the door just in case they needed it. "Did you get moved in?"

"My trunks are there," said Camille. "I stopped by long enough to confirm their delivery. I've been too busy at the paper to unpack." When they walked out the door, a blast of wind hit them in the face. "Oh, my. Nobody told me it gets this cold here."

"It doesn't happen too often, and it doesn't usually last long when it does. Sorry I don't have a buggy here to drive you over."

"I'll survive." She picked up the pace. "If we walk fast."

They turned the corner heading up the street toward Nola's. Ty positioned himself on the north side of her to try to protect her from the wind. "We won't be trying out that porch swing tonight."

"Sitting in front of a nice warm fire sounds much more appealing at the moment."

He reached down and caught her hand. "As long as it's with you."

She looked up at him and nodded, warmth lighting her eyes.

His fingers tightened lightly on hers. Right that minute, even a blue norther felt pretty good.

Chapter Fourteen

Ty brought in another load of wood, stacking it on the floor by the full wood box next to the kitchen stove. He had split a similar amount and brought it into the living room. "That should keep you nice and warm for a few days."

"Thanks." Camille stood near the stove, letting the heat warm her thoroughly. She had gone outside with him after dinner and held the lantern so he could see. They had worked at the side of the house out of the wind, so it wasn't bad. Her new coat kept her from getting overly chilled.

The vigorous exercise kept Ty warm. He had even slipped off his jacket halfway through the job.

Camille had been fascinated watching him chop the wood, particularly after he'd shed the suit coat. She had seen other men do the job, but hadn't really paid much attention to them. It had never occurred to her how much coordination and precision the task required. Not to mention the strength and stamina needed to provide such a large supply. He was a very competent man in so many ways.

"Bless you, boy." Nola, as she had insisted Camille call her, patted Ty's cheek with her wrinkled hand as if he were indeed a boy. "My bones told me we had a storm headed this way, but I didn't see Silas today to ask him to cut more wood for us. I think it's going to be a doozy the way my joints ache."

"You knew I was coming by and wouldn't let you freeze." Ty put his arm around her shoulders, hugging gently. "Now, I'm ready for that cup of tea and some of Hester's coconut cake."

"You go on into the living room and rest," said Nola. "Camille and I will bring in the tea and cake."

"I could use a little pampering. It's been a long day."

"Not without a bit of excitement, either." Camille smiled at him as she unbuttoned her coat. "Shall I write up the incident at the Tripoli for the paper?" She had no intention of trying such a thing. It would turn out to be far too biased.

"No need. By morning, it will be all over town anyway."

"Probably all over town already." Nola picked up a long knife to cut the cake. "You want a big piece, Ty?"

"Yes, ma'am. About half of it will do." He grinned and sauntered into the living room.

Nola cut him a generous piece of cake, but not half of it. "Don't want to give him bad dreams."

"He could probably eat half of it, given how hard he was working out there." Camille set the tea service, cups and saucers on a large tray.

"Admirable sight, isn't it? Watching a strong man chop wood. I always stopped what I was doing when my husband was tending to that chore." Nola paused in the middle of cutting another piece of cake, her expression wistful and a bit sad. "He looked so good swinging that ax. All man." She took a deep breath and focused on the task at hand. "I was always afraid he'd cut a foot off." She laughed, shaking her head. "We were married almost fifty years, and he never once nicked himself with that ax. The hatchet, either. But I was always afraid he would. 'Course half the time we burned cow chips in the fire instead of wood."

"Cow chips?" Camille picked up the tea tray.

"Cow manure that's dried hard from the sun. When we were first out here, we used buffalo chips, too. But the buffalo had been killed off, except for the few that were taken by some of the ranchers to keep them from becoming extinct. So we ran out of that fuel after about a year."

"I think I prefer wood or coal."

"Made a mighty good fire, and when there's barely any wood for ten miles around, you're thankful to have it." Nola set the plates, forks and napkins on another tray. "You'll have to come back for this, dear."

"I'll be glad to." Camille carried the tea into the living room and set it down on the center table. She went back for the cake, stepping out of the way so Nola could come into the room.

When she returned, the elderly lady motioned for her to sit on the sofa with Ty. "Why don't you take care of the tea for us?"

"I'd be happy to." She prepared a cup for Nola. "Sugar?"

"One spoonful, please."

Camille stirred a spoonful of sugar into the cup. "Cream?"

"No thanks."

She handed the cup and saucer across to her landlady. "Mr. McKinnon, how do you like your tea?"

"One spoon of sugar for me, too. No cream." There was a hint of admiration in his eyes.

It struck her that he was pleased because she could competently do such a ladylike task. I hope he doesn't expect the same thing when it comes to cooking, she thought. She poured her tea, adding a bit of sugar and cream, then handed the others their cake.

Ty took a bite. "Mm. As good as ever. Give my compliments to Hester."

"I will," said Nola. "I do enjoy her cooking. Almost as much as Jessie's. Now that woman knows her way around a kitchen."

"She loves trying new recipes. Cade says he never knows what to expect for dinner, especially when it comes to desserts. I don't think she's ever tried anything that wasn't delicious."

He polished off his cake, set the plate and fork on the table and turned toward Camille. "Did y'all get any news about how the legislature voted today?"

"On the fencing bill?" Camille had finished her much smaller piece of cake and set the plate down. When Ty nodded, she continued. "Yes. By the way Mr. Hill talked, I thought you'd probably heard. They finally passed the law. Fence cutting is a felony, punishable by one to five years in prison. The penalty for malicious pasture burning is two to five years in prison."

Ty whistled. "With the way the legislators have bounced around on the issue, that's stiffer than I'd expected. What about fencing in land that doesn't belong to you?"

"It's a misdemeanor. It has to be done knowingly and without permission. Those who build the fences have six months to remove them. Ranchers who build fences across public roads on their property have to place a gate every three miles and make sure it's in proper repair."

"It sounds like a fair law." Nola took her last bite, chewing thoughtfully.

"As long as the ranchers who have fenced in land they shouldn't have act quickly to take them down. If they procrastinate too long, it will cause more trouble," said Ty. "Cade and I are planning to fence in our place beginning next spring. It's costly to do it, but I think it will save money in the long run. We can keep track of our cattle a whole lot easier. Other ranchers' cattle won't eat our grass or drink up our water."

"What if we have a drought?" asked Nola. "What will you do with your stock then?"

"We'd have to find another range for them. Maybe lease land up north or out in New Mexico."

"Has there been much fence cutting around here?" asked Camille.

"No. Mainly because there aren't many fences. They've had some cutting down in Tom Green County. It's gotten bad in several other places. The small ranchers with no land started out cutting the fences of the big operators who had fenced in the public lands. I couldn't fault them for that. Seems like some rough characters have moved in expressly to cause trouble."

Nola shook her head. "I can't understand the arrogance of some of these big-money corporations thinking they can do whatever they want. In some places, they've fenced in other ranches, farms or even towns."

"That was what started it. Now some fellows just cut barbed wire whenever they see it, even if the rancher isn't causing any problems for anyone else."

"Mr. Hill had a telegram that fence-cutters were 'playing the wild' in Bastrop," said Camille. "They cut several miles of fence and left handwritten notices that they are free-grass fence-cutters and they'll cut the throats of any owners if they rebuild the fence. Do you think they'll follow through on their threat?"

"They might. There have been a few killings, but not many. I suppose it will take catching some of them and sending them to the pen to make them understand the law." Ty stretched his legs out in front of him in a comfortably relaxed manner. "Anything else of note?"

"If I tell you, you won't read the paper."

"I promise I'll read everything else."

"They're having a terrible flood in Ohio. Parts of Cincinnati and surrounding areas are completely submerged. They had lost telegraph communication with towns farther up the Ohio River. Thousands of homes and businesses are covered in water."

"Oh, my. Those poor people," said Nola. "They've lost everything."

"I think some were able to take their belongings with them. Where houses are only partially flooded, the police are patrolling in boats because they're afraid thieves will use boats and take advantage of the owners' absence."

"I wonder if the same storm is blowing in here tonight. If it is, we could be in for problems of our own." Ty glanced toward the window.

"Do you think Willow Creek will flood?"

"It could. But it's well away from any of the buildings, so I don't think it will cause too much trouble. Unless the water goes over the bridge. Then we won't be able to go out of town in that direction. If it floods, all the other creeks in the county probably will too. It'll be a mess."

"Well, I think I'll head on to bed in case we have some exciting weather in the next few days. Might not get to sleep as much tomorrow night." Nola stood, leaning on her cane. Ty stood also. "No need to play polite, boy, even if I did teach you to. Camille, just set the dishes in the kitchen with the rest. Hester will take care of them in the morning."

"Shouldn't I wash them?"

"No need. She's used to me leaving them for her. Gets testy when I don't. Says that's what she's paid for. You've had a long, busy day. You need to spend a few minutes with your beau without an old lady watching you like a nosy old hen."

Ty walked over and kissed Nola on the forehead. "Good night, sweetheart."

"You can flatter me all you want, rascal, but you can't have any more cake." She laid her hand on his face, her countenance softening and filled with love. "It's good to see you happy," she whispered.

Camille still heard her. Surely making him happy was a good thing. "Do you need me to get you another quilt?"

"I have an extra one at the foot of the bed. It should be fine. I'll see you in the morning, Camille. I hope you enjoy your room."

"It's lovely. I know I will."

"Has to be better than the hotel. Not nearly as noisy anyway."

"Simply being here is better than the hotel. Call me if you need anything during the night."

"I will, though I don't expect that to happen. But it is nice knowing someone will be here if I need help. Don't keep her up too late, Ty. She has to go to work in the morning." Nola winked at him and walked down the hall, her cane tapping lightly on the floor. Her bedroom was on the ground floor to the left of the kitchen.

Ty sat back down, moving a little closer to Camille than he had been before, but there was still a respectable space between them. "You two seem to get along well."

"I think we will. She's an interesting lady and very kind."

"Unless she catches you rollin' a smoke behind the barn."

"How old were you?"

"Fourteen. She plucked that cigarette out of my hand and stomped on it. Then she pulled the pouch of tobacco from my shirt pocket and ground it into the dirt with the toe of her boot."

"No lecture?"

"Yes, there was a lecture on the filthiness of tobacco. It probably lasted five minutes but seemed like an hour." Ty laughed and slipped his hand around hers. "It's funny now, but it sure wasn't humorous at the time, not when every cowboy on the ranch peeked around the barn to see what the ruckus was about."

"I bet it was a long time before you lived it down."

"A couple of years. By then I'd pulled plenty of other dumb stunts to give them fodder for their tales."

"What about Cade? Did he get into mischief, too?"

"Half the time he led the way. But if I got into trouble, he was always there to bail me out."

She looked up at him, resting her head on the back of the sofa. "I expect you went to his rescue, too."

"On occasion."

"Fourteen. Weren't you young to be working on a ranch?"

"No. I've seen boys as young as ten show up wanting to be cowboys. Sometimes they make it at that age, sometimes they have to wait a while." He was quiet for a few seconds, lost in thought. "I was eleven and Cade was thirteen when we came west."

She wondered if he was even aware of his fingers tightening around hers.

"Father was killed in the war. Mother died six months later. Cade blames himself for that. He did his best to take care of her. As far as that goes, I did, too. But there was too little food and no medicine." He looked at her, sadness and regret etched on his face. "Our mother was a true Southern lady like you. Her family had owned a small plantation in Georgia for four generations. Father was a lawyer and a businessman. Her parents had wanted her to marry another landowner, but she loved him desperately, so they relented.

"My grandparents had both died of a fever in the early days of the war. We stayed at the plantation for a while before deserters burned it to the ground. There wasn't much left anyway. The military on both sides had taken everything of use. We hid in the woods when the deserters came, then lived in a makeshift shack Cade and I put together. We'd gotten word about our father's death a week before the big house was burned. Maybe if the two hadn't happened so close together, Mother would have survived. But she'd lost too much. She didn't have the strength or the will to fight the sickness."

"She died of a broken heart," Camille said softly.

"I think she did. No matter how much she loved us, she couldn't go on without Father."

He had known so much heartache. Perhaps it had played a big part in making him the man he was. "How did you get to Texas?"

"Walked. We buried Mother and pointed our bare feet west. Sometimes we caught a ride in a farm wagon, but we walked most of the way. We'd do odd jobs whenever we could, usually just for a meal and a night's sleep in a barn. Some folks had us stay a while, though most only wanted us around for a few days. The Petersons in East Texas kept coming up with things for us to do. Mrs. Peterson said they had to keep us around long enough to fatten us up a bit."

"How did you meet Nola's husband?"

"We hooked up with one of his cowboys in San Antonio, and he took us out to their ranch in South Texas. They moved out here about six years ago. Cade and I were still with the Rangers, but we kept in touch with them and tagged along a year later."

"At the right time to start a town."

"First we established the ranch and worked it for about a year. When we heard the railroad would be coming through here, things started hopping." He grinned and released her hand, shifting a bit so he could look at her easier. "I decided I wanted to be in the thick of it."

"I expect Amanda was glad to move to town."

"Yes and no. She liked living out at the ranch, but she enjoyed being around people. Unfortunately, there weren't any houses or buildings. Our first town home and the first store were in tents. As soon as the railroad got this far, we shipped in lumber from Fort Worth and built a store and a house."

"In that order?"

"Nope."

A gust of wind rattled the window. "You'd better head on home," said Camille.

"Ready to get rid of me?"

"No, but I don't want you caught in the storm, either."

"I suppose you need to unpack." Ty stood and held out his hand. When she clasped it, he pulled her up beside him.

"Some, at least. It will take a few days to get settled." She tucked her hand around his arm as they walked toward the front door. "I sent one of my trunks over to Bonnie's." She lowered her voice to almost a whisper. "The dresses I used to wear to work. I didn't want to bring them here."

"Nola wouldn't pry. Doubt Hester would, either."

"Probably not, but she might get curious about a trunk that I never opened. Bonnie and I will eventually box them up and send them to an acquaintance in New Orleans. If she can't wear them, she'll probably find someone who can."

"You aren't going to keep any of them?" A second later, dull red crept up his neck and face.

She couldn't resist teasing him. "Why, Mr. McKinnon, are you interested in seeing what I wore to work?"

"No." He frowned and huffed, then glanced away. "Yes. But I shouldn't be."

His admission, however grudgingly given, was touching. In an odd way, it was also comforting. It told her jaded, cynical mind that he was as normal as any man, even though he lived by higher morals than other men she had known.

"I'll keep one or two. Perhaps someday I'll wear one for you." When he swallowed hard, she took pity on him. "My clothing wasn't nearly as immodest as one would expect. I was Angelique, the Angel."

"So you dressed like one," he said with a quiet sigh.

She wasn't sure if he was disappointed or relieved. "Well, I didn't have wings."

His lip twitched with the beginning of a smile. "So you were the demure gambler?"

"Most of the time."

He rested his right hand at the small of her back. "And other times?"

"A little less demure." She slid her hand around his neck. "But never vulgar. They would be appropriate for a fancy ball." Though she had never gone to one.

"Too bad the ladies gave up on the idea of a Leap Year Ball. Save one for New Year's. We'll throw a party."

"If I'm still here."

"I hope you are." His left hand joined the right one.

"So do I."

"If your gowns aren't scandalous, why do you want to get rid of them?"

"Every time I wore one, it would remind me of what I used to do. The two I might keep are brand new, so they probably wouldn't bother me that way." The wind rattled the window again. "You'd better go."

"I will directly." He lowered his head until his mouth was only an inch or two above hers. "But I need a proper send-off."

She put her other hand around his neck and whispered, "Good night."

"Dream of me." He captured her mouth in a toe-curling kiss, guaranteeing that she would do just that.

Chapter Fifteen

Camille awoke Thursday morning to a cold, pouring rain. By the time she left for work, it had lessened but was still coming down steadily. It kept up all day, prompting pleased smiles from the ranchers because it would provide good ground moisture for the spring grass. The townspeople were anticipating plenty of fresh vegetables from their gardens and pears and peaches from their fruit trees. Slipping and sliding across the muddy streets were novelties, invoking laughter and hearty teasing when an unfortunate cowboy landed on his backside.

By Saturday, however, the good humor and smiles had been replaced by frowns of worry. The rain had been relentless, turning the streets into a muddy bog which captured wagons, horses and sometimes people in its clutches. The creeks in the surrounding area overflowed, and Willow Creek lapped at the edges of the bridge.

Ty and Camille stood inside his store, gazing out the front

window at the dark, cloudy day. The streets were almost empty. Other than Camille and the employees, nary a soul had ventured out to McKinnon Brothers in the two hours they had been open.

They had decided the day before not to drive out to the ranch. It was just as well, since Cade had come to town to be with his family instead of taking them back home.

"Does it rain like this often?" Camille asked gloomily.

"No, and it doesn't last too long when it does. Maybe tomorrow will be nice and sunny."

"I hope so. We had rainy spells in San Antonio, and of course, lots of rain in New Orleans, but it wasn't this cold, dreary stuff."

Ty gently turned her away from the window. "I think I know someone who needs a distraction."

"Doing what? Stocking shelves?"

"How did you guess?" Resting his hand on her back, he propelled her down the aisle. "I have two boxes of books to unpack."

She slanted him a glance of disdain. "You want me to unpack books?"

His expression was filled with pure mischief. "Not a good idea?"

"Nope."

"Why, Miss Dupree, I thought you'd jump at the chance to do some hard physical labor."

Camille batted her eyelashes, exaggerating her Southern drawl. "Mr. McKinnon, I've never done physical labor, hard or otherwise."

He chuckled, guiding her into his office. She noted that he left the door open this time. It was the proper thing to do, but it made her wonder if there had been some talk or some questions after her visit on Monday. He pulled the extra chair over in front of the desk next to his, waiting until she sat down before he took his seat.

"Red Mulhany and I are thinking about building an opera house."

"I'm surprised he's interested after his experience with the Hamilton Performers Extraordinaire. You, either, for that matter."

"We've both been thinking about it on our own for about a year but hadn't mentioned it to anyone else. He thought he was getting a different kind of entertainment. I'm sure he wouldn't have brought them here if he'd known what they were like. We want to build something high-class, and bring in entertainment suitable for families as well as the cowboys."

"It's a wonderful idea. But won't it be expensive?"

"Yes. I'm looking for a few other people to invest in it. Red wants to run it. He and the missus go to plays fairly often in Fort Worth and Dallas. He has some good ideas, but I thought you might have some suggestions."

Camille had often gone to the theater, particularly in New Orleans, but she was surprised that Ty would even consider that she might have. "Let me see what you have in mind."

He unfolded a floor-plan sketch. "He's based this on one in Dallas. It's about the size that I think we could build and support here."

"What about boxes?"

He unfolded another sheet. "I think we could only do one row on three sides of the building."

"That should work. Then they could watch the stage if they wanted or check out who else is there."

"Which always seems to be important to some."

"The lobby seems large enough. So does the hallway around the boxes. Are you going to slope the stage or the main floor?"

"We haven't decided yet. Red's going to take a trip to Fort Worth and Dallas as soon as the weather clears up and see which one seems to work best."

She leaned against the back of the chair. "Red velvet curtains. Padded seats?"

"Only in the boxes."

"Benches on the main floor?" She frowned thoughtfully. "That could get uncomfortable in a long performance. Especially for women and children."

"We were thinking chairs that can be fastened together. Something with a shaped seat, but no cushion. Most of the cowboys and freighters scrub up when they come to town, but some don't. Plain wooden seats would be easier to keep clean."

She studied the drawings once more. "You might need to make the dressing rooms a bit larger, and the pit for the musicians. There should be room for a piano as well as a handful of other instruments. And you'll need to provide the piano." She leaned back again. "I hope you have several investors."

"Three so far. Red, Cade and me."

"Make it four."

"Camille, I didn't tell you about this to try to get money out of you."

She liked the soft, gentle way he said her name, and the fact that he spoke without thinking about whether it was socially proper or not. It was the way friends talked, not polite acquaintances. "I know you didn't, but I'd really like to be a part of this. An opera house can be so important to the community. Churches, schools, and local drama groups can all use it, too."

Ty searched her face. "You sound like someone putting down roots."

"Maybe. Even if I move on, at least I'll have contributed to something worthwhile." At the moment, staying in Willow Grove held great appeal, but she had learned long ago that life could deal a lousy hand when you least expected it.

She glanced at the clock hanging above his desk. "I should go. Nola is expecting me a little before noon. Hester is making chicken soup."

Ty smiled and folded up the opera house notes. "I assume you like chicken soup."

"Love it." Camille pushed back her chair and stood. "Then again, I like almost any kind of food. It's probably good that I don't know how to cook. I think I'd be far too prone to eating more than I should."

"It might not make any difference. Jessie loves to cook and she stays nice and slim." He stood, too, but didn't seem in any hurry for her to leave.

"She has two children to keep up with."

"There you go. Have a couple of young 'uns and you can eat all the time."

"That doesn't seem to work for some people."

"I suppose not." He paused, then met her gaze. "Do you want a family?"

Her heart skipped a beat. She was afraid to admit how much she longed for a husband and children. "Yes. Though I haven't been around kids very much. I don't know if I would be very good with them."

"Given how well you and Ellie hit it off on Sunday, I expect you'd do fine."

"Brad certainly didn't jump into the conversation."

"Never does. He's shy and likes to size people up before he starts talking to them. His pa treated him real bad. It took a lot of love and patience for Cade to convince him that he could trust somebody besides his mother."

"They certainly seem fond of each other, now. Oh, I almost forgot. I'd like to get a Bible. Do you have any?"

"Yes. Even have some that are still in the box."

"As in the boxes you wanted me to unpack?"

"Yep. But I have some on the shelf, too." He peeked out the office door. "Still no customers." Surprising her, he grabbed her hand, tugging her through the doorway. "Come on, we'll pick one out."

Laughing, she followed him for a few steps, then walked beside him when he slowed down. "I thought there was only one kind."

"Well, basically there is, the King James Version. But it comes in several styles and sizes." He pulled a large, heavy tome from the shelf. "Here is the pocket-sized version."

"Maybe a giant's pocket. It reminds me of the one we had when I was a child."

"It's a family Bible, the kind where you record all the marriages, births, deaths and other important events. Do you still have it?"

"No. Like yours, our home was burned, too."

Ty took a much smaller book from the shelf. "This one is the right size for everyday use. It's called a teacher's Bible, but I like it because it has maps and a concordance—an index of various words with a listing of some of the verses where they're found." He turned to the back of the book and opened it. "It doesn't list every word, of course, but the important ones, or at least the ones the publisher thought were important. A lot of times, it doesn't include all the verses where a word is found, like some of the bigger Bibles do. I don't know how they decide what goes in it." He closed the book and handed it to her.

When she opened it, she was surprised by how thin the paper was. "I'll have to be careful with it."

Ty nodded, his expression solemn. "The pages are stronger than they look. But you should treat it with reverence. Not because you're afraid you might tear a page, but because it contains the word of God."

"You truly believe that?"

"Yes, I do. The teaching found here has stood firm for almost two thousand years. Folks differ sometimes on the peripheral stuff—such as whether a sprinkling baptism is just as good as immersion." He glanced toward the front window at the pouring rain. "Today, you could go out in the street and do both. I figure God doesn't pay too much attention to those things as long as the core beliefs remain true to what Jesus taught. I think God looks on each person's heart, not what pew he sits in on Sunday morning."

"Should I start reading at the beginning?"

"Have you ever read any of it?" he asked gently.

Camille understood that he would not criticize if she admitted the truth. "No. We went to church when I was very small, but that pretty much ended when the war started. After that, neither of my parents had any use for church or the Bible."

"I'd suggest starting in the New Testament." He opened the Bible to the first page in that section. "It will tell you about Jesus. The first four books are about Him and His life. They were written by different men, close followers and His friends. Matthew and Luke talk about Jesus' birth."

"The Christmas story. My father had a friend who always told it on Christmas Eve." She smiled, remembering the incongruity of the scene. "Folks said that Preacher Sam had lost his faith, but I don't think he really did. Not all of it anyway. He would sober up on Christmas Eve and sit on a stool in the corner of the saloon. At eight o'clock, everyone would gather around, and he would tell us about Mary and Joseph and the baby Jesus. How the angel visited them both and told them what was going to happen. There was such reverence in his voice when he spoke. It took him over an hour."

"Then you're familiar with that part of the story. You might want to start with John." Ty opened the Bible to the Gospel of St. John. He pointed at the first verse. "When he refers to the Word and to the Light, he is talking about Jesus." He handed her the book. "The main thing is just to have an open mind and an open heart. Let God show you His truth from the scriptures."

She held the Bible carefully, curious to read it, yet a little frightened, too. Would the words scorn her as that fire-and-brimstone preacher in New Orleans had done? "How much do I owe you?"

"Nothing."

She started to protest, but stopped when he held up his hand.

"I want to give it to you as a gift. It means a lot to me."

"Thank you, Ty."

"You're very welcome. If you'll let me borrow it for a minute, I'd like to fill in the inscription page."

"All right. I'll get my things while you do it." They walked back to his office. She sat down in the spare chair and pulled on a pair of overshoes. She glanced at Ty as he sat down at the desk, a thoughtful look on his face. Taking her rubber coat from the rack in the corner, she put it on, buttoning it up as he bent over the desk and began to write. By the time she reached for her hat and gloves he was finished. She waited to put on the gloves.

He stood and handed her the Bible. "Here you go."

Camille opened it, flipping a couple of pages until she reached the dedication page, where he had filled in the blanks and added a few lines:

> This Bible is presented to Camille Dupree by her friend, Ty McKinnon, on February 9, 1884.
> May this book and the God who inspired it be a blessing to you. Psalm 25:1-6.

His words prompted a swell of emotion and tenderness, bringing a faint mist to her eyes. How had she ever become friends with this kind, caring man? "Thank you. Where is Psalms?"

"In the Old Testament. There is a table of contents in the front. I still can't find some of the books without looking up the page numbers." He adjusted her collar more securely around her neck. "Wait until you get back to Nola's to read the passage in Psalms."

She looked at the clock. "Oh, dear, I'm going to be late."

"Tell her you were keeping me company. That will pacify her."

"No doubt." Camille tucked the Bible into her bag and drew the top tightly closed. Pulling on her gloves, she picked up the umbrella and laughed. "I feel as if I'm armed for battle."

"You are—with the weather. Will you be warm enough?"

"Yes, my coat is lined with alpaca."

"I'll come by and pick you and Nola up in the morning for church. I've already reserved the surrey. Hopefully the top will help keep some of the rain off us." They started toward the front door.

"Maybe it will have stopped by then."

"I hope so." A minute later, he peered out the door as he opened it for her. "But it doesn't look too likely. Do you want me to go with you? That mud is awful slippery."

"And have you pull me down when you start falling?" She grinned cheekily over her shoulder. "No thanks."

"Maybe I'll drop by after supper."

She stopped and turned around to face him. "That would be nice."

"Yes, it would. I'll plan on it then."

Chapter Sixteen

Smiling with happiness, Camille carefully walked along the wet boards of the sidewalk until she turned up the cross street. She slogged through the mud, at times wondering if it would pull the overshoes right off her feet. The umbrella protected her head and shoulders, but water ran off the lower half of her coat. When she reached Nola's, she walked around to the back of the house, thankful for the covered porch that wrapped around it.

Nola threw open the door. "Lord have mercy, what a day. Use that hook there by the window to hang up your coat. Best for it to do its dripping out here."

"I'll say. I'm thankful I had it." Camille set her bag on a chair and propped the open umbrella in the corner so it could dry. Then she laid her gloves on a little table against the wall. Taking off her coat, she hung it up, staring briefly at the water streaming off of it. Sitting down in a chair by the back door, she pulled off her overshoes and left them on the porch. Gathering up her gloves and bag, she went inside.

"I have a nice pot of tea all made."

"Good. I'm cold and thirsty. Let me run my hat and gloves upstairs, then I'll be right down to help."

"No rush. The soup and cornbread will stay warm."

"It smells wonderful." Camille hurried up the stairs, placing her things in her room. She took the Bible from her bag, relieved to see that it hadn't gotten wet. Checking her reflection in the mirror, she smoothed her hair and adjusted a few pins before going back down to the kitchen.

Nola was ladling the soup into bowls. "The cornbread is on the warming shelf. If you want to set it on the table, then get these bowls, we'll be all set to eat."

When everything was ready, Camille paused while Nola sat down, then joined her at the table. She had already learned that her landlady said grace at every meal. Bowing her head, she folded her hands in her lap.

"Heavenly Father, we thank You for this food that You provided. We thank You for the rain, too, but You've already provided enough. You can turn off the spigot anytime. Please protect folks who live near the streams and creeks and anyone working out in the storm. In Jesus' name, amen."

"Amen," whispered Camille.

"So what's going on in town?" Nola buttered a piece of cornbread and took a bite.

"Nothing. There was hardly anyone there besides the shopkeepers. Ty didn't have a single customer."

Nola's eyes began to twinkle. "So did you visit a spell and keep him company?"

"I did." Camille took a spoonful of soup. "This tastes as good as it smells. Is it hard to make?"

"Nope. I'll have Hester show you next time. Just chop a few vegetables and throw them in with some chicken and water and let it simmer all morning. I often tell her to make soup on Saturday, so she can leave early. What is our illustrious mayor up to? Had any more run-ins with Miller?"

"None that he mentioned. Ty, Cade and Red Mulhany are making plans to build an opera house."

"It's about time. Should have started on that a year or two ago."

"Ty showed me some preliminary drawings, merely idea sketches. They appear to have thought things through. I'm going to put some money into it."

"Better make sure you have a say, too. I like that. Those men need a woman's input on this."

Camille paused to eat some cornbread. "Maybe Hester can show me how to make this, too."

"She could. Or I will, since I made this batch. It's easier than the soup, as long as you don't leave it in the oven too long."

"Well, either it's the best cornbread I've ever eaten, or I was starving." She grinned and dipped a corner of the bread into the soup. "Probably both."

She told Nola all about the opera house and listened to a few ideas the older lady had. She made a mental note to pass the information on to Ty. When they finished eating, she cleaned up the kitchen while Nola retired to her room for a nap. She didn't think it would be a good idea to leave the dirty dishes until Monday morning.

Camille went upstairs to her room. The night before, she had scooted the rocking chair over closer to the stovepipe which ran up one wall. It wouldn't be warm enough to stay very long, but it would do until she read the verses Ty had noted. Sitting down, she tipped the Bible toward the window to use the gray light coming through the panes and read his inscription again. She traced a fingertip over the words.

"He has beautiful handwriting. My friend," she whispered. It would be so easy to let him become something more. "Foolish and impossible." But it was equally impossible not to dream.

She checked the table of contents and found the page number for Psalms. Turning to it, she quickly found chapter twenty-five and began quietly to read out loud.

> Unto Thee, O Lord, do I lift up my soul. O my God, I trust in Thee: let me not be ashamed, let not mine enemies triumph over me. Yea, let none that wait on Thee be ashamed: let them be ashamed which transgress without cause. Shew me Thy ways, O Lord; teach me Thy paths. Lead me in Thy truth and teach me: for Thou art the God of my salvation; on Thee do I wait all the day. Remember, O Lord, Thy tender mercies and Thy loving-kindnesses; for they have been ever of old.

She had once asked Ty how to pray. He'd said he simply talked to God. Depending on how he was feeling, sometimes he prayed with great reverence. Other times he talked to God as if he were talking to his dearest friend—which he probably was. The verses Ty had given her were a prayer from whoever wrote them. She knew he intended them to be her prayer, too.

Camille considered the words of the psalm. If she said them as a prayer, she had to mean it. She had to have an open heart and an open mind. She looked out the window, watching the rain slide down the glass and thought of how Bonnie had changed since she'd left San Antonio. Though her friend didn't have all the answers, especially where Nate and his business were concerned, she seemed happier than she ever had, more at peace with herself and life.

Camille believed in God. She supposed she always had. She didn't know much about Jesus, but she was willing to learn. The real issue was whether or not she was willing to trust God and believe that He would show her His truth.

Taking a deep breath, she turned her gaze back to the scriptures, silently reading them as a prayer, until she came to verse four. "Shew me Thy ways, O Lord; teach me Thy paths," she said softly. Surprised by the yearning in her heart, she stopped, considering the unexpected depth of feeling. "Lead me in Thy truth, and teach me: for Thou art the God of my salvation; on Thee do I wait all the day," she whispered.

She finished verse six in silence, then went on to verse seven, even though Ty hadn't included it. "Remember not the sins of my youth nor my transgressions..." Her voice cracked and she drew a harsh breath.

Harlot! The preacher's shout and pointed finger of so many years ago burned through her soul.

Pain and shame filled her heart. Tears blurred her vision, but she continued reading softly, stopping at the end of verse eight. "...according to Thy mercy remember Thou me for Thy goodness' sake, O Lord. Good and upright is the Lord: therefore will He teach sinners in the way."

She sat quietly rocking for a few minutes, contemplating the things she had read. "Lord, I don't know much about You, but I want to learn. You know I'm a sinner, so I have to depend on You to teach me the way."

The chill in the room sent her downstairs where she spent the next few hours reading her new Bible. She read about half of John, then went back to the Psalms, skipping around, reading the chapters that caught her eye. Thumbing through the pages, she found the book of Proverbs.

That's where she was when Nola joined her in the living room by the fire. The older lady cast a knowing eye at the book in her hand and smiled. "A good pastime for such a dreary day."

"It's interesting." Camille hesitated, then decided that if Nola wanted to discuss the scriptures with her, she would quickly figure out that Camille knew little about them. "My parents weren't much for going to church. Last Sunday was the first time I've been in years."

"Better to start late than never go at all." Nola sat down in her favorite chair, picking up her own well-worn Bible. "Where are you reading?"

"John. And Psalms. Some of Proverbs, too." She stopped, wondering if Nola would think she was silly for jumping around so.

"I like to read the Psalms, too, even if I'm studying another book. They have a way of expressing a lot of the emotions we all feel at one time or another."

"The first verse of Proverbs says that Solomon was David's son. Is he the same David who wrote some of the Psalms?" Camille caught her lower lip between her teeth. Now Nola would realize how ignorant she was.

If her question came as a surprise, Nola didn't show it. "Yes. He was a king of Israel hundreds of years before Jesus' time. Did you ever hear the story of David and Goliath?"

"I think so. Goliath was a giant that David killed with a sling-shot?"

"That's right."

"My mother read the story to me when I was little. I remember because it was right before the war. She said the Confederacy was like David, and Lincoln and the United States were like Goliath. She believed God would make the South victorious."

"Most of us like to think that God is on our side in a conflict. I reckon sometimes He's the only one who truly knows who should win." Nola tilted her head, studying Camille's Bible. "That looks brand-spankin' new."

"Ty gave it to me. I was going to buy it, but he insisted on making it a present."

"Sounds like him. He has a generous soul, that boy."

"Yes, he does." And a kind heart, integrity, loyalty, a sense of humor and ruggedly handsome looks.

No wonder he was slipping past the barriers protecting her heart.

Chapter Seventeen

Ty didn't get to spend the evening with Camille after all. The back corner of the warehouse section of the store sprang a leak. He and Cade spent half the night moving merchandise, plugging the hole and diverting the water on the roof with a secondary makeshift gutter.

When he picked Camille and Nola up for church Sunday morning, he was tired, cranky and felt as if he were coming down with a cold. By the end of the service, he was sure of it. He practically had to stuff a handkerchief in his nose to keep it from dripping.

He helped Camille and Nola into the surrey, pausing to sneeze before he climbed in, too. "I'd planned to invite you ladies out to dinner, but I'm not fit for company." He turned away quickly, sneezing again.

"You look like you feel miserable." Camille tugged off a glove and laid her hand on his forehead. "You're awfully warm. Maybe you should see a doctor."

"It's just a cold. But about all I feel like doing is going home and sleeping the rest of the day."

"Which is exactly what you should do," said Nola. "Do you have anything to eat at the house?"

"Some canned goods, but Jessie will make sure I have plenty to eat. This morning, she was already talking about making me a pot of chicken soup."

"That's as good a cure as anything. Now take us on home so you can go rest."

"Yes, ma'am."

A few minutes later, he pulled up in front of Nola's house. He helped her down from the surrey, then gave Camille a hand while Nola waited by the gate, holding the umbrella over her head.

"You walk with Nola," said Camille softly. "I'll follow you."

"All right." He smiled, appreciating the way she looked after his old friend. Taking the umbrella from Nola, he held it above her and put his other arm around her waist. "Now, don't you decide to take a swim."

"Just about could. I think we've had enough rain, thank You, Lord."

"It could stop any time." Ty sniffed before his nose dripped. "But we'll start worrying and griping if it stays dry too long."

"No pleasin' us." Once they were on the porch, Nola led the way around to the back door. "Hold me steady, Ty, while I pull off these boots."

Ty held her arm as she put the heel of her boot in the bootjack and tugged her foot out of it. "Miss Nola, I reckon you're the only woman in town who wore cowboy boots to church this morning."

"Nope. Ada Nichols had some on, too. Us old ranch hens know a thing or two about slogging through the mud and the muck. I told Camille she should hie herself down to the store and get a pair, too."

Camille sat down in the chair and pulled off her mud-caked overshoes. They had only walked from the surrey into the church and back out again. "If this rain doesn't stop by tomorrow, these overshoes won't cover my shoes enough to do any good." She wiped her hands on a towel lying on the table. "With the boots and bootjack my hands wouldn't get all muddy." She met Ty's gaze with a smile. "I think you just sold a pair of boots, storekeep."

"We have plenty. Should find some to fit you." Ty helped Nola remove her raincoat and hung it up on the porch to dry. "Do y'all have enough wood?"

"Plenty. I had some coal delivered, too, in case we need it. So don't you fret about us. We may be womenfolk, but we can take care of ourselves." Nola smiled and gently patted him on the cheek. "We know how to holler loud and sweet if we need help."

"Well, the loud I can attest to." Ty grinned and pulled back, pretending she might take a swing at him—though it was something she never had done, even when he was an ornery kid. He ruined the fun by sneezing.

Camille stayed on the porch with him when Nola went inside. "Do you have some tea at home?"

"I think there's some in the cabinet. Nola brought it over when I had a cold a couple of years ago."

"It keeps for a long time. How about lemons?"

"Nope. But Jessie probably has some. Tea with lemon?"

"A bit of sugar, too. It's nice and soothing, especially if your throat is sore."

He grabbed his handkerchief, turned his head and blew his nose. "Sorry."

"There's no need to be sorry. Your poor nose. Do you have any Vaseline?"

"Down at the store."

"Come inside and I'll get my jar from upstairs. It will help your nose."

"I'll track mud in the kitchen."

"I'll clean it up. You don't need to wait out here in the cold." She tugged on his arm. "Nola won't care."

He knew she wouldn't. It was nice to be cared for. Very nice. So he let her lead him into the kitchen, but he took long strides to leave as little mud as possible. She parked him in front of a chair and ordered him to sit. Then she raced down the hall and up the stairs.

Standing in front of the stove, Nola watched in amusement. "Want me to rustle you up some dinner?"

"No thanks." He leaned his throbbing head on his hand. "I'm not hungry."

"You stop by and tell Cade to check on you later."

"Yes, ma'am." He heard Camille running down the stairs. "Don't break a leg on account of me," he called.

"Not to worry." She set the jar on the table. "A layer of this on your nose might help it from becoming raw. At least it will make it feel better. Use it often."

"I know that."

"But would you have done it?"

"Maybe tomorrow when I got some from the store."

"Too long to wait."

Ty nodded, then wished he hadn't because it made his head hurt. He stood and picked up the jar of Vaseline. "I'm heading home, ladies. I'll see you in a year or two when I'm better."

Camille followed him to the door. "Let us know if you need anything."

"I will." He needed a hug, but he didn't want to risk making her sick, too. Would have made him feel better, though. He was sure of it.

She tucked his coat collar around his throat, much as he had done for her the day before. "Take care of yourself. I'll stop by in the morning to see how you are."

"As much as I'd like that, you'd better not."

She rolled her eyes. “Because it’s improper.”

“Yes.” When she opened her mouth to retort, he shook his head, glancing at Nola. Thankfully, she had her back to them. But he was certain she heard every word.

“Then I’ll stop by Jessie’s to see if she knows how you are doing.”

“That would work.” He managed a smile. “Thanks for caring.”

“I do care, Ty,” she said softly. “Very much.”

His heart soared, despite the rest of him feeling lousy. “That’s good to hear. The feeling is mutual, you know.”

“I know. Now, git.”

Chuckling, Ty obeyed, picking up his umbrella from the back porch on the way.

He spent the next two days at home, taking it easy and catching up on his sleep, the lack of which had probably had something to do with getting the cold. By Wednesday morning, he was feeling almost human.

Walking into the kitchen, he glanced out the window and stopped, pushing back the curtain to admire the snow that had covered the ground overnight. There was only about two inches, but it sparkled like diamonds in the early-morning sunshine. Huge icicles hung from the eaves. The sky was clear and blue, with only a few scattered high clouds.

He cast a baleful eye at the canister of tea, deciding that he was more than ready for something else. Grinding some beans, he made a big pot of coffee. Promising his growling stomach that he would feed it, he scrambled some eggs and made toast.

After breakfast, he enjoyed another cup of coffee while he read his Bible. He spent a while praying, thanking the Lord that he was feeling better and for stopping the rain and sending snow instead. He asked God to be with his family and his friends, especially Camille as she sought Him. He also asked for wisdom in his relationship with her. As usual, he asked for the Lord's guidance in his business and running the town.

Deciding that he felt good enough to go to the store, he cleaned up, shaved off three days worth of whiskers, and dressed for business instead of lazing around the house. A squeal of laughter told him that Ellie and Brad had convinced their mama to let them play in the snow instead of going to school.

He put on his heavy coat, hat and gloves, and walked out the front door. *Smack!* A snowball hit him in the chest. Though the kids howled in amusement, neither of them had thrown the missile. Camille stood halfway between the house and the street, mischief and laughter frolicking across her face. He didn't think she had ever been more lovely.

"Can Ty come out and play?" she called.

"Not if you're going to nail him with another snowball." Ty checked to make sure she didn't have anything in her hands. "Maybe we should team up against the kids."

"Not fair," cried Brad ducking around the side of the house. Ellie raced after him. A second later, they peeked around the corner.

Camille tipped her head, glancing in their direction. "Brad's right. It wouldn't be fair. Though that was just a lucky toss, I'm sure your aim would be true."

"Don't count on it. However, my nephew is always the pitcher when the kids play baseball. So they would probably clobber us." Ty walked down the steps and across the yard, stopping in front of her. "How do you grow prettier every day?" he asked softly.

To his amazement, she blushed. "It's the snow."

"The snow?" His fingers itched to touch her cheek.

"This is the first time I've seen it, so I'm excited." She looked around at the sparkling whiteness. "I never imagined it would be so beautiful."

"This amount is nice to enjoy without causing too many problems."

"Could we make a snowman?" The wistful note in her voice tugged at his heart. "No, that's a silly question. You shouldn't stay out here in this cold." Suddenly she frowned. "Why aren't you still resting?"

"I'm feeling much better. Didn't you notice that I haven't sneezed since I came outside?" The cold was making his nose start to run though. Reluctantly, he pulled his handkerchief from his pocket and blew it.

She took hold of his arm and took a step toward the porch. "You need to go back inside."

He didn't budge. Her chin tipped up and a stubborn glint lit her eyes. Her concern for him was sweet. "It's just the cold air. Besides, I'm going stir crazy. Let's get Brad and Ellie to help us build a snowman."

"Is there enough snow?"

"It can't be too big, but it should work." If they used up all the snow in his yard. He looked at the corner of the house where the children had watched their exchange. "Come on, you two. We need some snowmen experts."

The kids hurried to join them. "I've only made one snowman, Uncle Ty," said Ellie. "I don't think that makes me a 'spert."

"I bet you remember how to do it, right?"

Jessie stepped out on the porch, buttoning up her coat.

Ellie nodded energetically. "But we need a hat and some stuff to make his eyes and mouth."

"I'll gather those up," said Jessie. "Brad, can we use your old hat? It doesn't fit anymore."

"The one we brought from East Texas." Brad turned toward his mother. "Not the one Daddy gave me."

Ty smiled at the boy, thankful for the love that had developed between Brad and Cade.

Ty showed them how to start rolling the ball of snow for the snowman's base. He stepped back, letting Camille and the children take turns pushing it across the yard. She enjoyed it as much as they did, maybe more. "That's big enough."

When all three of them glared at him in consternation, he laughed. "We can't use all the snow for that section. We have two more to go."

"But they're smaller," said Camille. "Aren't they?"

"Yes."

Camille stepped aside so Brad could start the next ball. "Jessie, you get to help with this one."

Jessie flashed her a grin and joined in the fun, laughing as much as her children.

"Let's make the head." Ty leaned down and made a small ball, rolling it across the snow in the opposite direction. "Your turn."

Pushing it farther, Camille slipped and almost fell down. Ty grabbed her around the waist, steadying her. He kept his arm around her after she straightened, holding her against his side. "We should do this more often."

"Play in the snow?"

"That, too." He grinned, wishing mightily that his kinfolk and all the neighbors weren't watching them. And that he didn't have the dregs of a cold. It wouldn't be wise to kiss her yet, even if they didn't have an audience.

Releasing her, Ty picked up the snowman's head and carried it to the base.

"Uncle Ty, you need to get his tummy, too." Ellie pointed to the middle ball, which was almost as big as the bottom one. "We can't lift it."

"I'm not sure I can, either." Ty rolled it back to where Mr. Snowman was taking shape, hefting it in place. "Now, the head. I bet you, Brad and Camille can pick it up."

Working as a team, the three put the snowman's head into place, shrieking and laughing when it almost rolled off.

Camille quickly righted it and pushed it down more firmly. "Mr. Snowman has no neck."

"Never saw one that did." Ty gathered up a couple of thin mesquite limbs for arms, while the others made a face, using buttons for the eyes and mouth and a rather shriveled carrot for its nose.

Jessie handed Brad his old hat, letting him do the honors of crowning Mr. Snowman. She gave Ellie a pair of old gloves to put on the ends of the sticks for hands. Handing Camille a long wool scarf, she smiled. "The finishing touch."

Ty laughed as Camille draped it around the snowman. "Isn't that Cade's?"

Jessie grinned impishly. "Must be. I found it in the drawer, and it's not mine."

They all stood back to admire their handiwork. Ty thought it was better than most.

"My first snowman," murmured Camille.

"My second." Ellie beamed with pride, then looked up at Camille with a frown. "You never made a snowman before?"

"I've never even seen snow before. I lived in New Orleans and San Antonio. It was always too warm."

"Then this is a special treat." Jessie rested her hands on the children's shoulders. "How about some hot chocolate?"

"Yes, ma'am," said Brad. "I'm kinda cold."

"Me, too." Ellie pretended to shiver and almost fell down. "I'm real cold."

"Camille? Ty? Would you like to come in for some chocolate or maybe some coffee?"

"None for me," said Ty with a shake of his head. "I need to get on down to the store."

"Thanks for the offer, but I need to get to work, too." Camille smiled at Jessie and the children. "Thank you for showing me how much fun it is to build a snowman."

"You can help us again next time." Brad smiled shyly.

"I'd be delighted to."

Ty offered her his arm. “Better hold on to me in case I lose my footing.”

“It isn’t bad if you walk carefully.” She curled her arm around his, gripping his forearm lightly. “I don’t think it’s as slick as the mud was.”

They walked down the street, admiring the snow and laughing at some lads having a snowball fight. Though the temperature hovered in the twenties, Ty barely felt the cold. “Did you have a chance to look at your new Bible?”

“I spent a good part of Saturday afternoon reading it. I started with the psalm you wrote in the dedication.” Tenderness softened her eyes. “You pointed me in a good direction.”

“I was hoping you’d think so.”

“I’ve read several psalms and some of the proverbs, too. I’m ready to start chapter fourteen of John.” A frown creased her forehead. “But I don’t think I’m going to like the rest of it. Jesus’ enemies are plotting against Him, and Judas is going to betray Him. Jesus told him to do what he had to do quickly and sent him off.” She stopped, her grip tightening on Ty’s arm as she looked at him. “Why did He have to die?”

“To save us from our sins so that one day we can stand before God, unblemished and pure. We could never be good enough on our own to do that. God didn’t make us perfect. He didn’t want millions of puppets worshiping Him. He wants us to love Him by our own choice, a true and honest love.

“Man is naturally a sinful creature. We give in to our own desires and emotions and are tempted and led astray by Satan. There is no way we can redeem ourselves from sin. We all deserve punishment. So God sent Jesus, His only son, to take our place, to be the atonement or sacrifice for our sin. He took our punishment for us, so that we have eternal life in heaven.”

“So all we have to do is believe in Him? Believe that Jesus died for us? Then we’ll be saved?”

"Yes. Though it needs to be a personal thing, not just a general acceptance that He died for the whole world. He gave His life for me...and you. It's the realization and acceptance that He loves you as much as He does anyone else. We have to make an honest commitment, too. We can't just accept the fact that Jesus died for us, say thank you very much and not try to live as He wants us to." His ears were getting cold, so he pressed her hand against his side and took a step, silently asking her to start moving again.

She didn't hesitate, but her grip remained tight on his arm. "How do you know how He wants us to live?"

"It's in the Good Book, too. After you give your heart to Christ, He sends the Holy Spirit to guide and comfort you. It's similar to your conscience guiding you, only better." He noted her frown. "It's a lot to try to take in all at once."

"Yes, it is." Her expression relaxed. "I asked God to show me His ways and to teach me, so I suppose He'll do it."

"He will. Unlike us, God never lies." Ty thought he saw her wince, but he wasn't sure. Maybe it was time to shift the conversation to another subject. "Do you have a busy day ahead of you?"

"Yes. I'm going to take the ads around so our customers can approve the final layouts. That should take the rest of the morning. Then I'm going to hit up a few people about revamping their advertising." She glanced at him with a twinkle in her eye. "Starting with you."

"Me? There's nothing wrong with my ad."

"No there isn't. But how long have you run the same one?"

"I don't know. Months, I suppose."

"So the people who have lived here a while probably don't even look at it. You need to do something to catch their attention, bring them into the store to buy things they didn't even know they needed."

Ty laughed at the way she said it, but her suggestion intrigued him. "I hadn't thought about it that way. And here I considered myself a good businessman."

She patted him on the arm. "You are a good businessman. But that's why you need me—to give you a fresh look at things."

"You certainly do that." He drew her to a halt before they stepped past a building onto Main Street. Brushing a strand of hair back from her cheek, he captured her gaze. "I'm beginning to realize that's only one of many reasons I need you."

Chapter Eighteen

Curled up in bed that night, quilts pulled up to her chin, Camille wondered how she'd made it through the day without a mistake. Her mind had drifted at the most inopportune moments, such as when the grocer was pointing out a change he wanted in his ad. He had been patient with her, but as she was leaving she overheard his muttered comment that she must be in love.

Was she? In the same way she once would have sized up the opponents around a poker table, she considered the feelings and emotions Ty evoked in her. Her heart soared whenever she saw him, sometimes merely at the thought of him. He made her smile and laugh. He made her think about what she wanted out of life.

"How would I feel if I left Willow Grove? If I left Ty?" That was the real question. The answer was swift and sure, bringing tears to her eyes at the mere thought. It would break my heart. She took a deep breath, releasing it slowly, swiping away the tears. "I'm in love."

Equally important, he seemed to be falling in love with her. Could it possibly work? Common sense told her it wouldn't. What would he do if others found out about her past? He probably would support her if there was talk about the gambling, point out that she had put that behind her and started a new life. Most of the people in Willow Grove seemed to respect her and approved of her job at the paper and what she had done there.

But if she told him about Anthony, would Ty feel the same? He was a kind man, but he didn't like liars. For all his goodness, he was a proud man. Given some of the things he had said about Amanda's character and high morals, she didn't think he would simply forgive and accept Camille's past transgressions. His wife had been a paragon of virtue, without fault or blemish. Could anyone truly be so pure?

"Of course not," she murmured. "Ty even said so himself." Yet he had Amanda on such a high pedestal he had forgotten any faults she might have had. "How can anyone—especially me—measure up to her?"

Her gaze fell upon the Bible lying on the table beside the bed. Amanda had been a strong Christian. If Camille believed also, would that make her more worthy of Ty? Maybe. But if she put her trust in Jesus for that reason, it would be false.

She thought about some of the things she had read, things that God had been teaching her through His word. "God, I do believe that Jesus is Your only Son and that He died for the sins of the world."

Then she heard a noise downstairs. Listening carefully, she decided Nola was up. She grabbed her robe and slid her feet into her slippers, hurrying down to check on her friend. Nola was in the living room, adding some wood to the fire. "Are you all right?"

"Couldn't sleep. This weather makes these old bones ache." Nola eased into a rocking chair close to the stove. "Sorry I woke you."

"I hadn't gone to sleep." Camille pulled another chair closer to the fire and sat down. She glanced at the mantel clock. Almost midnight. She'd been up since six. No wonder she was tired.

"Too cold in your room?"

"It's nice and warm under the quilts." She touched the tip of her nose. "I think I need a mitten for my nose."

Nola laughed. "Maybe I can teach you to knit one. Don't think I ever tried to make a nose warmer. Used to make nice wool socks. But that was a long time ago." The older lady studied her for a minute. "What's keeping you awake, child? Is it Ty?"

"Partly." Camille smiled. "I tend to think of him too much."

"Did you two have a spat? Is that the real reason he didn't come to dinner?"

"No." Just the opposite. "He needed to go home and rest. He looked tired. I'm afraid he overdid it today."

"He's tough. A good rest will set him straight again. It's good to hear that you're getting along. Does my heart good to see him happy again." Nola rocked back and forth. "So what's troubling you?"

"Jesus."

"Calling to you, is He?"

Camille hadn't considered it in that way. "I suppose He is."

"You're seeking and He's calling. Sounds like a good combination to me. Do you believe in Him? In what the scripture says about Him?"

"Yes." She hesitated. "For the most part. I believe He is God's only Son and that He died to save people from their sin."

"He didn't just die. He came back to life."

Camille stared at her. "He did?"

"Haven't gotten to that part yet?"

"No. I haven't been able to bring myself to read about His death. Only where He says it's going to happen."

"Well, after you read about that, finish up John. It talks

about him appearing to His disciples again. Each of the gospels tells about different episodes. It helps to read them all. If you read the last few chapters in each book, where it talks about the resurrection, it will give you a better understanding of what happened. The main thing to remember, dear, is that He loves you."

"I know the Bible says He does. But it's hard to believe." Camille lowered her gaze, her heart pounding in her chest. "I've done things I shouldn't have."

"We all have, dear. Still do for that matter. Just this morning I had to ask God to forgive me for wishing Grace Montgomery would fall on her backside in the snow. Preferably on Main Street in front of half the town."

Camille laughed and felt herself relax. "She can be annoying."

"That's putting it politely." She paused as if gathering her thoughts. "My point is that God loves me even though I had hateful thoughts about Grace. I'm sure He didn't approve of them, but I'm also sure that when I asked Him to forgive me, He did. Because He loves me. Scripture says that if we confess our sins to Him, He is faithful and just to forgive us and to cleanse us from unrighteousness. Doesn't matter if it's the first time you go to him or the umpteenth. You go on upstairs and ask Him if He loves you."

Camille tensed again. "Ask Him? He's supposed to answer? Out loud?" The thought scared her half to death.

"He will answer in whatever way suits Him. I haven't heard of anybody lately that He spoke to out loud." Nola laid her hand on her heart. "When He gives you the answer, you'll know it in here."

Camille stood and kissed Nola on the forehead. "Thank you for listening and for your advice."

"Got over seventy years worth of advice stored up." Nola chuckled and patted her hand. "I don't hesitate to give it, either."

"To everyone's benefit. Are you warm enough?"

"I'm fine. I'm going to sit here and think about my Henry for a while. Remember how we used to sit by the fire on cold winter nights, me mending or knitting and him reading to me." When she looked up, moisture glistened in her eyes. "That memory is easier to handle than lying in a cold, lonely bed without my man next to me." She caught hold of Camille's hand. "Hang on to Ty. Don't spend your life alone."

Camille gently squeezed her frail hand. "We'll have to see what happens."

"What happens will be a wedding if you encourage that boy. It's as plain as day that you're both in love."

"Well, whatever it is, it's certainly distracting."

Nola's wrinkled face brightened with a smile. "And fun to watch. I saw the glow in his eyes the first time he mentioned you. Now, get to bed. Mornin' will come much too early as it is."

Camille obeyed, but when she crawled into bed and pulled the covers up around her, she didn't ask God if He loved her. Her discussion with Nola had been somewhat reassuring, but she simply couldn't bring herself to do it. She'd never considered herself a coward, but she was in this. And in telling Ty about Anthony.

"I'm too tired now. Maybe we can talk about it tomorrow." Yawning, she mentally shook her head at her silliness for expecting God to talk to her. He hadn't even talked directly to Mary or Joseph. He'd sent an angel to speak to them.

But God wasn't to be put off.

Camille dreamed she was standing in the doorway of the White Buffalo Saloon. She wore a bright red dress that revealed far more bosom than any of her own dresses. The hem of the full skirt hit her at the knee, scandalously displaying her legs and several layers of petticoats. It was unlike anything she had ever worn.

It was late at night, and the streets were quiet. A man stepped out of the shadows across from her and walked forward, stopping in the middle of the street. He was dressed in a long white robe, like the one Jesus wore in a picture in Nola's big Bible. A light surrounded Him, and kindness and love shone in His face.

Jesus.

He nodded and smiled, holding out His hand. She started toward Him, but suddenly Anthony stood between them.

Her ex-lover's sneering gaze raked over her. "What do you think you're doing? God doesn't want anything to do with you. You're too wicked, too sinful."

Camille knew she was unworthy. Her fear of the Lord's rejection halted her. Yet, how her heart ached to know His grace and love! She stretched first one way, then the other, trying to see past Anthony. Though she couldn't see Jesus, the light still illuminated the darkness. But wait…was it growing dimmer?

"My Lord, don't leave me. I need You."

Instantly, Jesus stood in front of her. He again held out His hand. When she took hold of it, He smiled. Oh, that smile! Filled with love and forgiveness, its radiance washed over her, cleansing her from the inside out. Her vulgar red dress was transformed into a beautiful gown of white, long sleeves and high collar of the finest lace, the skirt flowing across the dirt street without a single spot or stain.

Jesus stepped to one side, pointing behind Him. "Do you see your sin?"

Camille searched for Anthony, but she could see nothing beyond the light of Jesus' love. "No. Your glory hides it."

"I have taken it away. It is no more." He turned her around toward the saloon. It, too, had vanished. "I love you."

Camille awoke with a start. Heart pounding, she sat up in bed, tears pouring down her cheeks. She should have been freezing, but she felt surrounded in warmth, cloaked in the love of Jesus.

"God, You do love me," she whispered, her heart overflowing in gratitude and awe. "Thank You." Some of the things that Nola and Ty had shared with her came to mind. "Lord, You know what's in my heart right now, but I'm going to say it anyway. I don't think I could keep it inside even if I wanted to. I believe Jesus is Your Son and that He died for me. For me. Oh, thank You, Lord. What a priceless gift!

"Please, Lord, just as You did in that beautiful dream, forgive me of my sins. Forgive me for all the times I gambled and for living with Anthony." She swallowed the lump in her throat. "Forgive me for being his mistress, for having sex with him." There, she'd said it in the plainest way she could.

"Help me to do what is right. Help me to live the way You want me to. Teach me Your ways. Help me always to put my trust in You. As the Bible says, abide in me and let me abide in You."

She wiped her cheeks on the edge of the sheet and snuggled down beneath the heavy layer of quilts. Closing her eyes, she was surprised by an unexpected yawn. How could she possibly sleep when her heart was so full of joy? She wanted to stay awake, to bask in the love of Jesus and the freedom of forgiveness. Instead, sleep slowly overtook her.

Her last conscious thought was of the sweet peace soothing her soul.

Chapter Nineteen

On Thursday morning, Ty stopped by the *Gazette*. Camille was at the front counter, discussing an ad with the new tailor. Figuring it might be a while, Ty unbuttoned his heavy coat. He picked up a copy of the *Fort Worth Daily Gazette* and thumbed through it. He had one back at the office but hadn't taken the time to read it yet.

It had rained heavily throughout North Texas. Dallas also had snow, sleet and freezing rain. The Houston & Texas Central was the only railroad centering at Dallas that was making anything resembling their schedule since the bad weather had set in.

Another article caught his eye. No mail from St. Louis and the east had been received in Dallas since Sunday. Trains were still abandoned on the Dallas branch of the Missouri Pacific, which had five miles of track and trestle underwater between Dallas and Denton.

Ty had already known about that since he hadn't received any shipments all week and had checked on them by telegraph. The article mentioned another area of railroad that was unsafe, and the Trinity River was over a mile wide at Dallas, submerging the pike road and the bottoms west of the city.

He glanced over the top of the newspaper, watching Camille. The new tailor was German and had a heavy accent, but she paid close attention and seldom misunderstood what he said. When she did make a mistake, her sweet smile quickly banished any frustration on the gentleman's part.

She looked different today. He couldn't quite pinpoint what it was, but she seemed to have a glow he hadn't noticed before. She glanced toward him and her smile grew softer, more tender. He caught his breath. She looked like a woman in love.

The tailor said something, drawing her attention again, and Ty lowered his gaze to the paper—right to a drawing of gums and teeth in the advertisement for a Dr. A. J. Lawrence, Dentist. Making a face, Ty closed the paper, folded it and set it on the counter.

Camille thanked the tailor for his business and looked at Ty. "Mr. Schroeder, have you met our mayor, Ty McKinnon?"

"Yes, he came to see me when I first opened the shop."

Ty shook the other man's hand. "It's good to see you again, sir. I trust you've had some customers since I saw you."

Schroeder nodded. "A start, but I can use more. This beautiful lady convinced me to advertise in her paper. Do you think that's a good idea?"

"A very good idea."

"Give it a few weeks, Mr. Schroeder," said Camille. "Maybe even a month if the weather doesn't clear up soon. With all the rain and snow folks have been staying close to home this past week."

"Once it warms up, everyone will be anxious to shop. I'll do my best to steer the gentlemen your way," said Ty.

"My thanks. Now I must get back to work. Good day, Mayor. Miss Dupree." Schroeder quietly left the office.

Ty moved down until he faced Camille. "Good morning." He was tempted to lean across the counter and give her a kiss. Maybe he should. After all it was Valentine's Day.

Her brow lifted delicately, and a knowing glint lit her eyes. "Good morning. You appear to be feeling better."

"I am." Ty rested his arms on the counter, leaning closer. "And you are incredibly lovely." He searched her face and eyes. "Different somehow."

"Really? It shows?"

"Something does." Ty nodded toward the inner office. "Is Ralph in?"

"No. He's touring town to see if there have been any damages from the rain and snow. Would you like to come into the office?"

"Yes." Ty walked around the end of the counter, nodded a greeting to the typesetter, and followed Camille into the office she shared with Mr. Hill. He caught a fleeting expression of surprise on her face when he shut the door. "Do you mind?"

"No." She watched him every step of the way as he crossed the room to stand in front of her. "God loves me," she said softly. "Jesus, too."

Joy swept through him. "That's why you're glowing this morning."

She laughed and hugged him. "I don't know about that. I just know I'm happier and more at peace than I've ever been in my life."

Of course, he put his arms around her and hugged back. "Do you want to tell me about it?"

"I couldn't sleep and then I heard Nola up, so I went downstairs. She couldn't sleep, either. This weather makes her ache, poor thing. We talked for a while." A sparkle lit her eyes. "A little about you. More about Jesus and God. I admitted that it was hard for me to believe that God loves me. She told me to go upstairs and ask Him if He loves me."

"Did you?"

"No, I was afraid. I don't know what I expected. I certainly didn't think He would talk to me or anything, but if I asked and nothing happened..."

"It would have been very painful."

"So, I told God that maybe we could talk about it today. Isn't that awful?"

He chuckled and pulled her a tiny bit closer. "We all do that on occasion, especially when we figure it's something He wants to deal with and we don't want Him to. So you talked to Him this morning?"

"Yes, but in the middle of the night, too. This sounds crazy, but I think God figured I might not ever work up the courage to ask Him if He loves me. So He took matters into His own hands."

Ty listened in amazement as she told him about her dream, how Jesus had come to meet her and take away her sins. His eyes misted as he considered God's mercy and grace by reaching out to her in such a personal way.

"I woke up right after the dream." Her voice dropped to barely more than a whisper. "I felt as if He was right there with me. I felt His love surrounding me." Moisture glistened in her eyes, but Ty sensed they were tears of joy and reverence. "I still feel Him with me." She laid her hand on her heart. "In here."

"Then it's the joy of the Lord that I see in your face, in your smile." He gathered her close and held her gently. "That's the most beautiful testimony I've ever heard."

She laid her cheek against his chest. "I love Him so much, Ty. I knew I felt empty inside, but I didn't realize how big that hole was until He filled it."

"That I understand. I still remember the night I asked Him to be Lord of my life. I haven't been the same." He eased away from her. "This seems kind of minor, now, but I have something for you."

Reaching inside his suit jacket, he took out the card he'd spent half an hour selecting at the store. It didn't say exactly what he wanted it to, but all the others said too much. Though his feelings for Camille grew deeper every day, he didn't know if he was in love with her. He definitely wasn't ready to say anything about it.

"Happy Valentine's Day." He held out the simple brown envelope containing the card.

She stared at the envelope, then lifted her gaze to meet his. He couldn't begin to discern the emotions sweeping across her face.

"A Valentine?" she whispered. "For me?"

"Yes." He hoped she wasn't expecting something declaring his everlasting love. *God, please don't let her be disappointed.* The last thing he wanted to do was hurt her.

Her fingers trembled slightly as she took it from his hand. "No one has ever given me a Valentine before." She opened the envelope and carefully slid out the card. Her mouth formed a silent "Oh."

He desperately wished he'd found one that said something better than accept this tribute of my sincere regard.

"Ty, it's beautiful," she said in hushed awe. She traced her fingertip around the paper lace and bright flowers. "How can they make something so delicate without tearing it?" Pausing, she read the printed sentiment, then the simple wish for a happy day and his signature that he'd put on the inside.

Ty cringed. "The wording is a little lame. It doesn't quite say what I wanted it to."

"It's perfect. I treasure your regard, Ty. I truly do. If it were more sentimental, I wouldn't have believed it. After all, we've only known each other two weeks."

"Is that all? It seems like forever."

"Yes, it does." She looked at the card again, pleasure written all over her face. "Thank you." Throwing her arms around his neck, she surprised him with a kiss.

"Maybe I should give you one of these every day."

"Nope. Then it wouldn't be so special." She moved backward a step and turned toward her desk. Propping the card against a couple of books, she admired it with a happy smile.

Ty wished he could always make her so happy. "I'd intended to bring you a box of chocolates, too. But the last shipment was smashed, and the new order hasn't arrived." He withdrew a small bag of stick candy from his coat pocket. "These will have to do."

Camille laughed and took the bag from him, opening it eagerly. "It will do nicely—at least until more chocolates arrive. Thank you, kind sir. Would you care for one?" She held the open bag toward him.

"No thanks. Might spoil my dinner. Speaking of which, would you like to eat at Trotter's with me? They're having their grand opening today."

"I'd love to."

"I'll come by a little before noon. I've already reserved a table, so we shouldn't have any problem getting a seat." He buttoned up his coat and moved to the door.

She followed him, giving him a sweet smile as he left. He didn't realize until he opened the door to the store that he had been whistling a jaunty tune since he left the *Gazette*.

They fell into a comfortable routine of dining together at noon and attending church on Sundays, along with Nola. He still ate at Nola's every Wednesday evening and visited there many other evenings as well. Sometimes they played dominoes or simply chatted. Other times, when Camille had a particular question or had come across something in the Bible that she didn't understand, they spent the evening discussing it.

After over a week of freezing temperatures, the weather warmed up and the snow and ice melted. The trains from the east finally began running to Dallas again, and he was able to replenish his dwindling supplies at the store.

Camille wrote an interesting and humorous article for the paper about her experiences in the snow, as well as those of other folks. People complimented her for days. He wasn't sure who was prouder—her or him.

He watched her blossom in her job, praised God as Jessie and other new acquaintances became friends and admired her loyalty to Nate and Bonnie. It was difficult to imagine that she had spent most of her life in such an opposite fashion.

Ty took her out to the ranch, chuckling as she willingly fed the chickens but refused to gather the eggs. He didn't blame her a bit. Those old hens liked to peck. He taught her how to drive a horse and buggy, an adventure that took them far enough from the house and curious eyes to steal a few kisses.

The next Sunday morning, after a particularly moving sermon, the minister asked if anyone wanted to accept Jesus or to come forward and publicly acknowledge their belief in Him for the first time. Camille was the second person down the aisle. He wasn't the only one to notice the radiance on her face as she shared about finding Jesus and the joy He brought her. No one could doubt that her testimony was heartfelt.

March arrived with unusually warm days and the promise of the coming spring. As the days passed, Ty's feelings for Camille deepened, and he accepted the undisputable fact that he was in love. He couldn't be positive about Camille's feelings, though she certainly seemed to hold him in high regard and deep affection. He wasn't quite ready to take the leap and proclaim himself. Perhaps he was a coward, but he simply wanted to enjoy their courtship a while longer.

One day he quietly realized that he was no longer angry or bitter toward God over Amanda's and the baby's deaths.

The ache was still there, but he supposed that would always be with him. For the first time since he'd lost them, he truly believed life was good.

And it was only going to get better.

Chapter Twenty

On Monday, March tenth, Ty saw Cade and Jessie off on the train to Dallas where they were to attend the Cattlemen's Convention. Early that evening, Nate threw open the door to the store, rattling the glass. "Ty, your livery is on fire!" He only paused long enough to shout the warning before running next door.

Ty dropped a stack of shirts, bolted out the door and down the street, followed by Ed and everyone else in the store. His heart lurched at the sight before him. Flames shot up the wagon-yard side of the building, engulfing practically the whole wall. The terrified shrieks of the horses pinned in their stalls spurred him to run with all his might.

Two horses raced out the large open doors, followed by the stable manager. Joe stumbled and fell to his knees, coughing and gasping for air. Several bystanders hurried to his aid, dragging him away from the fire.

Ransom and Quint met Ty thirty feet from the blaze. "I have to get the horses out." Ty ripped off his jacket and dunked it in a nearby water trough. "Has anybody gone for the fire wagon?"

"I see them coming." The bell on the hand-drawn wagon announced the impending arrival of the fire hose. Ransom shed his jacket and dipped it in the water, too.

Quint grabbed it out of his hands. "I'll help Ty. You get people organized. They've never had to fight a fire."

Ransom nodded and started giving orders. "Make way for the fire wagon. Move away from the hydrant. Give them room to hook up the hose. You men, get some buckets and blankets." He pointed at a handful of other men. "Get those wagons and buggies out of the yard."

Ty threw the wet jacket over his head. Out of the corner of his eye, he saw Quint do the same. *Please, God, protect us. Help us get those animals out of there.* He took a deep breath and using a wet coat sleeve to shield his face, he rushed through the doorway. Quint was right behind him.

The smoke was thick and dark, but the spreading flames cast an eerie glow throughout the building. When he was forced to take another breath, the intense heat and smoke stung his lungs. He jerked open the door to the first stall, stepping back out of the way as Dusty raced for safety. Another horse followed right behind him.

At the next stall, he had to slap the horse with his jacket to get it moving in the right direction. The third horse had almost broken the stall door down. As Ty's fingers closed on the latch, she kicked the door and almost knocked him off his feet. "Easy girl."

Dragging in a smoky breath, Ty wished he'd kept his mouth shut. Coughing, he fumbled with the latch, stumbling back out of the way as it swung open and the horse dove out. For a second, she went the wrong way, then spun around, slamming him against the stall wall, before she raced out the main doors.

Ty groaned and grabbed the doorjamb to keep from falling.

Two other horses raced by.

"You all right?" Quint appeared at his side, then doubled over with a fit of coughing.

Ty straightened. "Yeah. Go." He pushed Quint toward the door and waited a few seconds to see if he could make it. When he figured he would, Ty felt his way through the thick smoke to the last stall. Buttercup. Joanna Watson's sweet little mare, the most docile, shyest horse of the lot. Though she stomped and cried out in fear, she'd backed into the corner. She didn't budge when Ty opened the door.

He took the wet coat from over his head and shoulders, and eased into the stall, holding back a cough with every ounce of willpower he possessed. He threw the coat over her head, covering her eyes, grabbed a fistful of mane and led her toward freedom.

The heat scorched the back of his hands and his neck. Unable to breathe, he pulled an edge of the coat over his mouth and nose, hoping it would filter out some of the smoke. It was enough to keep him on his feet as they made for the door. Water streamed from his raw eyes. Through the haze of smoke and tears he barely could see the outline of the big double doors.

He heard a crackling overhead and looked up. Fire swirled along the roof, chunks of burning wood dropping down into the hayloft above them. A fiery board fell, hitting his arm. He jerked away, clenching his teeth against the pain and dodged the board as it hit the ground.

They cleared the doorway, the horse dragging him from the building when his legs turned to rubber. Fighting for air, Ty was vaguely aware of hands reaching for him, arms going around his waist to hold him up and of being pulled away from the smoke. Someone threw a rope around Buttercup's neck and led her to safety.

Collapsing on the ground, Ty sat up, struggling for air. Every breath seared his lungs and triggered more coughing. Suddenly, Camille was beside him, kneeling in the street. She handed him a cup of water, then helped him hold it to his mouth and drink. He repaid her kindness by coughing and spewing water all over her. "Sorry," he rasped.

"Don't be." Putting her arms around him, she held him close, letting him lean on her for support. "You're safe. That's all that matters." He felt her shudder. "I was so afraid you wouldn't come out of there."

He looked up at her face, his heart aching at the tears rolling down her cheeks. "Don't cry, sweetheart," he whispered. It was all he could manage. Resting his head on her shoulder, he closed his stinging eyes.

"Don't tell me not to cry, Ty McKinnon. You scared the life out of me." She sniffed and angrily wiped her nose on her sleeve. "A woman has a right to cry when the man she loves goes dashing into a burning building."

It was a second before her words sank in. It took a great deal of effort, but he looked up at her face again. "You love me?"

"Yes, I love you." Scowling, she sounded downright mad about it. "More's the pity since you'll probably always go charging into fires or helping Ransom chase after desperadoes, bent on being a hero."

"Couldn't let the horses die." Ty touched her cheek with his fingertips, leaving a trail of black soot. He couldn't let the moment pass. She was right. He might have been killed in that livery, and she never would have known what was in his heart. "I love you, too, Camille."

"Oh, Ty." She hugged him fiercely. He couldn't hold back a groan.

She let out a squeak. "Ty, you're hurt. Your arm is burned. Where's the doctor?" she cried. "He's hurt!"

"It's not that bad." Ty looked down at the long, wide burn on his arm. Then again, maybe it was. He twisted around to look at the livery stable. Flames shot high into the air. All four walls were ablaze. Somehow, the fire had jumped across the alley, embers carried on the wind or falling debris, he supposed. The saloon and billiard hall on the corner was completely in flames. He watched in horror as the fire crept along the boardwalk, igniting a second store. Trying to stand, he glared at her when she held him down. When did she get to be so strong? "I need to help."

"You need to stay right here." Looking around, she yelled, "Somebody get a doctor." Her voice gentled. "Ransom and the others are doing all that can be done."

"Quint?"

"He made it out okay. He's still coughing some, but he's helping with the fire hose anyway. Thank goodness, here comes Dr. Thomas." She waved frantically. "Over here."

The good doctor knelt beside them, nodding when Camille pointed to Ty's arm. "Sorry. You'd think with three doctors in this town a man could get treatment quicker. But broken bones and new babies don't adhere to a schedule." He frowned when Ty coughed and grabbed his side. "You got another burn?"

Ty shook his head. "Horse knocked me into the wall. It's not cracked. Had cracked ribs before and this isn't the same."

The doctor leaned down, pulling up his shirt, gently pressing his side with his fingertips. "No obvious break and no cuts. You're likely to have a hefty bruise. Come over to the office where I can properly tend to that burn."

"Not now. I need to stay here until the fire is out." He dragged in a breath and was thankful when it didn't trigger another round of coughing.

"Then let me wrap it. That will at least keep it from getting dirtier. Don't you try to man the hose. Take plenty of deep breaths, even if it hurts. Try to force that smoke from your lungs." He took a bandage from his bag and carefully wrapped it around Ty's forearm. "I'll check Quint out before I head over to the office. Can't see as anyone else needs me. The minute you can leave, you hightail it over to the office so I can clean that up proper."

"Thanks, Doc." Ty watched the fire for a few minutes after the physician walked away. "I need to send Cade a telegram. Fine way to start off his week. Hope I can convince him that he doesn't have to come home right away." He stood with Camille's help, though he didn't really need it. "After I talk to Ransom, I'll let Cade know about this. Then I'm coming back here."

"All right."

He looked at his love, wondering why she had suddenly become so docile. "No fussin' at me?"

"It wouldn't do any good. But I'm staying right with you to make certain you do what the doctor ordered."

"Good." Ty caught her hand and together they walked over to where Ransom was supervising the battle. They were concentrating on keeping the fire from spreading. It appeared they had succeeded. The flames dwindled in Mr. Schroeder's new tailor shop, but, like the saloon, it was a total loss.

"Do you know what caused it?" asked Ty.

Ransom made a quick appraisal of his condition before answering. "A ranch freight wagon cut the corner too sharp going into the wagon yard. It was loaded high with buffalo bones. One of them must have been sticking out and struck the lantern hanging from the eaves, the one lighting the way into the yard, and knocked it down. The driver was pulling two wagons and didn't notice it. By the time he parked the wagons and climbed down, flames were already racing up the side of the building. He sounded the alarm and tried to douse the fire with his coat, but a spark flew through the window and lit a pile of hay inside the building."

"And it spread too fast." Ty surveyed his ruined building. At least he had insurance and other means of livelihood. With all the liquor in the saloon adding fuel to the fire, he hoped the proprietor had insurance. He caught sight of Mr. Schroeder, standing forlornly off to the side. He glanced at Ransom. "Thanks for taking charge."

"That's what you pay me for. It'll probably burn half the night, but I think we can keep it under control."

Ty nodded and walked over to speak to the tailor. Camille went along, staying right by his side as she'd promised. "Mr. Schroeder?"

The man turned his head, the despair in his eyes highlighted by the flames. "It's all gone. Everything. How will I support my family?"

"You don't have insurance?" Ty figured he knew the answer already.

"No. I've made suits for fifteen years and never needed insurance."

"I'll pay your losses, Mr. Schroeder."

Schroeder's mouth fell open. "Why?"

"That was my livery stable." Ty choked as a cough caught him by surprise. It took a few minutes to catch his breath. "Since the fire started there, I feel responsible. I trust you'll be fair in the estimate of loss. We'll start working on it tomorrow."

The tailor scrutinized him a long time before he replied. "You're a good man, McKinnon. I accept your offer."

They shook on it, then Ty and Camille looked around for the saloon keeper. He was holding the nozzle of the fire hose at that moment.

Ty approached the man carefully. He had a reputation for a hot temper, though he and Ty had always gotten along. "Jake?"

Jake Forrester glanced in his direction and turned the fire

hose over to someone else. "Nasty business." He glanced at the bandage on Ty's arm. "You all right?"

"Yeah. Gotta let Doc fix it up after a while. Do you have fire insurance?"

"Yes. Too many bullets flying around on Saturday nights not to. I'll be out of business for a while, but it should cover the whole thing."

"That's good to hear."

"We 'bout got the fire out. You'd better go let Doc tend to that arm. Wouldn't do for it to get infected."

Ty studied the remnants of the fire. "It will need watching all night in case it flares up again."

"We'll handle it. You go take care of your wound and get some rest. I've heard that smoke in the lungs can cause pneumonia if you aren't careful."

"I'll stop back by after I see the doctor." Ty slipped his arm around Camille's shoulder. She put her arm around his waist, being careful not to press on his hurt side. Oblivious to the interested glances from those still watching the fire, they walked down the middle of the street, holding on to each other.

Chapter Twenty-One

Harvey Miller stood in the back of a wagon, waving his fist in the air. A small crowd had gathered to hear what he had to say. Camille slowed her pace along the boardwalk, stopping at the edge of the group to listen.

"Ty McKinnon is a dangerous man," decreed Miller. "He almost burned down the whole town."

"He didn't start the fire. Everybody knows that," Red Mulhany called back, shaking his head.

"His negligence caused it." Ty's political opponent shook his fist again, emphasizing every word. "Anyone with a lick of sense would have known better than to hang a lantern outside a livery stable. His irresponsibility makes him responsible."

Several people frowned as if trying to decipher what he'd said.

"Willow Grove needs a mayor with common sense. A mayor with vision for the town, not one whose stupidity is going to ruin it."

"Then they certainly don't want you," muttered Camille. A couple of men nearby heard her and grinned, nodding their agreement.

"McKinnon only cares about himself. He doesn't care about the good people of Willow Grove. He wants to take over the town, to run it to suit his needs, not yours." Miller pointed across the street at McKinnon Brothers. "He already has the largest store for fifty miles, but is he satisfied with that? No. He starts a stage line and builds a livery stable. We already had a livery. We didn't need another one."

"Then how come the wagon yard was full this morning?" hollered a rancher from west of town.

"There are more people in town today than usual," said Miller with a condescending smile. "Came in to see the destruction for themselves. Destruction caused by Ty McKinnon. I'm sure you found an adequate place."

"There were more people here on Saturday than today," said the rancher. "Both days I had to park my wagon here on the street. And I didn't give you permission to stand on it."

Miller ignored him. "Now I hear that McKinnon wants to build an opera house."

A murmur went through the crowd. Judging from the numerous pleased expressions, Camille decided most folks liked the idea.

Miller frowned at the reaction. "An opera house is just another name for a variety theater. If McKinnon has his way, before you know it, we'll have indecent theatrics right here on Main Street."

"You ever been to an opera house, Miller?" asked city councilman Tom Carmichael.

"Of course not. McKinnon's partner is Red Mulhany. We all know what a fine upstanding citizen he is." He sneered at Mulhany. "A saloon owner who brings indecency to our fine city."

"I apologized to my neighbors for that mistake," said Mulhany. "Don't forget that the ordinance Mayor McKinnon and the current city council passed sent them skedaddlin' out of town."

"And has kept others from stopping here." Sheriff Starr walked through the crowd toward Miller. Camille noted with amusement that the people moved out of his way without hesitation. "You've done enough speechifying for today."

"I most certainly have not. Willow Grove needs to realize how corrupt and irresponsible McKinnon is. He'll ruin this town—if he doesn't burn it down first."

"That's enough, Miller. Climb down from that wagon or I'll haul you down myself."

"You can't make me stop. Free speech is an American right."

"Disturbing the peace is an American wrong. I've had three complaints about you already this morning from the proprietors of these businesses, and one from the owner of this wagon. Next time you want to sling mud, do it in front of your own store."

Grumbling, Miller climbed down from the wagon. "My store is at the end of the street. I need to be where I can talk to more people."

"There's an empty storefront right over there," said Starr, pointing to a vacant building nearby. "Fork over the extra rent so you can move up here."

"What about the others who lost their businesses last night?" asked Miller. "They should receive recompense from McKinnon since the fire was his fault."

Camille gritted her teeth. She could barely refrain from marching up to the windbag and slapping him.

"Don't pretend to be concerned about me, Miller." Jake Forrester scowled at him. "Everyone knows you'd like to ride me and every other saloon owner out of town on a rail.

But to set the record straight, I had insurance. I'll start rebuilding in a week or two."

"What about the shoemaker? Did he have insurance?" Miller's arrogant demeanor was disgusting.

"I am a tailor, not a shoemaker." Schroeder's disdainful glance spoke volumes about what he thought of the other man's clothing. "I do not have insurance."

"There you have it. A man ruined by McKinnon."

"No, you're wrong," said Schroeder. "Mr. McKinnon has already given me more than enough to replace everything that was lost and to start over. Would you have done the same?"

Miller sputtered. "I wouldn't have caused a fire in the first place."

With that comment, the crowd dispersed. Camille didn't think Miller had won any votes. Still, the audacity of trying to blame the fire on Ty infuriated her. Half the businesses in town had a lantern of some type hanging outside their door. They provided light for people walking down the boardwalk in the evenings and served as a beacon when the stores were open.

Camille decided to stroll to the end of the street to see if Harvey Miller's business had a lamp outside the door. Sure enough, it did. Closer inspection revealed that it wasn't fastened to the wall as securely as it should have been. It wouldn't take much of a bump to knock it down.

Her ire rose with every step back to the *Gazette*. She stormed into the office, ready for battle.

Mr. Hill took one look at her and laid down his pen. "What has you so riled up?"

"Harvey Miller." She jerked the long hatpin from her hat and plucked the fancy creation of spring silk flowers from her head. Poking the pin back in it, she set it on the corner of her desk. "He's trying to blame Ty for the fire."

"That's ridiculous."

"He says Ty was negligent by having a lantern hanging from the eaves. He was spouting off about how Ty could have burned down the whole town."

A gleam lit the old newsman's eyes. "What are you going to do about it?"

"Write an editorial. Point out the absurdity of his accusations. Miller's whole campaign is based on smearing Ty."

"Good point. You should mention that." Hill leaned back in his chair, obviously enjoying their exchange and her fervor.

"He doesn't have any good ideas for improving Willow Grove."

"Close the saloons."

"True." Camille paced around the room. "That would be an improvement, but half the other businesses would go under without the ranch trade. I doubt he could get the city council to go along with it." She sat down in the chair behind her desk. "It seems to me that a man needs more than one issue to campaign on."

"He should, but it's not too unusual. I don't think Ty has anything to worry about from Miller. Ty has done an excellent job as mayor and folks know it."

"Would it be wrong for me to write something?"

"No. I think we're in agreement about who is the best candidate. We'd be remiss if we didn't bring Miller to task on his mudslinging. Things haven't been done that way in the past around here. I think most folks don't want it to continue."

She spent a good part of the day composing her editorial, scribbling thoughts that seemed perfect until she re-read them. After tossing out sentences, even paragraphs, she decided it was the best she could do. Still, she read it through one last time.

With less than three weeks left until the election, mayoral candidate Harvey Miller can't seem to climb out of the mud. Though he slings it left and right, he only sinks deeper into the mire. In his latest tirade, he had the audacity to blame his opponent, Mayor Ty McKinnon, for Monday's fire. He proclaimed to the small crowd gathered around his impromptu stage—someone else's wagon—that McKinnon's negligence caused the fire and could have burned down the whole town.

What was this grave negligence on the mayor's part? He had a lantern hanging from the eaves of the livery to illuminate the way into the wagon yard. Normally, no person or vehicle would come close to it. It took the unusual circumstances of a large wagon load of buffalo bones with a wayward rib at the top to do the damage.

It is true that two other businesses were destroyed in the blaze. The losses at the Silver Dollar Saloon were covered by insurance. McKinnon is completely taking care of all costs incurred by Mr. Schroeder, the tailor. This was agreed upon right after the fire, long before Miller declared that McKinnon should be held liable.

Though Miller wanted his listeners to think he was concerned about the victims of Monday night's fire, it was obvious that he merely wanted McKinnon to pay for the damages. He held no sympathy for McKinnon in the total destruction of his livery.

Instead Miller declared that the mayor did not care for the people of Willow Grove, that he only wanted to take over the town. How did he reach this preposterous conclusion? He pointed to McKinnon's successful businesses as proof that the mayor was only interested in himself.

This reporter is fairly new to the town, but I have been told by numerous people that the McKinnon Livery was a much-welcomed addition. It was obvious this morning by the overflow of vehicles from the remaining wagon yard that it is needed. I personally can attest to the benefit of the stage line, since that is how I came to Willow Grove. But Miller believes that neither of these enterprises have anything to do with serving the people of Willow Grove.

Which begs the question—how does Harvey Miller propose to serve Willow Grove if he is elected mayor? As far as I can tell, he has campaigned on one issue, closing the saloons. But if he were successful at that, would he simply sit back and do nothing else to improve our city? Perhaps Miller spends all his time and energy attacking his opponent because he has nothing of substance to offer Willow Grove.

As for the safety of our town, the lantern mount hanging outside the door of Miller's business is badly in need of repair. No wayward buffalo bone would be required to dislodge it from its precarious perch. A tall cowboy or a lady with a parasol would do.

She handed it to Mr. Hill, waiting impatiently as he read through it.

"Good job." He handed it back to her. "Give it to Brian to set the type. Then we'll sit back and see if it does any good. I don't expect Miller to come up with any new ideas. He doesn't have the intellect for it." He grinned and leaned back in the chair. "If nothing else, it will give folks something to chew on. Might even sell a few extra papers."

Chapter Twenty-Two

Friday evening, the editorial was the talk of the town when Ty and Camille took the kids to the train depot to welcome Cade and Jessie home.

As Ty had anticipated, Cade inspected him carefully, then gave him a big hug. "You just about scared the daylights out of us with that telegram," he said gruffly. "I was all set to come home the next morning until we heard back from Quint."

"Checking to see if I told you the truth?"

"I thought you might gloss over the details. Turned out I was right. How's your arm?"

"Sore. But Doc says it's healing nicely. It will leave a scar."

"Another battle wound," said Jessie quietly. "Ransom said both you and Quint went in after the horses."

"You wired Ransom, too?" Ty looked at his brother in surprise.

"I did that." Jessie hugged Ellie to her side. "I figured

Quint would be honest about your condition, but he might not quite come clean about his own."

Quint and Ransom walked up and joined the homecoming. "I told it true," said Quint, giving his sister a hug.

"Nobody bothered to send a telegram asking about me." Ransom pretended to be hurt.

"We decided somebody had to be in charge. Since Ty and Quint were busy risking their necks, that most likely was you."

"We missed all the excitement," said Brad, walking on the other side of his mother as they strolled toward downtown. "Miss Lydia wouldn't let us come down here. She made us watch it from the house."

"Which was very wise." Camille smiled at him gently. "I bet you could see the flames from the house, couldn't you?"

"Yes, ma'am. They shot way up in the air."

"It was scary." Ellie danced around in front of her parents. "We thought the whole town was going to burn up."

"For a little while, I thought that, too," said Ty. "Believe me, honey, you weren't the only one who was scared. If it hadn't been for Ransom, Quint and the other men fighting the fire, the whole place might have gone up in smoke."

Cade sent him a piercing look. "You didn't lend a hand fighting the blaze?"

"Doc told me not to, didn't want me aggravating my arm."

"Or his side or his lungs," muttered Camille.

"Shh." Ty lightly nudged her side with his elbow.

"Camille, you might as well tell us the whole of it." Jessie frowned at her brother-in-law. "Ty won't." She turned her annoyed gaze on Quint and Ransom. "I'm not sure about these two, either. I'd rather hear it from you than Mrs. Watson."

Ty took one look at Camille's face and didn't bother to protest. If she didn't spill the beans now, she would later to Jessie. Women.

"Quint came out of there coughing his head off, and he made it clear quicker than Ty. Besides a burning piece of the roof hitting Ty on the arm, he was slammed against the wall by one of the horses. He didn't break any ribs, but he has a giant bruise. Not that I've seen it, of course. He told me about it. He had breathed in so much smoke that the only way he got out of there was by hanging on to the last horse and letting her blindly drag him out."

"Blindly?" asked Cade.

"He had to put his coat over her eyes. I'm amazed she knew which way to go. Ransom was heading toward the door to try to rescue him when they appeared."

Ty didn't know Ransom had been ready to go in after him. He shot his friend a grateful glance. "Buttercup knew where to go because I was guiding her. I was just too rubbery-legged to walk."

"Doggone it, little brother," roared Cade. "I can't leave you here by yourself for a day without you trying to get yourself killed."

"Getting killed wasn't exactly what I had in mind." Ty grinned at his brother. "Buttercup was too scared to run out on her own. Had to have some persuasion and comfort. I reckon it was fortunate for me that she did. My legs might have given out either way."

The burned-out livery and other buildings came into view. Jessie gasped and Cade let out a low whistle. "It's a miracle it didn't spread farther," Cade said quietly.

"A miracle and the new water mains we put in last fall. Without that hydrant and the hose from the fire wagon, I hate to think how far it would have spread."

"It looks better now than it did." Quint nodded to where the saloon had stood. "Forrester has been hauling away debris for the last two days. He said the insurance man was here this morning. They'll be sending him his money next week. Is Schroeder going to rebuild, Ty?"

"No. He's decided to rent a place so he can get his business up and running quicker." Ty shrugged, looking at Cade. "We now own another lot."

"You paid him for what he lost in the fire?" asked Cade.

Ty nodded. "He didn't have any insurance. Once we get the lot cleared, we shouldn't have a problem selling it. We ordered everything he needed to run his shop through the store, so that cost wholesale. I don't think it will be too bad."

They discussed rebuilding the livery for a few minutes while Jessie and Camille kept the kids out of the wreckage. While they were standing there, several people walking by complimented Camille on her article.

"You put that blowhard Miller in his place, Miss Dupree," said Mrs. Watson, who had ventured down to the depot with Joanna to see who had come in on the train. "I can't imagine how he thinks he can actually beat Mr. McKinnon. Not after all the good things the mayor has done for our town."

"Thank you, Mrs. Watson." Ty moved beside Camille, putting his arm loosely around her waist. He didn't even think about it until he saw the other lady's shrewd eyes take note of it. He left his hand resting at Camille's waist, knowing that if he pulled away, it would only cause more speculation. He turned his attention to Joanna. "How's Buttercup?"

"Her eyes are still a little red, but she was perkier this morning and eating better. Doctor Thomas has been checking her every day. He says he doesn't usually treat animals, but he's sure done right by her. He says she should be right as rain in a week or two." Tears welled up in the young woman's eyes. "I can't thank you enough for rescuing her, Mr. McKinnon. I don't know what I would have done if she'd died in that fire. I don't think I could have stood it."

"She rescued me, too, Miss Joanna. If I hadn't been able to hold on to her, I might not have made it. She carried me out the door."

Joanna's mouth fell open. "So she's a hero, too?"

"She certainly is. I'm real glad to hear she's going to heal up. Now, if you folks will excuse us, we need to let Cade and his family get on home."

"Of course. Jessie, you come by next week for a nice visit and tell me all about your trip to Dallas. I'll invite some of the other ladies over, so you won't have to repeat yourself so many times."

"Thanks. I'll look forward to it." Jessie smiled politely until Mrs. Watson turned away. Then she rolled her eyes. "I should have known I'd have to give as much of a report as Cade will."

"Only about different things." Cade reached down and picked up Ellie, making her squeal with delight. "Is Miss Lydia cookin' supper, or do I have to eat another meal in a restaurant?"

"She's cooking supper. A big pot of red beans and corn-bread." Ellie hugged his neck and planted a noisy kiss on his cheek. "We'd better hurry up 'cause I'm feelin' mighty hollow."

"I am, too," said Cade.

"That's nothin' new." Ty loved ribbing his brother whenever he got the chance. Mainly because Cade teased him just as much. "We're coming to supper, too, so you can tell us about the convention."

"And Jessie can tell Lydia, Nola and me about the things that interested her," said Camille.

"You saying my wife isn't interested in cattle raising?" Cade grinned at Camille.

"I expect she's interested, but I doubt she spent all her time in Dallas listening to men talk about cows."

"You're right about that." Somehow Jessie moved over beside Camille, and Ty found himself walking along with his brother, Ransom, Quint and Brad.

"You've just been outflanked." Chuckling, Ransom hit the back brim of Ty's hat, nudging it forward.

"Careful or I'll have you fired." Ty dodged when Ransom reached for his hat again. "You're full of it today. You bored again?"

"Yep. The only fun I've had all week was ordering Miller down off that wagon. Here I go hiring me a deputy and all the desperados decide to behave themselves."

"No doubt we'll have more business tomorrow." Quint ruffled Brad's hair and received a grin from the boy in return. "A few drunks, a few fights. No more fires, I hope."

Amen to that, thought Ty. "From what I've seen, George Hutton seems to be doing a good job as marshal. Is he working all right with you?"

"No complaints here," said Ransom. "Things have been so quiet, he's been pretty much occupied with the outhouse patrol."

"Town smells better, too," added Quint. He cast a baleful eye toward Ty. "If you'd talked me into that job, I would have shot you by now."

"Figured as much." Ty grinned at his friend.

"Ransom needs a woman to keep him hoppin'," said Cade.

"Now that I have a little free time on occasion, I have more women than I know what to do with. 'Would you like to come to dinner, Sheriff Starr?' 'Here's a nice cake for you, Sheriff Starr. I made it myself.' 'Oh, you lost a button on your shirt. I can sew real good.' Then there are the more blatant invitations to drop by for the evening, no meal included."

"Prissy must have set her sights on you." Ty watched Camille and Jessie laugh at something, though they were too far ahead to hear the men's conversation. Or if they could hear it, he doubted they were paying attention to it. Judging by some of Jessie's hand motions, they were probably discussing some of the fancy gowns the women had worn to the ball.

"She tried. But I told her straight out that I wasn't the least bit interested."

"Did that stop her?"

Ransom made a face. "Not so far."

"You'll have to get serious over someone else, like Ty did," said Cade. "That's what got her off his trail."

"Haven't found anyone as intriguing as Miss Dupree."

Ty glanced at him out of the corner of his eye, wondering if there was some hidden meaning in Ransom's comment. Had his friend been checking up on Camille?

"I don't think I've ever met a woman who writes the way she does," said Ransom.

"I can't wait to see this article everyone is talking about." Cade had a speculative gleam in his eye. "I gather it has something to do with Ty and Miller?"

"As usual, Miller was bad-mouthing Ty, trying to blame him for the fire," said Ransom.

"How in the world could he blame Ty?"

"It's a long story, one I expect Ty and Camille will tell you. The short version is that Camille heard the speech and blasted him with both barrels. From what I hear, he's mad as a rained-on rooster."

That shifted the discussion to the upcoming election and Miller's tactics. That topic didn't last too long since Miller's ways were all too familiar to them.

"Asa came by the store this afternoon. He's over at the house now." Ty stepped around a big hole in the street, mentally making a note to tell the street sweeper to fill it in. "Said we had four new calves this week. All healthy and strong."

"Looks like I got back home just in time. Longhorn and Hereford mix?"

"Three of them. It appears Hercules is earning his keep. The other one was pure longhorn."

When they reached Cade and Jessie's, Asa's wife Lydia had supper ready and waiting. "I thought you'd like some plain fare tonight. Figured you've been eatin' high on the hog all week." She set the big pot of pinto beans flavored with salt pork on the table. Two plates of cornbread followed.

"You figured right." Jessie sat down between her children, holding their hands.

The rest followed suit until there was an unbroken circle around the table, heads lowered, eyes closed while Cade asked the blessing. It was a tradition Jessie had started after she and Cade married. At first, it had troubled Ty because it made him think of Amanda and little William. But he had gradually come to be simply grateful for the family he had left. Now that Camille often was seated beside him, it made the prayer time extra special.

"Heavenly Father, we thank you for this food that Lydia has so kindly prepared. We ask you to bless it to our bodies. Thank you for a good trip to Dallas and back, and for keeping our family safe while we were gone. We especially thank you for protecting Ty and Quint during the fire, and that no one was seriously injured. In Jesus' name, amen."

"Amen." Ty thought the mingling of everyone's voices as they affirmed the prayer must be music to the Lord. Such a simple word, but it proclaimed the thanks of many hearts.

"Tell us about the convention." Ty took a piece of cornbread and passed the plate to Camille. Lydia dished up bowls of beans, which were passed to each person at the table. "Any important business decided?"

"The detective service is working out well. They're covering an area from Chicago and St. Louis west to Dodge City and south to the Gulf. It's been so successful at recovering stolen cattle and breaking up bands of rustlers that they're going to extend it. Supposedly, the detectives and inspectors are doing such a good job that rustlers will steal the cattle of ranchers who don't belong to the association but leave association members' cattle alone, even if they're side by side on the range."

"That seems a stretch." Quint paused, doing a quick check of the available cornbread and took another piece. "Hard to determine brands in the middle of the night." He knew what he was talking about. When he had infiltrated the rustlers the year before, he had had to go on raids with them or else they would have shot him as a spy.

"What about the land board's rent increase on leasing state land? Was the association able to persuade them to come down on the price?"

"No." Cade buttered a piece of cornbread. "They're still insisting on eight cents annually per acre of unwatered land and twenty cents an acre for watered land. I don't think I heard anybody who was willing to pay that, but neither was there a consensus of what was fair. The suggestions ranged from four cents an acre for all land to as much as ten and twelve cents. Some men are threatening to take their herds to New Mexico, Wyoming, Colorado or even old Mexico. Others, particularly C. C. Slaughter, declared that they would fight the land board by every legal means possible. There were some who thought folks should wait awhile and see if it didn't all work out."

"That seems a bit simple-minded to me," said Ty before he took a bite of beans.

"I think it is. But I'm not for moving our herds anywhere else. Reckon we'll have to wait a while and see if something can be done through the legislature. I'm all for building up the state school fund but driving the ranchers out of the country won't do that."

"What about ranches changing hands?" asked Camille. "Mr. Hill said that ranches are often bought and sold at these conventions."

"I heard of a few. An Englishman, the Earl of Aylesford, bought a ranch twelve miles north of Big Spring. He got title to twelve sections and the lease to twenty-nine sections."

"How much stock?" asked Ty.

"Sixteen hundred head of cattle. I didn't hear any number for the horses, but there are bound to be some. He paid seventy-five thousand for it."

"Sounds like a fair price. We're getting a passel of Englishmen and Scots in West Texas. Doesn't bother me, since they like to spend money at the store."

"There was also a presentation from a company that makes refrigerated rail cars for hauling meat back east. Though that has to be a boon for the meat-packing plant in Fort Worth, I can't see them ever handling all the cattle Texas has to offer."

"Jessie, what did you do while Cade was at the meetings?" Lydia poured Asa another cup of coffee.

"Shopped and visited with some of the other ladies. The meetings didn't take up all the time. One afternoon Cade and I went for a carriage ride around Dallas. Carriages were provided free for anyone who wanted to go. It was quite a procession." Jessie cut Ellie's cornbread in half so it was easier for the little girl to eat. "I never saw such a line of buggies and carriages. I heard they used up almost every one that was for hire. Many private ones had been loaned for the drive, too."

"How was the banquet and ball?" Camille dabbed her mouth with a napkin, making Ty smile inwardly. She even managed that task in a ladylike manner.

"The banquet was elaborate. I've never seen anything like it. The room was fifty by two hundred feet, brilliantly lit by electric lights and gas jets. The decorations were amazing. There were great swags of evergreens along the walls and huge wreaths of lovely flowers. There were numerous cattle, deer and antelope horns hung on the walls, with pretty bouquets of flowers in the center of each one. They also had many pictures and paintings on the walls."

"Don't forget the cows hanging from the ceiling." Cade winked at Ty.

"Cows?" Brad's gaze narrowed. "Are you joshin' us, Daddy?"

"Not exactly. The cows and steers weren't real. They were miniature and bronzed."

"What's miniature mean?" Ellie swallowed quickly before her mother reminded her not to speak with her mouth full. "And what is bronzed?"

"Miniature means small, something that isn't life-sized. Bronze is a type of metal."

"So they had metal cows hanging from the ceiling?" Brad's spoon was poised halfway to his mouth. "Did they look like the real thing?"

"They had a good resemblance." Jessie smiled at Cade. "But the decorations I liked the best were a lone star and a good luck horseshoe made out of flowers. They were suspended from the ceiling and were very beautiful. It smelled wonderful, too. In the very center of the room, they had made an enormous five-pointed star out of evergreens. They had six long tables loaded with food. They seated five hundred people at a time. It was all very impressive for this small-town gal."

"It sounds impressive for anyone," said Camille. "I never saw anything like that in New Orleans."

"That's because Texans always do things bigger and better." Ty relaxed, enjoying the company of the people he loved. Without a doubt, Camille Dupree was included in that category. *Maybe I'll take her to the convention next year,* he mused.

When the implication of that thought hit him, he almost choked on a mouthful of beans.

Chapter Twenty-Three

Almost two weeks later, Camille skimmed some of the out-of-state newspapers for fillers to take up the extra space. They didn't need to use as many of them as they had in the past, but customers actually complained about the cut. Folks liked those little tidbits gleaned from across the country.

When the door opened, she looked up, smiling as Ty came into the *Gazette* office. "Good afternoon. What brings you by?"

"Why, I wanted to see your smile, of course." He glanced at the two men setting type and laying out ads. "What are you doing?"

"Finding bits to fill in small spaces. We're also going to make a short column of some of them."

"Like the one last week that said all goods manufactured in the New Jersey state prison had to be stamped as being made there?"

"That's right. I suppose some people wouldn't want to buy things made in a prison."

"It wouldn't bother you?"

"Not if it was good quality. Here's one: 'The great Los Angeles meteor has been dug up and is scientifically described as about the size of a Saratoga trunk.'"

Ty laughed and turned slightly, relaxing against the counter. "That sounds like a scientific description I'd come up with. Any more?"

"Dakota has a pretty fair chance of becoming the thirty-ninth star in the flag."

"Every part of the country should be a state, not a territory."

"Here's one from overseas. 'Eight hundred vagrants, a score of them men whose ages ranged from ninety to ninety-nine years, were arrested in a single week toward the close of last month in Paris. Many asserted that they had not slept on a bed for thirty years.'"

"So that's the secret to a long life, but not a very comfortable one." Ty pulled a sheet of paper from his coat pocket. "I do have some business to attend to. Need to change my ad."

Camille pretended to be shocked. "Changing it twice in one month? My goodness."

"You showed me the error of my ways. Here's the list. Y'all can draw up the ad however you see fit."

She took the paper with a grin. "You are mellowing out, aren't you?"

"I'm trying."

"But it's not easy when you're used to being in charge. Let me see what wonderful things you have in stock. 'Two thousand yards lawn, styles good, colors warranted at seven cents a yard.' I'll have to come see what I can find. 'Combination suits, ten beautiful styles, all wool. Twenty-five shades handsome brocade satins at sixty cents. Fifteen styles ladies' linen and lace collars.'"

She laid the sheet on the counter, skimming her finger over the list. "'Gent's linen collars. Gent's summer merino undershirts. Lenolian matting, both American and English. Ten pieces Brussels carpet, styles entirely new.' You did get in a large shipment. This will make a good ad, but we may have to increase the size."

"Suits me."

"You are so accommodating."

"I like to make you happy," he said softly.

Camille's heart skipped a beat at the warmth and tenderness in his eyes. "You do. I've never been happier."

A light cough drew her attention to the layout man. "I have Fuller's ad done, Miss Dupree, if you want to take it over for final approval."

"Thank you. I'll take care of it right away."

"I need to get moving, too," said Ty. "I have to sort out some things for the city council meeting tonight. Wish I could cancel it. I'd rather spend the evening with you."

"With Nola out of town?" Camille had seen her off on the train that morning for a trip to visit her sister in Dallas for a few days. Nola had been worried about her with all the flooding.

Ty glanced past her into the office where Mr. Hill was working on an article. Shifting so his back was to the other men, his gaze dropped to her mouth. "It should be warm enough to sit out on the porch swing tonight," he said softly. "I don't think it would be too improper for me to call as long as we stayed outside where folks could see us."

"If it's cool I could wear a shawl."

He leaned a little closer, whispering, "I'll keep you warm."

She caught her breath, longing to be alone with him. "What about the neighbors?"

"It gets dark early."

She picked up the list and fanned her face, making him laugh. "Go to your meeting. It's safer for both of us."

"Yes, ma'am." His face drooped into a hound-dog sad expression. "But not nearly as much fun."

"I know." She leaned closer, too, turning so only he could see her face and hear her whispered words. "I love you."

"I love you, too. If we didn't have an audience, I'd kiss you until your legs turned to jelly."

Just the thought of it made her knees weak. "They already are."

Heat flared in his eyes. "I'll come by after the meeting. We'll stay on the porch. That won't give the neighbors too much to talk about."

"All right." She wondered if she'd be able to do a speck of work the rest of the day.

After he bade the others goodbye and left, Camille went into the inner office for her hat. She smiled at Mr. Hill when he looked up from his work. "Finished?

"Yes. And so am I. I think I'll take the rest of the day off." He looked weary.

"Are you feeling ill?"

"No, but I am tired. Too much excitement this last week. I'm going home and sleep for a while."

"There's no need for you to come in tomorrow. That article is the last one we need for the paper this week. There is a city council meeting tonight, so I'll save some space for the report." She frowned in concern. "Why don't you stop by the doctor's on the way home?"

"Won't do any good. He'll tell me the same thing he has before. I already have all the medicine and tonics that I need." Mr. Hill stood and slowly slipped on his jacket. "I'll rest easy knowing you're overseeing things here. I may not come back to work until next week."

"We'll manage. If I have a problem or a question, I'll come see you. Tell your wife hello for me."

"I will. You're a good partner, Miss Dupree," he said with a smile. "Hope you stay with it when you and Ty get hitched."

Blushing, she laughed. "I don't have any plans to quit anytime soon. As for getting hitched, we'll have to see how that goes. He hasn't mentioned it yet."

"All in good time." Mr. Hill put on his hat and left the office slowly.

Carrying her hat, Camille went to the office door. "Brian, would you keep an eye on Mr. Hill? See that he makes it home all right?"

"Yes, ma'am." The young man hopped up, quickly taking off the apron that protected his clothing from the ink. "I'll catch up with him."

"Thank you." Camille pinned her hat in place. Taking the ad for Fuller's, she quickly walked the few blocks to the grocery store. "Good afternoon, Mr. Fuller. Would you care to look over your ad?"

The grocer nodded and gave some instructions to one of the clerks, then turned his attention to Camille with a friendly smile. "You appear to be in good spirits today."

"It's a warm, sunny day. Not a drop of rain in sight."

Mr. Fuller chuckled and took the ad from her. "Hasn't been any rain in sight for a couple of weeks. I'm of a mind that the mayor has something to do with the sparkle in your eyes."

"You could be right." Camille smiled and left it at that.

The grocer checked the ad, going over it carefully. "Don't see any mistakes. As long as everything I ordered from Fort Worth comes in on Thursday, business should be good."

"At least the trains are running pretty much on schedule now."

"Finally." He handed the ad sheet back to her. "Thought they never would get back to normal."

"I suppose they had to repair the tracks that were flooded."

"Shouldn't have taken this long. Wouldn't surprise me if they decide to hike the shipping rates to make us pay for it."

"Well, they shouldn't. Freight is expensive enough already. Thank you for your business, Mr. Fuller."

"I'm the one who should be thanking you, ma'am. Business has picked up since I started advertising the weekly specials. You're an astute young lady."

"I simply know how I like to shop, and I think many women are the same. We like bargains. Have a good day."

"You, too, Miss Dupree. Give my best to Mrs. Simpson when she comes back from Dallas."

"I will." She left the store, thinking how easily everyone seemed to know everyone else's business. It was one trait of living in a small town that she didn't like. But she supposed she'd better get used to it. She stopped for a few minutes to watch the men Ty had hired to clean up the mess from the fire. He had one crew working on the livery and another hauling away the debris from the tailor shop.

On the way back to the *Gazette*, she felt a prickling of unease across the nape of her neck. It wasn't merely the feeling that someone was watching her. That happened every day. But this time she sensed danger. She scanned the street but could see nothing to cause it. Though she couldn't explain it, she couldn't shake the foreboding that settled over her.

Hurrying back to the office, she gave Brian the ad. She didn't bother to remove her hat, since it was almost time to go home. She read the article Mr. Hill had written, first for content, then again to study how he put the whole thing together. He was a very good writer, with the ability to make the reader question and ponder. Her style was very different from his, but she had learned a great deal from him.

She considered dropping by his house on the way home to see how he was feeling, but decided against it. He didn't need her interrupting his rest.

When she arrived at Nola's, Hester had a pot of stew waiting. They ate, chatting about the day's happenings.

"Are you sure you want me to take the next few days off?" asked Hester as she cleared the table.

"Yes. Unless there is something you specifically want to do around here while Nola is gone."

Hester laughed as she filled the dishpan with hot water. "Miss Nola likes to oversee things. She wouldn't like it much if I started any major cleaning without her here."

"Then enjoy a few days of leisure. I'm no authority on housework, but I assume it will soon be time for spring cleaning." Camille's mother had been keen on turning everything upside down and inside out in the springtime. Though her mother hadn't done any of the cleaning herself, she had run the campaign with the precision of an army general.

"We don't usually start that until April. Miss Nola likes to wait until it's warm enough to air out all the quilts and pack them away. I'll enjoy some time to myself. Give me a chance to tidy up my own house and sew up a new set of kitchen curtains."

Hester finished the dishes while Camille read the daily *Fort Worth Gazette*. They had an agreement with them to use some of their articles, particularly ones dealing with the state legislature and happenings in Austin. The editor of the Fort Worth paper was a staunch supporter of the open range and free grass. Since local opinion was mixed on the subject, Mr. Hill and Camille were careful about which articles they put in their paper. They sometimes included stories about West Texas, such as the one she'd spotted the week before about laying out the streets in the new town of Midland.

"I'm finished, Miss Dupree. Let me know if you need anything before Saturday." Hester hung her apron up on a peg on the hat rack by the back door.

"I will. Relax a bit while you're off."

"That's not in my nature, I'm afraid. Though I do have a new book to read. Maybe I'll spend a little extra time with that."

After the housekeeper left, Camille went upstairs and laid out her clothes for the next day. She had gotten into the habit because she still moved rather slowly in the mornings. "I should have gone to see Bonnie tonight instead of tomorrow night." Though she doubted her friend would mind if she dropped by unexpectedly, she decided against it. *I'd hate to be there if Ty's meeting ends early,* she thought. Picking up her Bible, she went back downstairs to read and wait for him.

She went into the living room and lit the lamp. A second after she set the chimney back into place, she heard a faint noise from behind her. Heart pounding, she spun around—and gasped at the sight of Anthony Brisbane. Tall and blond, he was as handsome and dapper as ever.

"Good evening, Angelique." He rose smoothly with a happy smile. "The years have been gracious to you. You've grown even more beautiful."

"What are you doing here?" Camille fought to control the quiver in her voice.

A slight frown creased his brow. "I came to see you, of course. I heard you'd followed Nate and Bonnie out this way." He stopped in front of her, tracing his fingers down her arm. "I've missed you, my sweet."

She shifted away from his touch. "I'm not your anything, Anthony. Except a memory."

"A pleasant one, for the most part. I treated you badly, Angel. I regret that. No one has ever made me as happy as you. I was a fool to walk out on you and stupid to throw away your love." He closed his hand lightly around her upper arm. "I'd like to regain what we lost."

Camille twisted out of his grip and stepped away. "There is nothing to regain. You took advantage of my fear and grief over my father's death. You never loved me. You only wanted a roll in the hay and the notoriety that came from being the man who won the Angel's interest."

"Not merely interest. You loved me passionately."

"I never loved you. I thought I did, and you broke my heart because of it. But now I know what true love is." She lifted her chin, meeting his gaze defiantly. "What we shared was lust and a trifling affection. Nothing more."

"I cared for you." His face twisted in anger.

"You didn't care enough to make me your wife. You shamed me, made me the brunt of gossip and scorn."

He shrugged as if her hurt didn't matter. "You joined me willingly. People talked about you all the time anyway."

"It wasn't the same. It was one thing to be a gambler. Quite another to be a mistress." She took a deep breath, silently asking God to help her, to guide her. "I have a new life here, Anthony. A respectable one."

"Doing what?"

"I'm part owner of the local newspaper."

He snorted in disbelief. "A leopard can't change its spots, Angel. You're a born gambler. Gambling is in your blood, just like it was with your old man."

"No, it never was. I walked away from gambling when I came here, and I've never once felt the urge to go back to it. I've discovered how nice it is when people treat me decently. I'm a new person. I've found Jesus, and He cleansed me from my old life. My old sins."

"You got religion?" He laughed in her face. Then his gaze suddenly narrowed. "You said you're in love." Grabbing her hand, he checked her empty ring finger. "You aren't married, so you must be sleeping with him on the sly."

Camille shook her head in disgust. "Not everyone lives by the same low standards you do. Some men have integrity and honor. They aren't only interested in getting a woman into bed."

"That's not all I'm interested in. When I came here, I was willing to marry if you insisted on it. Now, I don't think I am," he said sullenly.

"Good." She started toward the door, but stopped when she heard him sit down on the couch. Coming back, she tapped her foot impatiently. "Leave, Anthony. Take the next train out of Willow Grove. East or west, it doesn't matter. Just leave."

"No. I have business here."

She didn't like the sound of that. "What kind of scheme are you planning?"

He appeared offended, but it was false. She knew him far too well to be fooled by his acting.

"I've gone respectable, too. I'm a representative of the Great Western Fire and Casualty Company. Since the town recently had a fire, folks who didn't have insurance are bound to see the need now."

"I don't believe you."

"You'd better. I won't take kindly to you costing me money."

She didn't miss the underlying threat in his tone. "The people here are good and honest. Don't swindle them out of their hard-earned money."

"I won't." Anthony jumped to his feet, startling her. "I sell insurance. They protect their homes and businesses, and I make a tidy commission. If I'd known legitimate business was so profitable, I might have tried it years ago."

He sounded believable, but she caught the little twitch in his cheek. He was such a smooth liar that the twitch didn't always show. But when it did, it was a sure sign that he wasn't telling the truth.

"You could never do anything legitimate, Anthony. You like the challenge of fooling people and the excitement of getting away with it. The thrill of the game attracts you as much as the money. If you don't leave town on the morning train, I'll tell Sheriff Starr what you're up to."

She braced for his anger, expecting him to rail at her. Instead, a calculating gleam lit his eyes, sending a shiver of dread down her spine.

"Does your lover know about your past?"

"Yes. And he's not my lover."

"What about the good, honest townspeople? Do they know you were a gambler?"

"No. Ty is the only one who knows."

"Ty? As in Ty McKinnon, the mayor?" Anthony always sized up a town before he plied his trade, particularly the law and others in authority who might cause him problems.

"Yes."

He studied her intently. His uncanny ability to read people served him well in his profession. And with her. She had never been able to fool him even with a partial truth. "But you didn't tell him about me."

"No." Though she spoke firmly, her heart sank. Now he had her in his power. She anticipated his next words.

"Keep your mouth shut, and I won't say anything to him about our love affair. You tell anyone, and I'll make certain that the esteemed mayor and everyone else learns about your past. All the intriguing details. That would make mincemeat out of your *good* reputation." He sneered as if the very thought of her living a decent life repulsed him. Stepping closer, he gripped her arms painfully. "That goes for Nate and Bonnie, too. If they talk, you'll pay. Don't cross me, Angelique, or you'll be sorry. Very sorry."

Releasing her with a shove that sent her stumbling backward, he grabbed his hat and walked toward the door. He turned, glancing around the living room. "Nice house."

His hateful expression sent fear washing over her. He had changed, become harder, with a mean streak she had never seen.

"Hope you have fire insurance. If you even say good morning to the sheriff, you'll need it."

Chapter Twenty-Four

Heart pounding, Camille sank into the nearest chair before her legs gave out on her. Her thoughts were so jumbled she couldn't think straight. "What am I going to do? Why, God? Why did Anthony have to come here? After all these years, why did he decide he wanted me now?"

Your sins will find you out. The minister's words from the previous Sunday echoed through her mind. "But You've forgiven my past," she whispered on a sob. "Those things shouldn't count anymore. He's going to destroy my life again. It's not fair."

After a few minutes and a good cry, she regained her composure and decided to go see Bonnie. She hurried to her friend's house, leaving so quickly that she didn't think about taking a shawl or jacket for the walk back. When she arrived at the Flynn's, she was surprised to find Nate there.

"I'm trying to spend more evenings at home," he said as he stepped back and opened the door wider. "Come on in."

His smile changed to a frown as she walked into the living room and he got a good look at her face. "What's wrong?"

"Anthony is here."

"You've talked to him?" Bonnie put her arm around her waist and led her over to the sofa.

"He sneaked into the house after Hester left. When I came downstairs, he was waiting in the living room."

"What does he want?"

"Me." Camille took a deep breath, forcing herself to settle down. "At least he said he did. He changed his mind when I told him I wasn't in love with him and never had been. He pouted like a little boy."

Bonnie made a face. "That's Anthony. If he doesn't get his way, he sulks."

"He won't stop with that this time. He's different."

"How?" Nate paced back and forth across the room.

"Colder, harder. Mean. I think he's done worse things than steal from people. He says he's here as an insurance salesman for Great Western."

"Surely you don't believe him?" asked Bonnie, her expression incredulous.

"Of course not, and he knows it. But if I say anything to anyone—or if you do—he'll tell Ty about us. The whole town, too. He threatened to burn Nola's house down if I so much as bid the sheriff good morning."

"That little weasel. I ought to teach him a lesson." Nate looked around as if seeking something he could smash.

"It won't help. If you beat him up, he'll have you arrested for assault."

"And spread all kinds of rumors about Angel anyway, likely embellished to tarnish her reputation more."

"So we sit back and let our neighbors be swindled?" Nate sat down across from Camille. "That's not right."

"I know it isn't." Camille closed her eyes. Though Nate wasn't a Christian, he had strong convictions about what was right and wrong. But his life and everything he held dear wasn't at stake. Hers was. She looked at Bonnie, then Nate. "Give me a chance to figure out what to do. How to explain to Ty."

"Don't take long. Folks will be more forgiving about something that happened in the past than they will about losing their money."

"I understand. But Sheriff Starr isn't going to arrest him merely on my say-so. If he starts asking questions, Anthony will know I'm to blame. I'm afraid he might actually try to burn down Nola's house." She shuddered.

"Lord have mercy, you're serious." Bonnie's face paled. "Do you think he might try to kill you?"

"No. But I don't think he would have any qualms about setting the house ablaze. Then he would turn around and use it as another reason to persuade people to buy insurance."

Nate stared at the floor for a few minutes. "I think you should see the sheriff in the morning. Starr's a good man. He's not one to pry more than is necessary, and he doesn't gossip. He'll know how to check up on Anthony without the weasel suspecting it. You wouldn't have to tell him everything. Only that you were acquainted with Brisbane in San Antonio and that he was suspected of being a swindler. Give him the idea to see what he can find out."

"Why couldn't you do that, honey?" asked Bonnie. "So Angel wouldn't have to be involved."

Nate shook his head. "She has to do it." He looked at Camille. "He needs to know about Anthony's threat to burn down the house. Only you know how much to tell Starr about your relationship with Anthony."

"I don't want to tell him anything."

"You have to."

"I know." She glanced at the mantel clock. If she went on home, she should have time to freshen up and gather her wits before Ty came by. "I'll work it out. If nothing else, I'll leave Willow Grove and you can tell the sheriff about him."

"Don't you dare," scolded Bonnie. "You can't up and leave Ty like that."

"It's cowardly, but easier than seeing his face when I tell him about Anthony. Or seeing what happens if Anthony decides to spread rumors about me. It's not only me I'm worried about. It's less than a week until the election. I don't want to think about what such a scandal would do to Ty's chances."

"You don't have to worry about Ty winning the election. He has it sewn up. And you aren't a coward, Angel." Nate stood when she did.

"Well, I don't feel very brave."

Bonnie took her hand and squeezed it. "Trust in the Lord. Let Him lead you through this."

Camille wished it were that easy. She had been trusting God in this new life of hers. And what had happened? Her old life had come back to tear everything apart. "I'm trying, but He seems very far away right now."

"Don't give up on Him. I don't understand what's going on either, but the Bible says that if you love the Lord, all things happen for good. Even when it doesn't seem like it."

Camille tried to take Bonnie's words to heart as she walked home. "Heavenly Father, I'm so afraid. You've blessed me so much here in Willow Grove. I love it here and don't want to leave. I can't bear the thought of leaving Ty. I love him so much. I don't want to hurt him or bring him shame. Lord Jesus, please make Anthony get on that train tomorrow. Send him to Australia or some place as far away."

Ty waited impatiently on Nola's front porch. He figured Camille had gone to see Bonnie, anticipating that his meeting would last longer. Sitting on the swing, he had a good view of the street and spotted her as she turned the corner.

He waited to stand and show himself until she reached the gate. When she spotted him, she practically ran to meet him.

"I could get used to that kind of welcome." He put his arm around her shoulders as they walked up the steps. He thought he felt her tremble but decided he was imagining it. The evening was cool, but not that cold, especially after a brisk walk.

"I'm sorry I wasn't here. I went to see Bonnie."

"Figured as much. We resolved a couple of issues but had to table everything else until we have more information." He started to sit down on the swing, but she shook her head.

"Let's go inside."

"That's probably not wise." Not only because the neighbors might talk.

"I don't care. I want to be away from prying eyes." She scanned the street and nearby houses. Curling her fingers around his arm, she tugged him toward the door. "Please, Ty. I don't want to sit out here."

"All right." Maybe if he did as she asked, she'd tell him what had her spooked. He followed her inside, closing the door. Light from the kitchen lamp filtered down the hallway, casting the living room in a faint glow. "Do you want me to light the lamp in here?"

"No. The neighbors are more apt to see you with it on."

Ty tossed his hat on a table and caught her hand, drawing her to him. Leaning against the door, he pulled her into his arms. "What's wrong, sweetheart?"

She shrugged, then snuggled close, resting her head on his shoulder, burying her face against his neck. "I want to hold you and kiss you without an audience."

"I'm not fond of puttin' on that kind of a show for folks, either." He kissed her forehead and ran one hand up and down her back. She put her arms around him, holding tight. Too tight, almost as if she couldn't bear to let him go. "Camille..."

She looked up at him, searching his face. He thought he saw deep sadness in her eyes, but it could have been a trick of the light. "I love you," she whispered. "You mean more to me than anything."

He heard heartache in her words, in her voice. "Sweetheart—"

She kissed him. Passionately. Urgently. Desperately.

Whatever he meant to say vanished in a rush of emotion, need and desire. He was incapable of coherent thought, aware only of the woman in his arms and the love taking flight in his heart. "I love you, too," he murmured between kisses. "So very much."

He buried his hands in the chignon at the nape of her neck, scattering hairpins across the floor. When the heavy locks drooped, he worked the other pins loose until her hair flowed freely over his hands and down her back. He had longed to see her hair down, to feel its softness against his skin. Lifting his head, he threaded his fingers through the silky strands, starting at her temple, sweeping down the length until he reached her elbow. "So beautiful."

Cupping her face with both hands, he kissed her, intending it to be slow and sweet, to guide them back from danger. But the passion burning between them could not be so easily contained. The kiss went on and on, building in intensity. He felt her knees buckle as she sagged against him, gripping his shirt for support. Somewhere in the back of his mind, he noted that his knees were weak, too, and if he didn't find some place to sit, they would wind up on the floor.

Drawing her with him, he maneuvered to the sofa and eased her down, sitting beside her. "I have to leave."

"I'll behave." She laid her head on his shoulder, resting her hand on his chest. Her breath was hot against his throat. "I promise."

"I don't think I can. If I don't leave now, I'll be staying the night." He held her close. "And neither of us would be too proud of ourselves in the morning."

"Forgive me," she said softly, reaching up to brush his jaw with her fingertips.

"There's nothing to forgive. I knew what was liable to happen when I walked through that door."

"Don't hate me."

Leave it to a woman to worry over the oddest things. He caught her hand, kissing it gently. "I'm glad you're passionate, Camille. It would be a sorry situation if I loved a cold fish." He started to kiss her goodbye but thought better of it. "I have to go to Fort Worth in the morning to look at a builder's work, to see if the quality is good enough for our new city hall. But I'll be back on the evening train. I'll see you then." He rubbed his knuckle beneath her chin. "Don't fret, sweetheart. It will give you wrinkles."

"Heaven forbid." Her voice almost sounded normal. But not quite. That little wobble nagged him all night long.

Chapter Twenty-Five

By noon the next day, Anthony had set up shop in a corner of the Barton Hotel lobby. Camille had seen other salesmen do the same, paying rent for the table and space. She wandered by on her way to the small bookstore and newsstand inside the hotel. The sign displayed behind him bore the name and logo of the Great Western Fire and Casualty Company. If it was fake, it was a good one. Or else he'd stolen it from someone.

Despite several customers waiting in line, Anthony watched her cross the lobby. A few of the men noticed him staring, glanced in her direction and nodded good-naturedly. They found nothing amiss with him looking at an attractive woman. But they were unaware of the anger seething behind those deceptive eyes.

Purchasing copies of the Chicago and New York newspapers, she left the hotel without looking at him again. She had walked the floor most of the night, alternately begging the Lord to send him away and crying out her anguish because God had allowed him to come here at all. She tried so hard to trust Jesus to take care of it, but she couldn't see how anything good could come from the situation.

Leaving the hotel, she knew what she had to do, though it might cost her the man she loved and the respectable life she had found. Ducking between the blacksmith shop and the carriage maker's, she walked down the alley that ran behind the buildings on that side of the street. When she reached the sheriff's office, she knocked on the back door, praying that Ransom was there alone.

He opened the door with a stern expression that quickly became a friendly smile. "This is a nice surprise. Usually when someone knocks on the back door they want to break somebody out of jail. I don't have anyone in the calaboose, so that must not be it." He stepped back so she could go inside.

"Would you mind if we talked here?"

"No." He frowned and quickly surveyed the empty alley. "How can I help you, Miss Dupree?"

"By quietly checking with Great Western Insurance to see if Anthony Brisbane works for them."

"He's over at the Barton."

"Yes. I was acquainted with him in San Antonio. He's a charlatan, Sheriff Starr. At least he was then. He says he's reformed, but I doubt it. If he's still in the game, he's bilking quite a few people out of their money. I went over to the newsstand a few minutes ago and there were five men waiting to see him."

"I appreciate you telling me." As he studied her face, Camille decided Anthony had finally met his match. Sheriff Starr was also good at reading people, probably better. "You say you talked to him?"

"Yesterday. On one hand, he proclaimed that he's changed his ways. But on the other, he threatened to burn

Nola's house down if I talked to you. It was a veiled threat, but I believe a real one."

"You obviously didn't tell Ty about this. If you had, he wouldn't have gone to Fort Worth."

"No. I didn't want him storming over to the hotel and raising a ruckus."

"Would have done more than that, I expect. I'll wire the insurance company. I had to sign so many affidavits about the fire that I know the address. In the meantime, I'll keep an eye on Brisbane. He won't even know it." His grin surprised her. "It'll give me a chance to polish up my surveillance skills."

She smiled despite her worry. "I think you miss being a detective."

"I do. Sometimes I feel like I'm gathering cobwebs stayin' in one place."

"Everyone says you've done a good job as sheriff."

"Always give it my best. Did you hear that the train is running about six hours late?" When she shook her head, he continued, "They have to fix some broken track this side of Weatherford. Won't be in here until after midnight."

Then she had one more night's reprieve. I'll tell him tomorrow.

"I'll send that wire right away," said Starr. "If we're lucky, we'll hear something in the morning. Are you afraid to stay at Mrs. Simpson's alone?"

"No. I don't think he'll bother me for now. Once he puts a scam in motion, he focuses totally on it."

Starr's eyes narrowed. "You know him well."

Heat filled her face as she nodded. "Please don't say anything to Ty."

"That's between you and him."

"Thank you."

"A word of advice as a friend. Be honest with him. The simple truth is usually best."

"Sometimes the truth isn't simple."

"And sometimes it's not nearly as complex as we think it is. Keep your guard up."

"I will." Though she hadn't felt the need to constantly be on guard for the last few months, she hadn't forgotten how. She supposed some things always stayed with you. Perhaps some sins, too.

The next morning, Ty was late leaving for work. He hadn't gotten home until after three o'clock, so he slept later than usual. It hadn't helped much. He was as grumpy as a bear with a thorn in its paw. He decided to go straight to the *Gazette* and see Camille. That should brighten his morning.

Unless she was still in that strange mood. He'd tossed and turned all night long on Wednesday, worrying about her. He couldn't shake the feeling that something was wrong. She wasn't easily upset, but she clearly had been that night.

A block before the newspaper office, he ran into Ransom. "You're looking mighty serious this morning."

"Have some serious business to attend to. I'm on my way to the Barton to arrest a fraud."

"Who?"

"Anthony Brisbane. He's posing as a fire and casualty insurance salesman for Great Western. Miss Dupree tipped me off that he has a history of swindling, so I wired the company and checked. Sure enough, he doesn't work for them."

"Camille knows him?" That could explain why she was troubled Wednesday night. But why didn't she share her suspicions with him? What was she hiding? Ty got a sick feeling in the pit of his stomach.

"Said she was acquainted with him in San Antonio."

"How well acquainted?"

"Didn't say exactly." Ransom hesitated, and Ty's stomach began to burn. "Well enough that he threatened her if she talked to me."

Ty saw red. Intent on teaching the man a lesson, he started toward the hotel. He took three steps before Ransom grabbed his arm, bringing him to an abrupt halt.

"You probably should mosey on over to the *Gazette* and let her do some explainin'." Ransom released his arm.

"I'm going with you. Nobody threatens my woman and gets away with it."

"I'll take care of him. You go see Camille."

"Later."

Ransom shrugged. "All right. But we're going to arrest him for fraud, not to beat the living daylights out of him."

"He threatened her."

"If you make a scene, everyone in town will know it. And they'll wonder how she knew such a scoundrel in the first place."

"Then I'll go along as your backup. Where is Quint, anyway?"

"Talking to a couple of ranchers who lost some horses over the weekend. Ty, I think Camille has a history with this hombre. She knows how he works. Could she have been involved in his operation?"

"No. I'm positive she would never do anything like that."

"Why?"

Ty didn't like being backed into a corner. He'd promised to keep her secret, but he couldn't have Ransom thinking she was a criminal. "She was a professional gambler," he said quietly. "Who took pride in the fact that she never cheated. Nate confirmed it. The one time we talked about it, she impressed on me that she didn't hold with cheating of any kind."

"Good enough." Ransom started across the street with Ty in step beside him.

At the hotel, Ty let Ransom go ahead of him, keeping a clear view of Brisbane as he walked toward him. Though Brisbane had a customer, he quickly spotted the sheriff. When he glanced at Ty, recognition flickered across his face. So he knows who I am, thought Ty. Which probably meant he knew about his relationship with Camille.

"Good morning, Sheriff." Brisbane stood. His gaze flitted toward the doorway, but Ty had already moved to block any chance of escape in that direction. Ransom was in a position to stop him if he tried for the back door.

"Anthony Brisbane, you're under arrest for defrauding the people of Willow Grove."

A wild look flashed in Brisbane's eyes, and Ty remembered that he wasn't wearing his revolver. He tensed, waiting for the man to make his move. Brisbane flicked his wrist, but Ransom drew his Colt before the Derringer slid completely out of the criminal's sleeve and into his hand.

"Put the gun on the table, nice and slow," ordered Ransom, pointing a pistol at his chest.

Glaring at him, Brisbane complied.

"Ty, check to see if he has anything else up his sleeve. Or anywhere else."

Ty felt along both sleeves, then frisked him—none too gently—as well as checking his boots. He found another pistol in his coat pocket and one tucked into the top of a boot. Since Brisbane wasn't wearing a hat, he didn't have to worry about one being stashed there.

"This is ridiculous, Sheriff. Did Angelique Dupree tell you I was a fraud? Oh, wait, I forgot. She goes by Camille here."

"Miss Dupree informed me that you were a known swindler in San Antonio."

A shocked murmur went around the room. Ty glanced around at the crowd in the hotel lobby. The group was growing larger by the minute.

"You took the word of a card shark?" sneered Brisbane. He looked around. "That's how Camille Dupree made her living in San Antonio—playing poker in saloons."

Several of the ladies gasped and the men muttered among themselves.

"Shut up, Brisbane." Ty took a threatening step toward him.

"What's the matter, Mayor? You don't want these good people to know the truth about your mistress?"

"She's not my mistress," growled Ty, moving toward him.

"She was mine." Though Brisbane didn't raise his voice, his words carried throughout the hushed room. "Too bad she's been holding out on you."

Ty landed one good punch to Brisbane's jaw before Ransom shoved him aside. "I told you not to pulverize him." He handed Ty the Colt. "Keep him covered while I cuff him. Don't shoot him unless he tries to get away." Ransom walked around behind Brisbane and slapped a handcuff on one wrist. Brisbane wiped the blood off his mouth with his other hand.

The man's words ricocheted through Ty's mind. Mistress...she was mine...mistress. "I don't believe you."

"Why would I lie about it?"

"To pay her back for telling the sheriff about you."

"She has a birthmark on the side of her right hip. Almost looks like a butterfly." Brisbane winced when Ransom jerked his other arm behind his back and fastened it in the handcuffs. "She shouldn't have any qualms about showing it to you. There's no telling how many other men have seen it."

Ransom grabbed Brisbane's arm and hustled him toward the door.

"Hey, Sheriff, how do you know he's a fake?" called one of the men who had been waiting to see him.

Ransom paused. "Because I sent a wire to the insurance company. They never heard of him. Ty, collect everything he has here. We'll search his room later. See if we can't return everyone's money. I asked Great Western to send us a real salesman. When he gets here, I'll confirm that he's legitimate."

The room erupted in excitement as Ransom hauled Brisbane from the hotel. Ty gathered up everything he could find lying on the table. Even though he knew he should be the one to take care of it, he desperately wished Ransom hadn't asked him to.

Most of the chatter was a blur, but some comments jumped out at him. *Do you think he knew about her? She sure had him fooled. Maybe not. Who knows what happened when they were alone? ...was after his money. How could he get mixed up with someone like that? I'd get mixed up with her in a minute.* That was followed by laughter.

Ty grabbed a stack of papers from beneath the table and fled. His head was spinning, his heart pounding, and his temper rising by the second. He stomped down the boardwalk to the sheriff's office and threw everything on Ransom's desk. Without sparing his friend or Brisbane a second glance, he stormed off down the street.

By the time he reached the *Gazette*, he was furious. He hit the door so hard it bounced off the wall. "Is she here?" He glared at Brian.

The young man gulped and nodded. "In the office."

Camille opened the inner office door. The color drained from her face when she saw him.

Ty motioned to the typesetter. "Get out."

Brian scrambled for the doorway, scraping his back against the frame as he scooted by Ty.

"Is Hill in there?"

Camille shook her head. She stepped back, disappearing into the office.

He followed, slamming the door shut. "Is it true? Were you Brisbane's mistress?"

Her breath caught, and she closed her eyes for a heartbeat. When she opened them, they were filled with deep sorrow.

It didn't do a thing to ease his wrath.

"Yes."

"What were you going to do? Let me discover your lie on our wedding night?"

"I didn't lie to you."

"You didn't tell me, either," he shouted.

"What was I supposed to say? By the way, I was a man's mistress? I'm not pure and innocent?"

"I should have known better, given your background. Play in the gutter and you get dirty." When she flinched, he ignored it. "How many other men have there been?"

"None." Her chin lifted defiantly.

"You expect me to take your word for it?"

"There's no way to prove it. I've been honest with you, Ty, in everything but this."

"Why not this?"

"Because I knew how you'd react. How you'd feel."

"How can you know how I feel? I loved you. I believed in you. And trusted you." He turned away from her. If he didn't do something physical, he would explode. He shoved some books off the desk onto the floor and spun back around. "You deceived me. You've made me a laughing stock. The whole town probably knows about it by now. Brisbane made it clear to everyone in the hotel lobby. He even described the birthmark on your hip." He hadn't thought she could grow paler, but she did. "Guess he wanted to prove to me that he knew all about you," Ty said bitterly.

"In the hotel lobby?"

"Loud and clear. I expect everyone there heard everything. Too bad I was so noble Wednesday night. Then none of this would have been a surprise."

She sank in the chair, gripping the edge of the desk. "I've tried and tried to think of a way to tell you." When she looked at him, tears shimmered in her eyes. "But I knew I'd lose you. You're too good for me, Ty. In my heart, I've always known it. I didn't want to hurt you, but I couldn't keep away. I love you."

He snorted in disbelief. "You don't deceive someone you love. You lay all the cards on the table."

"I was nineteen years old. My father had just died, and I was all alone except for Nate and Bonnie. I'd never met a smooth talker like Anthony. He promised to marry me. He knew exactly how to persuade me to do his bidding."

Ty thought of her passionate responses and despised Anthony Brisbane even more. "I bet he did," he said sarcastically and succeeded in putting a little color back in her cheeks. "How long were you with him?"

She ducked her head. "Six months. I finally realized he never intended to marry me, so I left."

"Slow learner. Like me. Well, I'm wiser now." His chest ached, his heart breaking all over again. He couldn't think straight, couldn't get beyond the anger and pain. "Tell Nola I won't be coming to dinner anymore. I'll only deal with Hill when it comes to the paper. You can shop somewhere else—if you can find anybody who will accept your business. Might have to go down to the district. You should feel right at home."

She stood, turning her back on him and walking to the window. "You have every right to hate me, but I don't have to listen to your insults. Not here. Get out of my office, Ty."

He left, still angry, but more subdued than when he had arrived. She was right. He'd gone over the line. But he'd be dragged through prickly pear cactus before he apologized. He was the wounded party, not her.

The pitying and speculative looks he received on the way back to the store didn't help a bit. As he walked down the store aisle toward his office, Ed's concerned expression told him that he had already heard. "I don't want to be disturbed."

"Yes, sir."

Ty quietly shut the door to his office, hung up his hat, and leaned his forehead against the door, barely feeling the coolness of the wood. "Why God? Why did You bring her into my life?" Moving back from the door, he sat down, slumping in his chair. "Why do I have to go through such pain again? Wasn't once enough? Are You testing me? Testing my faith? If You are, You know that right now it's not real strong. A man can only get knocked down so many times before he starts doubting that You care."

That wasn't quite true. He believed with all his heart that Jesus loved him enough to redeem his sins. But he was having trouble trusting Him to be Lord of his life, to be in control. "Sorry, Lord, but You don't seem to be doin' all that great a job."

He wrestled with his conscience over that, but he couldn't help but feel that way. He also felt a little guilty for taking so many verbal jabs at Camille. "But she deserved them for not telling me the truth." Thinking what a disaster it would have been to marry her and then find out about her past made him sick. "Thank You that that didn't happen, Lord."

About an hour after he had returned to the store, someone knocked on the door.

"Go away."

The door opened, and Jessie peeked inside. "No." She walked in, shutting the door gently behind her. "I just heard what happened. You must feel awful."

"Lousy."

She came over and gave him a hug, then sat down on the guest chair. "It's hard to be humiliated in front of the whole town."

Ty nodded. She'd experienced it, too, in the East Texas town where she'd lived before coming to Willow Grove. It must have been terrible when her husband had been shot and killed in bed with the mayor's wife. Especially since Jessie worked as housekeeper for the mayor and his wife at the time.

"I assume it's the hot gossip."

"All over town. Mrs. Watson made a special trip to see me."

"Fishing for anything you might know, while telling you the news," said Ty.

"Of course." Jessie picked a piece of lint off her skirt. "Did you know she had been a gambler?"

"Yes. I found out the first Saturday morning she was in town, the day of the box supper. I saw her at the White Buffalo talking to Nate. She had come to Willow Grove to work for him. Her daddy had been a gambler. She took his place when he got sick. After he died, she kept at it. Her middle name is Angelique. She was known as the Angel."

"The Angel," mused Jessie. "I can see why men would call her that. So you knew about it the night of the box supper?"

"Yes. I had a feeling she wanted to do something else, be someone different." Ty squirmed a little. "I think the Lord gave me that insight. After she went to the supper and found out how it was to be treated like a respectable lady, she decided to give gambling up. I didn't feel good about keeping you in the dark, given how things were with your first husband. But I promised not to tell anyone about it. I'm sorry."

"I'm glad you didn't tell me. If you had, I never would have given her a chance. I wouldn't have gotten to know her, to love her, both as a friend and a sister in the Lord. She's not the same woman who came here on that stage, Ty."

"I don't know about that. If she's so changed, why wasn't she honest with me? Why didn't she tell me about Brisbane?"

"I expect she was ashamed. But enough talk for now. I have supper ready, and I want you to come share it with me and the kids."

"I'm not in the mood to be with anybody right now, Jess."

"Of course you aren't. Which is exactly why you need to be with your family. Now come on before the biscuits dry out." She snagged his hat from the rack and held it out to him. "Your other option is to eat at the restaurant, and I hardly think you want to be there tonight."

"Good point." He stood, taking the hat. "Did you say anything to the kids?"

"No. Ellie's too young and carefree to understand. I'll talk to Brad later. Given the way his father gambled and played around, he'll understand. He probably would have understood years ago. It's better if I explain it to him before he hears something from one of his friends."

Ty nodded, though he wished the youngster didn't have to know about such things. He supposed it was a good lesson for his nephew to learn—that you can't trust a woman, no matter how nice she seems.

They walked toward the front door, passing Ed on the way. "Will you lock up tonight?"

"Sure thing, boss."

When Jessie opened the door, she stopped and put her hand on his arm to halt him, too. She nodded toward the street with a frown.

It only took him a second to see what she was looking at. Camille had left the *Gazette* and was walking down the boardwalk in the direction of Nola's. Her carriage graceful and her head held high, she didn't speak to anyone.

But they spoke to her, both in words and actions. A couple of ladies hastily held their skirts aside as she walked past so her dress would not touch theirs. One of them made a comment, too, but he was too far away to tell what it was.

The men were another story. Some of their calls could be heard across the street—whistles and invitations to go to their rooms. Those who were silent openly leered at her.

"Poor Camille," whispered Jessie.

Ty agreed with Jessie, but anger and pride kept him from going to Camille's side.

A few minutes before she reached the sheriff's office, Ransom stepped outside, surveying the street. As she passed the office, he joined her, putting himself between her and the street as they walked down the sidewalk. The men's harassment stopped instantly.

Just like that, she finds another man. He's welcome to her. But Ty sure hated losing his old friend.

Chapter Twenty-Six

Ransom escorted Camille all the way to Nola's front door. Other than telling her that he would see her home, he'd been silent the whole way. Pausing on the front porch, she turned to him, wondering why he had done it. "Thank you."

"You're welcome." He looked out across the yard, frowning when he spotted the neighbor next door peeking out the window. "I figured there might be trouble if I didn't escort you. Didn't want you shootin' somebody."

"It might have made me feel better."

"Momentarily." He rested his hand on his gun belt. She suspected it was an old habit. "I told Ty not to go with me. Then I let it slip that Brisbane had threatened you, and he was determined to rectify the man's error. Maybe if he hadn't been there, Brisbane would have kept his mouth shut. He seemed to know about you and Ty."

"Anthony probably would have said something anyway, just to spite me. He came to Willow Grove for two reasons—to pull the insurance swindle and because he thought I'd jump at the chance to be with him again." She shook her head, still amazed at the man's audacity. "After all these years, he thought he could just waltz back into my life. He didn't take my rejection well."

"It would probably be best if you lie low here at the house for a few days. Give things a chance to settle down. By the middle of next week, it will be old news."

"You know that's not going to happen. Even if people do find something else to gossip about, Ty won't forget." Or forgive. She took a deep, shaky breath. "I'll have to settle accounts with Mr. Hill and talk to Nola tomorrow. But the sooner I leave Willow Grove, the better it will be for everyone."

"Don't be in too big a rush to hightail it out of here. Give Ty time to cool off."

"That will take years. I wounded him deeply."

"You wounded his pride more than anything else. When he gets over being mad and embarrassed, he'll figure out that you're worth keeping."

"But I'm not."

Ransom muttered a mild oath under his breath. "Don't think like that. You're as good as anyone else in this town, as fine a lady as any who warm a pew on Sunday mornings."

"You're very kind, Ransom. But I'm not good enough for Ty, not good enough to be the mayor's wife. If I leave town, maybe he'll still have a chance to win the election."

"If he has any sense, he'll realize that you're more important than being mayor. He'll figure out what a lucky man he is to have your heart."

"I can't blame him for being mad enough to spit hot coals."

"It wasn't the best way to hear about it." Ransom checked the street again. "Ty's been walking the straight and narrow for several years now. He's forgotten that life isn't always so upright and proper. I'm your friend, Camille. What's happened doesn't change that."

"Thank you. But you're Ty's friend, too."

"Doesn't mean I have to agree with him. We've been at odds before and our friendship survived." He stepped back, resting one foot on the top step. "If anybody bothers you, let me know. Lock your doors."

"I will."

He nodded, turned and walked back across the yard and toward town.

Camille went inside, locking the door after she shut it. Leaning against it, she closed her eyes, finally allowing the tears to fall. She didn't know if she would have made it home if Ransom hadn't come with her. Though she doubted any of the men would have actually tried anything, she didn't know if her courage alone would have carried her far enough.

"Miss Dupree..." Hester's soft voice startled her.

Gasping, Camille opened her eyes, looking at the housekeeper. She stood in the kitchen doorway, wearing her apron. "I thought you weren't coming back until tomorrow."

"I wasn't." Hester came into the living room. "Until I heard what happened."

Camille wiped her eyes and braced for a put-down. "I know you want me out of the house. As soon as I pack, I'll go to Nate and Bonnie's."

Hester frowned, resting her hands on her hips. "I don't have any say whether you go or stay. That's up to Miss Nola. I came over here to fix your supper. Didn't figure you'd be eating with Mr. McKinnon tonight."

"Or any other time." The painful thought took away her breath.

"I wouldn't count him out yet if I were you. He'll come around, just you wait and see. Men are all the same. Get in a snit over something, rant and rave for a few days, then come wandering back just like nothin' ever happened."

Camille wondered how a middle-aged spinster knew so much about men, but she was too wrung out to question her. She took off her hat and set it on the table in the hall. Following the housekeeper into the kitchen, she sat down and dutifully choked down an egg, a few bites of ham and a biscuit.

"Thank you, Hester. I needed the food and the company."

"I'm surprised Mrs. Flynn isn't over here."

"She's in bed with a sick headache." Which meant she would probably be too sick to move for two or three days. "Nate came by the office this morning and told me, before everything happened."

"Do you want me to stay?"

"No, you go on home. I think I'll go to bed. I'm exhausted."

"I'll be over in the morning, usual time."

"Good night. Please lock the doors when you leave." Camille trudged up the stairs and changed into her nightgown.

She curled up in bed, but sleep eluded her. *Heavenly Father, please be with Ty. I hurt him so much. I should have told him at the beginning. He might have stayed a friend, but he wouldn't have let it go farther than that. He would never have been hurt this way.*

Would it have been better never to have known his love? Despite the ache in her heart, she didn't think so. He'd changed her life. She wouldn't be the same if they'd only been friends. She'd probably still be gambling, cynical about all men, without an inkling of the love of Jesus. Or about what love truly meant—both to give and to receive.

Perhaps when the pain dulled, she would be able to remember only the good things about their relationship. Maybe when I'm Nola's age it will be better, she thought sadly. If I can get through all the years between now and then. She cried and prayed and asked for God's forgiveness over and over, until she finally felt into an exhausted sleep.

When she straggled downstairs early the next morning, Jessie was waiting in the kitchen with Hester. Camille wanted desperately to turn around and race back up the stairs.

"You look awful," Jessie said, with a sympathetic smile.

Her comment was so unexpected, it made Camille smile. "I feel awful."

"Did you get any sleep?"

"A little." Camille poured herself a cup of coffee. When Hester offered her a plate of biscuits, she shook her head. "I'll eat in a little while."

"Holler when you're ready. I'll go dust the living room." Hester picked up her feather duster and a cloth and left Jessie and Camille alone.

Camille sat down at the table. "How's Ty?"

"About the same as you, I expect. He ate supper with the kids and me last night, but he didn't stay very long. I saw him ride out at the crack of dawn with a pack horse."

Camille set the cup down with a thud. "He left town? The election is only four days away."

"I expect that election is the last thing on his mind right now. When Ty needs to relax or think—or when the world is closing in—he goes out on the range and camps. Cade said he stayed out there for weeks after Amanda and the baby died, but since then he only goes for a few days at a time."

"At least he can escape some of the uproar."

"Unlike you." Jessie helped herself to a biscuit. "You're welcome to go out to the ranch with me if you want."

Camille's eyes misted over. "How can you say that after what I've been?"

"I know what it's like to be manipulated by a worthless man, to be sweet-talked into a disaster. The only good that came from my first marriage are my children. What you did wasn't right, not in God's eyes or in the view of a lot of people. But you were the one to end it, weren't you?"

"Yes. When I realized he wouldn't marry me."

"Then you did all you could. You can't erase what happened. All you can do is learn from it and not repeat the mistake again."

"Believe me, I'll never make that one again." Camille took a drink of coffee, debating whether to say anything else. "And the gambling?"

Jessie pursed her lips and shrugged. "Ty said your father was a gambler. He encouraged you?"

"He taught me and set me up in his place when he became ill."

"How old were you?"

"Seventeen."

"I'm sure you had plenty of customers."

Camille thought she detected a faint note of bitterness in Jessie's voice. "Never an empty chair at the table. I'd like to think that all of them could afford it, but that's doubtful."

"You aren't planning to start up again, are you?"

"Heavens, no. I could never go back to it."

"Good. Then that's in the past, too. Dead and buried as far as I'm concerned. I expect quite a few folks around here feel that way, especially the ones who have had any dealings with you." Jessie pushed back her chair and stood. "I need to go out to the ranch and tell Cade what's happened. Do you want to come?"

"No, thank you." Camille stood, too. "I don't think your husband will be as forgiving as you are. I've hurt his brother. Cade won't take that lightly."

"He'll roar at first." Jessie pushed the chair back up to the table. "But I can calm him down."

"I'm planning on leaving tomorrow. I'll talk to Mr. Hill and then to Nola, when she gets home today, square things away with them."

"Where will you go?"

"I haven't settled on it. Maybe to San Francisco. I've never been to California."

"Don't leave yet. Give Ty a week, if you can stand to stay here that long. If you can't, please let us know where you'll be. I believe he'll come around. He loves you, Camille. He's been happier these past two months than I've ever seen him. Because of you, he's finally healed from the death of his family. At least as much as anyone ever heals from something like that. Trust God to soften Ty's heart and his pride."

"When Bonnie found out Anthony was in town, she reminded me that all things work together for good for those who love Jesus. Ty and I both love Him, so I'm trying very hard to believe that, to trust Him to make it happen. But it seems impossible for good to come of this."

"For one thing, you saved a lot of people from that swindler. Some have already expressed gratitude for that. For another, Ty knows your secret. Better for it to come to light now than later. I assume it was something you meant to tell him but couldn't figure out how?"

"No matter how much I knew I needed to, I couldn't bring myself to do it."

"So God had to force your hand," Jessie said quietly.

Camille gasped softly, holding on to the back of the chair. "He did, didn't He?"

"I suspect He has some things to teach Ty, too. We all have things to learn, and my dear brother-in-law is no exception. So don't go running off right away. Give God the time to finish what He's started."

Camille took a deep, steadying breath. "One week. If it takes longer than that, God will have to send Ty after me."

Ty rode south toward the ranch but kept on going when he reached the road leading to headquarters. It was too soon to see Cade. He was too raw for a lecture from his big brother.

Cutting across the range, he eventually wound up at the top of a ridge and set up camp in one of his favorite places. This time he didn't talk to Amanda. Somehow in the past month, he had lost the need to feel close to her. He had finally let her go, which only added to his emptiness.

He made himself comfortable, leaning back against a rock in the lacy shade of a lone mesquite tree. The land dropped steeply for about two hundred feet before descending more gradually to a broad valley. Antelope mingled with a dozen longhorns grazing in the grass down in the valley. A hawk soared overhead searching for its breakfast. A sparrow darted from branch to branch in a bush nearby, and a scissortail landed in the tree above him.

Gazing out across the vast land, he waited for the peace that always came when he was out on the range, away from people and the demands of town life. Today was no different, despite the turbulence in his mind and soul. The natural quiet and beauty of God's creation soothed some of his tension.

"Maybe this is what I need all the time. To be out here where things don't get so muddled. Don't have to put up with people. Just ornery longhorns."

He considered withdrawing from the election, selling the store and moving back to the ranch. It sounded mighty appealing. Folks wouldn't elect him now anyway, not after he'd been so foolish over Camille. Harvey Miller would be having a grand time with that.

Who'll build the opera house? Red could handle it. Ty would still contribute; otherwise they wouldn't have enough money. But that was as far as his involvement could go, especially since Camille was a partner in the project.

"I should have known she had a man in her past. A woman couldn't live in that situation and stay untouched." He hadn't wanted to see it, to think about it. If she'd just told him about it, been honest with him, maybe it wouldn't have bothered him so much.

Later in the morning, Ty saddled Dusty and wandered down into the valley. He rode for a while, taking a look at the cattle, and following a little stream simply to see where it went. He found a small wild plum thicket. The plums were just beginning to form, so he made note of where they were located, planning to come back later to gather them.

Thoughts drifted through his mind unbidden, even as he tried to focus on his surroundings. It would be a sorry end if he got lost and died of thirst on his own range. What would he have done if she had told him about Anthony? He mulled on it as he rode back to camp, concluding that it depended on when she told him.

Unsaddling Dusty, he discussed the matter with the horse. "If she'd told me right up front, I probably would have kept my distance." Dusty snorted and looked back at him as if he didn't believe a word of it. Ty glared at him and lifted the saddle from the animal's back. "You're right. I couldn't have kept my distance from her if I'd tried."

He ate some jerky about noon and rolled out his bedroll, settling down for a much needed siesta. Lulled by the warmth of the sun and the peaceful surroundings, he slept for a couple of hours. And woke up crankier than ever. He'd dreamed of Camille. Her smile, her sweetness, her kiss. Nothing of her dishonesty or his humiliation. Even his own mind was betraying him.

Taking a small hatchet from his pack, he went in search of firewood. There was plenty of dead wood lying on the ground, but he looked around until he found a dead bush he could hack to pieces. Chopping it up and carrying the wood back to camp worked off some of his irritation. Enough that he spotted and appreciated the sight of the first wildflowers of the season.

He rode bareback down a trail made in earlier times by buffalo hooves as the animals had gone down to water. The trail led to a spring of clear, fresh water. Dusty had a long drink while Ty filled his canteens. Returning to camp, he fed the horse some oats and built a fire. Supper was a can of pork 'n beans, crackers and coffee.

And loneliness. He had spent most of the day at various tasks to keep himself busy and sometimes occupy his mind. Now he had nothing to distract him from his thoughts.

Deciding to read the Bible, he opened it randomly to the Psalms. Psalm thirty-two was at the top of the page, so he began there:

> Blessed is he whose transgression is forgiven, whose sin is covered. Blessed is the man unto whom the Lord imputeth not iniquity, and in whose spirit there is no guile.

Maybe something else. He looked over at Psalm thirty-one, his gaze landing on verse seventeen.

> Let me not be ashamed, O Lord; for I have called upon Thee: let the wicked be ashamed, and let them be silent in the grave.

He didn't want her to be in her grave, just ashamed. He continued with verse eighteen, "Let the lying lips be put to silence—" That seemed appropriate. "—which speak grievous things proudly and contemptuously against the righteous."

Well, he thought, she didn't say anything proudly or contemptuously. And it wasn't against me.

Are you righteous?

A shiver crawled over him. The thought seemed to come directly from God himself. "Only through Jesus. I'm not righteous on my own." Ty swallowed hard. "But reckon I'm acting like I am. She wronged me, Lord. She deceived me. She's the one who is wrong here."

He decided Psalms wasn't the right place to read tonight. He flipped over to the New Testament, the Bible falling open to chapter six in Matthew. It was about worshiping the Lord in private, not in front of others to gain their admiration. Ty figured he was pretty safe on that score, even if he was active in church and folks knew of his beliefs. There was a difference in living God's way and flaunting it for the whole world to see. He did fine with that chapter until he reached verse fourteen.

> For if Ye forgive men their trespasses, our heavenly Father will also forgive you: But if ye forgive not men their trespasses, neither will your Father forgive your trespasses.

Ty groaned and slammed the book shut. He didn't want to forgive her. He looked up at the heavens, spotting the first star of the evening and sighed heavily. "It isn't so much that she wasn't pure and innocent like Amanda was when I met her. It isn't even because she gave herself to another man." That one stung, even if he had no right to be jealous of someone she knew before she met him. "Her not telling me about him hurts."

He stopped to consider why it hurt so much. "Because I didn't want any secrets between us." Frowning, he rubbed the back of his neck. He certainly hadn't told her everything about his past. About all the women he had known before he met Amanda, before he gave his heart to Jesus. "She couldn't trust me enough to tell me. She knew I'd go off half-cocked in self-righteous indignation."

It hurt because he had been humiliated in front of the whole town. "That's the crux of it, isn't it? The woman I love isn't who I thought she was, and I found out when everybody else did. The upright, honorable Mayor McKinnon got mixed up with a woman with a checkered past. I've been knocked off the pedestal, smashing my pride. That's what this is mostly about, isn't it, Lord? My pride."

Feeling contrite, Ty leaned his head on his bent knees. "Forgive me, Lord, for my pride. Forgive me for judging her, for hurting her." Tears burned his eyes as he remembered her walking down the street the day before, head held high. He didn't know how she did it. He was suddenly deeply ashamed because he had let her walk alone, and grateful to Ransom because he hadn't. "She's been hurt far more by this than I have. Jesus, please comfort her. Show her how much You love her. I've failed her, so I can't fault You or Ransom if he steps in to take up the slack. But I hope I get a chance to redeem myself, or at least to help her."

Still troubled, not by his own misery now as much as what she must be going through, he lay down on his bedroll and continued to pray. "Please keep her safe, Lord. Keep her in Willow Grove until I can make amends." He kept praying until sleep overtook him, with his last conscious thought being that he would follow her to the ends of the earth to try to win her back.

Chapter Twenty-Seven

Ty's first impulse Sunday morning was to ride to town and apologize to Camille, but he decided he needed additional time alone with the Lord. He had more fences to mend between himself and the Father before he went charging in to rescue the princess.

In the late afternoon he headed to ranch headquarters. He tied Dusty to the hitching post in front of the house as Cade stepped out the front door.

"How are you?" Cade waited on the porch, studying him intently.

"Not bad considering I've been wrestling with the Lord for a couple of days."

"Did He win?"

"I think so."

"Good. Come in and tell me about it."

"Only if you'll feed me something besides pork 'n beans."

"You know Jessie sent some grub out with me. How does leftover pot roast sound?"

"A meal fit for a king. Or a repentant man."

"I think the second one will be better company."

"I'll go tend to Dusty while you warm up supper."

After he returned to the house and they ate, Ty told his brother about what happened in town. They migrated to the living room where they discussed the things he had worked through with the Lord's help. Then he told Cade what he planned to do.

Cade relaxed in his big chair, sipping the last of his coffee. "Reckon I'll go to town with you tomorrow. That's one day I don't want to miss."

On Monday afternoon, Ty walked quietly downtown. He'd arrived home about noon and cleaned up before heading off to make his last speech before the election. Being in front of a crowd normally didn't bother him, but today his hands were sweaty and his heart pounded. He had some important things to say to one special person. He hoped the rest of the townspeople would take his words to heart, too, but Camille's response was the only one that truly mattered.

Ty pulled his watch from his pocket. If Miller had started on time, he had been talking for about fifteen minutes. Judging from the pained faces of the large group around the specially built stage, his opponent had been particularly venomous. It appeared that just about everyone in town had turned out for the show.

"What kind of man is Ty McKinnon?" shouted Miller. "He pretends to be a God-loving man, but at the same time, he steps out with a woman who lived with another man—without the benefit of marriage—and who made her living as a gambler. In saloons, mind you, not a little bet on canasta or dominoes when the ladies got together for tea. She spent her nights cavorting with men."

Ty curled his hands into fists as he worked his way through the crowd toward the stage.

"Now, some folks say McKinnon didn't know about her past. Didn't know she'd been a man's mistress. But I say he should have checked into her background before he started courting her. As acting mayor of Willow Grove, he had an obligation to the citizens of our town to pursue a woman of high morals, not one of ill repute. His association with her shows poor judgment and a lack of character. Can you imagine the disgrace he would bring to Willow Grove if he actually married her?"

"That's not any more disgraceful than you are, Miller," shouted someone in the back. Ty couldn't see who it was, but it sounded like Quint.

Several others shouted their agreement.

"And she kept us from losing our money to that faker."

Ty walked slowly up the steps to the platform.

A murmur went through the gathering. "Thought you'd run out on us, Mayor. Good to see you."

"Should have stayed gone," shouted someone else. "Don't need the likes of him running our town." A brief argument broke out before the others shushed them into silence.

Miller turned around, glaring at Ty. "Go sit down. I'm not done."

"Yes, you are. You've said way too much already." He stared at his opponent, his gaze hard and unrelenting. "Shut your mouth and get off this platform or I'll throw you off."

About half the crowd cheered.

Miller spun around toward Ransom, who stood at the foot of the steps. "You heard him, Sheriff. He threatened me. Throw him in jail."

"If I threw everybody in jail who has threatened you in the last couple of days, they'd be stacked up three deep. You've had your say, Miller. Get off that platform or I'll haul you to the calaboose for annoying me."

"You can't do that."

"Try me."

Mumbling under his breath, Miller sent Ty a hateful look, then went down the steps, edging past Ransom.

Ty walked to the center of the stage, surveying the throng. He spotted Cade and Jessie standing with Camille and Nola across the street in front of the newspaper office. She didn't leave. Relief swept through him, quickly followed by sorrow because she'd heard Miller's vile comments. How that must have hurt her.

He waited until no sound could be heard except the faint whisper of the afternoon breeze. "I stand before you a sinner."

A shocked gasp rippled through the crowd.

Ty pointed at the minister of his church, knowing the good man wouldn't be offended. "Just like you." Then the blacksmith. "And you." One by one, he pointed to various people in the crowd, many of them strong Christians. "We are all sinners. To some of you, the sins of Miss Dupree's past are worse than your own. But they aren't. Not to God." He pinned Miller with his gaze. "In God's eyes, the gossiper or slanderer is just as guilty as a murderer or thief."

He looked around at the assembly again. "We're all sinners, saved by God's grace, saved by the love and sacrifice of Jesus. Even Camille Dupree. She found salvation after coming to Willow Grove, and Jesus wiped her slate clean. He made her a new person. I challenge anyone to find fault with her behavior since she arrived here.

"I challenge each of you to look into your own hearts, your own past and see if any of you can stand in judgment of Miss Dupree. 'Let him who is without sin cast the first stone.'" Ty looked over the crowd at Camille. She was wiping tears from her cheeks. "I'm certainly not worthy of judging her." He looked at Harvey Miller again. "And neither are you." Amazingly, Miller's face turned red, not out of anger but shame.

"I'm not going to expound on the things I've done as acting mayor. You know the good and the bad. Overall, I think

I've done a good job, and if you elect me, I'll continue to do the best I can. But one thing you do need to know." He looked back at Camille and rested his hands on the podium to keep them from shaking. "I love Camille Dupree with all my heart. I intend to marry her if she'll have me. If she can forgive me for being a hypocrite and an idiot." Smiling through her tears, Camille nodded vigorously. "If any of you have a problem with that, then you can vote for Harvey."

"Heaven help us if Miller wins," hollered Mr. Hill.

Most of the crowd broke into loud cheers and applause as Ty ran down the platform steps. A path opened up for him as he made his way to Camille, receiving several pats on the back in the process.

To his eternal relief, she welcomed him with open arms. Holding her close, he leaned down and spoke into her ear. "Will you marry me?"

"Yes." Then she squeezed the stuffing out of him.

Laughing, Ty let loose with a rebel yell. He didn't need to do anything more to announce their engagement. Cade gave them a joint hug before Jessie wiggled in to do the same.

Ty shook hands with those around him, keeping one arm around Camille the whole time. He hugged Nola with the other arm and kissed her forehead. "Thank you for not letting her run."

"You have Jessie to thank for that. Though I had my say on it, too."

Ty met his sister-in-law's gaze. "Thank you."

Jessie winked and put her arm around her husband.

As soon as they could leave, Ty and Camille slipped into the *Gazette* and went into the inner office. He noticed that Mr. Hill pulled the entrance door closed and stood guard outside. Ty drew her into his embrace and kissed her gently.

"I assume this means you forgive me," he murmured.

"And you forgive me." She framed his face with her hands. "I'm so very sorry."

"So am I." He kissed her again. "How soon can we set the wedding date?"

"We can set it right now. But I think we should wait a few weeks for the wedding."

"Why?"

"Last night I dreamed we were married in a beautiful meadow of wildflowers."

"We don't have meadows out here. We have prairie. Open range."

"That will do."

Ty laughed quietly. "Yes, it will. In a few weeks, the range will be wearin' its spring coat of many colors."

Her expression grew solemn. "I want a small, quiet wedding. Just family and close friends. Maybe at the ranch."

"Fine with me, as long as I get to run away with you afterward, go some place where I can have you all to myself."

"We can't be all by ourselves. We need someone to cook."

"A minor detail. Have I told you lately how much I love you?"

"I believe you mentioned it, in your quiet shy way." She smiled dreamily. "I believe you said it was with all your heart."

"Yes, ma'am. And all the rest of me, too."

Two weeks later, Reverend Brownfield, Ty and Camille stood before his family and their closest friends a short distance from the ranch house. God had decorated the scene for the wedding by covering the surrounding prairie in wide ribbons and bouquets of blue, purple, pink, white, red and yellow. No one could remember such a proliferation of wildflowers in the county. Cade stood up with Ty, and Bonnie with Camille.

Reciting their vows with tenderness and conviction, they promised to love, honor and cherish each other for the rest of their lives. Radiant with joy and love, Camille's eyes grew a little misty as Ty slipped the wedding band on her finger, then shifted her two-week-old diamond engagement ring from her right hand to join the band on her left.

Glancing up at him as she slid his wedding band on his finger and said her vows, she noted moisture in his eyes, too. *Thank you, Lord, for this man, for the love You've given us. For healing the hurts of the past and the present.*

"I now pronounce you man and wife." The minister beamed at them. "You may kiss your bride."

Ty happily obeyed, kissing her gently, but with the promise of the passion awaiting them. When he ended the kiss and raised his head, he looked into her eyes, his own shining with love. "Good morning, Mrs. McKinnon."

Camille sighed, her heart overflowing. "My, that sounds nice. Good morning, Mr. McKinnon."

Cade slapped Ty on the back. "Now that you two have gotten acquainted, give the rest of us a chance to congratulate you." He picked his brother up in a giant bear hug, making them all laugh. Camille saw the tenderness in the big man's action, and his joy over his brother's happiness.

The others gathered around them in a flurry of hugs and good wishes. As the commotion died down, Cade whistled to get their attention. "There's food up at the house." He looked over at the newlyweds with a grin. "If you two walk slow, you might get a few minutes to yourselves. I'll have Jessie save you something to eat." Like a true cowboy, he herded everyone else toward the house.

Ty and Camille stayed where they were, savoring the moments alone. He caught her hand, kissing the back of it. "Have you read Ecclesiastes?"

"No. Old Testament?"

"Yes. In chapter three it talks about life. There are quite a few different things mentioned, but some of them stand out to me more than others. I remember thinking about the verses the night you and I went to the box supper and walked down to the creek. They weren't in quite the same order as in the scripture, but they fit us and our situation. 'To every thing there is a season, and a time to every purpose under the heaven...a time to weep, and a time to laugh; a time to mourn, and a time to dance...a time to heal...' We've been through those, though we missed the dancing. We'll have to make up for that. Now, it's our turn for the best one."

"Which is?"

"A time to love."

"May it last a lifetime." She put her arms around him.

"Amen."

A gentle breeze sprang up, rustling the grass and turning the flowers into waves of delicately shimmering color. In her heart of hearts, in the quietness where Jesus had first whispered her name, Camille knew God was giving them His blessing, both now and forevermore.

A small article appeared in the *Gazette* on Friday regarding the wedding:

> On Wednesday last, Mayor Ty McKinnon, serving his first full term since his landslide victory, and Miss Camille Dupree, associate publisher of this paper, were married at the McKinnon Ranch south of the city.
>
> No church or home could have been more gloriously decorated for the plighting of the troth between these two fine people. The setting for the nuptials, the open range about a hundred yards from the ranch house, was painted in a rainbow of banners and bouquets by God's own hand.

After a honeymoon to San Francisco, the happy couple will reside here in Willow Grove and continue with plans for the building of the new opera house and city hall.

Some folks were put out at the shortness of the piece, but word quickly spread that Miss Nola was privy to all the details and would gladly share them.

After all, it was high time the town had something good to talk about.

* * * * *

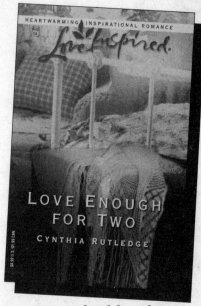

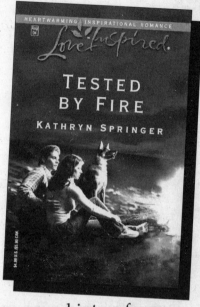

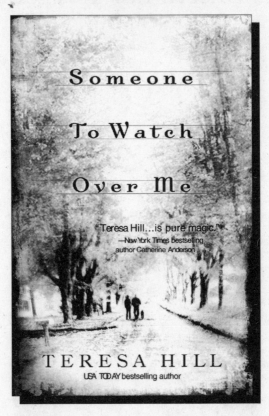